120 DAYS...

M. STRATTON

120 days...

Copyright August 2015 by M. Stratton
Cover by Covers by TOJ Publishing (http://tojpublishing.com/)
Edited by Hot Tree Editing (http://www.hottreeediting.com/)
Formatting by Integrity Formatting

All rights reserved. Except as permitted under the U.S. Copyright Act of 1976, no part of this publication may be reproduced, distributed, or transmitted in any form or by any means, or stored in a database or retrieval system, without prior written permission of the author.

The scanning, uploading, and distribution of this book via the Internet or via other means without the permission of the publisher is illegal and punishable by law. Please purchase only authorized electronic editions and do not participate in or encourage electronic piracy of copyrighted materials. Your support of the author's rights is appreciated.

120 days... is a work of fiction. Names, characters, places, and incidents are either the product of the author's imagination or are used fictitiously. Any resemblance to actual persons, living or dead, events, or locales is entirely coincidental with the exception of the names and stories given freely to M. Stratton to be included in this book and listed as 'guests' at the resort by the loved ones of family members who have died.

Paperback:
ISBN-13: 978-1515258384
ISBN-10: 1515258386

Dedication

To my parents who every day kick cancer's ass.
Your amazing attitude inspired this story.
I can only hope it inspires others to never give up.

To all the people who have cancer,
who have kicked cancer to the curb,

and

to those who are no longer with us,
but have fought as hard as they could,
for as long as they could,

you are more than your diagnosis.

To all the family, friends and caregivers
of these individuals, who have stood by them
and cared for them.
Thank you.

Prologue

Everything can change in a moment and Ethan McGregor's life was about to be changed forever.

Ethan McGregor paced around his office overlooking the San Francisco Bay. With one phone to his ear, he barked out orders for the deal he was going in for the kill on. This was the biggest one of his career and sure to double his already impressive net worth. He glanced down at the cell phone in his other hand and scowled; he'd missed another call from his brother.

No one would recognize the child he was, the one who used to run around the middle-class neighborhood near San Francisco, California with a goofy smile on his face as he and his friends had adventures. Nor would they recognize the one who was born after his parents' death when he was nineteen. Having quit community college to get a job in order to take care of his twelve-year-old brother, his life forever changed. The brothers were close until Evan went off and joined the Army as soon as he was able to be on his own. Once alone, Ethan used his street smarts to start making money and used that money to make more, until he became the go-to guy, for those looking for the right investment property, in the Bay area. He never looked back at the child, or teenager, he used to be; it was always onward to the next deal. His childhood memories were long and painful, so he chose to rarely visit them.

His assistant, Jodi, peeked her head in. He frowned at her, frustrated at the interruption. Shaking his head, he turned his back to her and continued his conversation on the phone. She walked around to stand right in front of him and looked at him with a raised eyebrow as if to say, 'Get off the phone, now.' He wondered if women were just born instinctively knowing how to use their facial expressions to get what they wanted without having to utter a word.

He spoke quickly, trying not to let his aggravation at his assistant show in his tone. "Peter, I have to go. You know what I want, get it done, or don't call me back." Hitting the disconnect button, he looked at her. "What?"

"Your brother is here."

"My brother?" Ethan blinked a few times and looked down at the cell phone still clutched in his other hand. His heartbeat picked up speed wondering if something was wrong. Since Evan had joined the Army, they only saw each other about once a year and only talked on the phone every few months.

"Yes, you remember Evan, don't you?"

"I know who my brother is, but what's he doing here?" His frustration came through in his voice. Frantically, he hoped his brother was only in town for a day or two. He had too much to do and couldn't be bothered to spend days playing family.

"Wanting to see you for some odd reason.

Although, I don't know why. It's not like you're pleasant to be around." She folded her arms across her chest.

"I don't pay for your backtalk," he all but growled at her.

"No, that's a free bonus for you. I'm the best assistant you've ever had. The only one who'd put up with you this long. Now, I'm showing your brother in." She turned and stormed out of the room, but not before she closed the door with a small slam.

He hated to admit it, but she was right. Before Jodi, he'd gone through assistants like they were disposable razors. Not only did she put up with his shit, she was also damn good at what she did. She kept him in line, and his employees too. Hell, he figured she could run this place without him and he'd still make money.

"Hey, bro," Evan's calm, smooth voice came from the door. "Sorry to bother you."

Ethan started speaking before he even turned around. "No prob–" His voice froze in his throat. He hadn't seen his brother in over a year, but he looked like shit, too pale and too thin. "What the hell is wrong with you?" The muscles in his legs tightened with the urge to go to him. It seemed the big brother protective instinct was still there.

He gave him a small smile. "It's good to see you too."

"Seriously, Evan, what's wrong? Have you been sick?" It made him uncomfortable looking at him. This wasn't the brother he knew and loved.

"You could say that." He pointed to the couch. "Do you mind if I sit down?"

"Of course not," he said. "Bad case of the flu?"

A short laugh burst from Evan's lips. "I wish. No, it's cancer."

120 DAYS...

Ethan couldn't speak. It felt like all of the air had been sucked out of his lungs. He reached backwards with a shaking hand to find his desk so he could lean against it before he fell. "Damn." This couldn't be happening, raced over and over in his head. "Are you sure?"

"Oh, yeah, there's no denying it."

He tried to form words, but it took a moment before they could move past the lump in this throat. "How... how long?"

"How long have I had it? Does it matter? There's nothing more that can be done. They've given me the typical, four-to-six weeks to live."

"There's got to be something that can be done." Ethan pushed off his desk, and with anger radiating from him, he walked around it, forcibly opening his laptop and quickly pulling up a search engine. "I don't want you to worry about the money. I've got it covered. We'll go to the best doctors; we'll go over to Europe. I'm always hearing about experimental drugs over there, and how they work wonders. What type of cancer is it? I need to know to find out who to go to."

"Stop, Ethan, just stop. It's too late."

He couldn't understand how his brother could be so calm. "No, no, I won't accept that." Ethan looked down at his hands; they were shaking so bad, he couldn't type. Clenching his fists, he looked over at his brother. "There has to be something." He felt like he was begging and hated it.

Evan spread his hands and raised a boney shoulder. "I'm sorry. There isn't."

"Dammit!" Standing forcefully, Ethan's chair rolled backward, crashing into the wall, and he slammed his fists on his desk. "No, you're wrong."

For the first time, impatience creeped into Evan's

voice. "Ethan, I'm not some kid. I'm an adult, and have been for some time. I know the questions to ask, I know the second opinions to get. Trust me, there is nothing else to be done."

"What has been done?"

"Nothing, it was too late by the time they caught it."

His shoulders slumped. "Four-to-six weeks?"

"Yes."

Trying to blink back his tears, Ethan ran his hands over his face trying to hide them from his brother. "Okay, fine, then I'll take some time off. I know I haven't been there for you in years, but I can be now." He grabbed his chair, righted it and sat back down, bringing his calendar up. In his mind, he thought if he could spend some more time with his brother, he might be able to find something else for him to try, anything to save his life. "I can rearrange my schedule. It's not a problem." He had to focus on something beside the fact that his only relative was dying.

When Evan slowly stood up and walked over to where he was sitting, Ethan tried to ignore how frail he looked. An image of the two of them running around the backyard together when Evan was six and he was thirteen flashed through his mind. It was the first time Evan had been fast enough and sneaky enough to catch him at the game they were playing.

Evan's thin hand trembled over his on the keyboard. "Stop. You already took care of me once. I'm not going to have you do it again."

"I'm your brother, what else am I supposed to do?"

"What you've always done, your own thing, work. You don't need to worry about me." Evan walked back over and sat down on the couch.

"No, you're not going to get your way. I'm going to be there for you. I'm the only family you have and I should be there."

"I'm not your responsibility anymore. I haven't been for fifteen years. You live your life."

"I'm not going to accept that." He started typing again. "I'm going to contact this guy I know. His father had cancer. They flew him to somewhere overseas. They cured him. He's still alive. I'll get the name of his doctor and we'll charter a flight and be over there within the day."

"Ethan, it's my life, and I say no. Nothing is going to change the outcome. We're all going to die. Cancer has made it so I can determine how I'm going to die, and it's not going to be experimental treatment after experimental treatment. I'm going to live it the best way possible for as long as I can."

"Fine, but then at least let me live it with you." Now that Ethan knew his brother was dying, he could see exactly how sick he had become. He'd tried to hide it with a bulky sweater, but looking closely, Ethan could see the difference.

"You don't understand. You've already taken care of me. I'm not going to ask you to do it again. You quit school and got a job you hated to take care of me. You've already sacrificed for me. I don't want you to remember me so sick that I can't do anything for myself, or even if I can remember who you are at the end. Ethan, death is never pretty. No, I'm going away to die. This is our good-bye."

"No." Ethan couldn't believe what he was hearing. His gut twisted that his brother was giving up. Ethan threw his hands in the air with frustration. "Just like that? Now? After all of this time you just show up here and say you're going off to die and I'm just supposed to accept it? Well, I don't. This"—he jabbed his finger on his desk—"...this is not our good-bye."

Evan smiled sadly. "It has to be. I don't have much time left. Already I tire out so easily. I'm going to go out and do everything I possibly can, while I'm still able to. Then I am going to die with as much dignity as I possibly can."

They looked at each other, Ethan in disbelief that this was the last time he would see his brother. It all seemed so surreal, like a nightmare. He closed his eyes, praying he'd wake up in his bed. Not in his office with his brother telling him he was dying of cancer. When he opened his eyes, nothing had changed. "Please..."

Shaking his head, Evan smiled sadly at him. "I'm only going to say this one more time, Ethan. This is my choice. I need you to understand, and I need you to not try to find me. Don't send private detectives looking for me, because you won't find me. We have the chance to say good-bye to each other, to remember one another as we stand here now. No regrets about what hasn't been said, and you don't have to watch me wither away and die. I can't be worried about you, and how you're going to react to seeing me like that, yelling at the doctors and nurses. This is my time, my last weeks. Let me live them as I see fit. Think of it as my last wish, one that you can easily fulfill."

"But you're my baby brother. I'm supposed to take care of you."

Slowly, Evan stood up, walked over to him, and put his cold hand on Ethan's shoulder. "I'm sorry. Thank you for everything, truly, thank you. When I was a kid and Mom and Dad died, you didn't have to stick around and raise me, but you did. Because of you, I'm the man I grew up to be. Not perfect, but a hard worker, kind of an asshole, but the 'When I give my word, it means everything' kind of guy. Just like you. All I need from you is a promise you'll slow down a bit, enjoy life, think of something besides work and maybe try some things you never thought you would ever do. Live. Live for me." He squeezed his shoulder. "Goodbye, brother."

Ethan's voice wouldn't come as he watched his brother slowly walk toward the door, fear and panic rising up through him. It couldn't end like this. Leaping to his feet, Ethan quickly caught up to him. Grabbing him in a bear hug, his body racked with silent sobs, he squeezed his eyes shut. "I love you," he whispered. There was nothing more he could do. "God, I love you."

120 DAYS...

away, his last wish, but he cou'' to the door he knocked. W the worst scenarios w thought for sure he w door, needing his h frustrations out neighbor came was vacant. After find hi one F

87 days later . . .

As soon as Ethan exited the lawyer's office, he leaned up against the hot brick wall, tipping his head back and hitting it hard. He welcomed the pain. It matched what he was feeling in his heart. Listening to the lawyer drone on and on about his brother's will was strange.

After Evan had shown up in his office to tell him he'd been diagnosed with cancer and say good-bye, Ethan's life wasn't the same. For the first month afterward, he threw himself into work, closing deal after deal, gambling on investments, demanding more, and each time, he came out ahead. But the thrill, the excitement was never there. Always in the background was the image of his brother, knowing he was out there dying. Alone.

One night after work, he found himself outside his brother's apartment. He knew he'd asked him to stay

dn't anymore. Going up
hen no one answered, all
ent through his head. He
as lying on the other side of the
lp but unable to call. Pounding his
on the door, he didn't stop until the
out and told him no one lived there. It

hat, he ended up hiring a private detective to
m, but he was unsuccessful. So he hired another
, and then another, the best money could buy.
van had disappeared off the face of the Earth. No one could find him. He really meant what he'd said about not wanting Ethan to take care of him, or find him. All he could think of was he was really gone. They would never laugh together again, or fight, play, or just talk ever again. Even though he was still alive, somewhere, he wasn't ever going to be able to hug him again. His mind wouldn't leave the fact he'd wasted so many years away from Evan.

Remembering as a kid how much Evan looked up to him, chased after him, wanted to be him when he grew up, Ethan was overcome with grief, yet the tears wouldn't come. He didn't know what to do next, so he buried himself in work, again, until one day the call came. His brother had died.

The tears he'd never allowed to have power over him, for all those months, finally broke loose and ran down his cheeks. He was truly, for the first time in his life, alone in the world. There was no one to share the grief with.

With the back of his hand, he wiped at his eyes. He didn't have time for the emotion, he had an appointment to get to, and there was no putting it off any longer.

Getting in his car, he clutched his brother's journal

in his hands before carefully placing it on the seat next to him. This was all he had left. He'd skimmed through it up in the lawyer's office. His brother had documented his death journey, and Ethan's plan was to read it.

DAY 1

ETHAN-

I'M MAKING THIS JOURNAL FOR YOU, HOPING YOU WILL KNOW AND UNDERSTAND WHY I HAD TO DO THIS. I HOPE THIS WILL BRING YOU PEACE AND CLOSURE AFTER I'M GONE.

YOU ARE MY BROTHER, YOU RAISED ME, AND WE'LL ALWAYS BE A PART OF EACH OTHER.

I LOVE YOU,

EVAN

Ethan's red-rimmed eyes took in the rising sun the following morning. He'd spent all night reading about his brother's last eighty-three days alive. On paper, he sounded like he was as happy as someone dying from cancer could be; though, he had to wonder about this ranch, this Last Resort. Exactly what was it, and what was their deal, their scam? No way could they do everything they did. It had to be too good to be true. He knew Evan had a list of charities he gave his money to. He wondered exactly how much went to Last Resort. He wanted to call the lawyer to see exactly when Evan had changed his will, and was it during his stay at Last Resort, or before he went up there, but it was too early to make the call. He made a quick note to call him in a few hours.

Needing to be proactive, he started doing his own research on Last Resort. On the surface, everything looked on the up-and-up, but there was no way a place like that existed only to help people. There had to be more to it. They had to be in it for the money. His mind whirled with all the different ways they would be scamming dying people out of their life-savings.

Leaning back in his chair, he thought. Since everyone there was dying, it wouldn't be hard to make them feel like they were given everything they wanted, but in reality, were they? The news was filled with stories of nursing home or caregiver abuse and money disappearing. This would be no different. He remembered back to the time after his parents had died and the neighborhood they'd lived in, the only one they could afford. Everyone was running one scam or another. You learned pretty quick how to read people and know when they were flat out lying or only stretching the truth.

He paced around the room, trying to think of what his next move should be. Something was pulling him toward the place where his brother died. He needed answers and he knew the only way to get them was to go there himself and ask. There was no way he was going to rely on someone else's information, open to interpretation.

Knowing his instincts would be valuable in this situation, he needed to figure out exactly how he was going to play it. He'd learned years earlier, you need to show a certain amount of cards to make the other person feel at ease, like there was no way you could be lying to them. You gave less information than you took from them and you showed no mercy. That was how he'd built his wealth.

He walked back to his laptop and clicked on the *Job Opportunity* section of their website. They were hiring for a few different positions. He wasn't qualified to be a nurse or a chef, but the general caregiver description sounded like something he could do. They needed someone who could drive the guests around, help with planned activities, spend time with the guests and do some light maintenance around the place.

Stopping, he snapped his fingers and knew just what to do. Going into his room, he started to pack clothes, ones he didn't often wear. Jeans and t-shirts replaced his suits, which cost thousands of dollars. Boots replaced Italian loafers. As luck would have it, Last Resort was looking for a new employee, and he was going to be it. This way, he'd be able to see firsthand where his brother spent his final days and find out exactly what kind of scam the owner was working.

Chapter 2

Samantha Truman looked out the window at the sunrise, said a silent prayer, and gave Elizabeth Munns' hand a squeeze before setting it gently down on the bed. She knew Elizabeth couldn't feel anything anymore; she was gone, but she still deserved to be treated with dignity. The melanoma took this sweet twenty-year-old's life, and it broke Sam's heart.

Carefully and systematically, she went through her checklist, knowing what to do, when to do it, and how to do it by heart. When everything was as it should be, she sat down in the chair and picked up Elizabeth's hand again and held it while waiting for the coroner to arrive.

This had been an especially hard week on her, this loss, so close to the last, was always difficult. Elizabeth had made it one-hundred-and-seventy-six days, better than the average, but that still didn't change the outcome. The outcome was whomever showed up at the Last Resort, died at Last Resort.

It was a sad fact of life that so many people ended up with a terminal disease and had no family to depend on, no one to be there for them during their final days. Or they had family, but didn't want to burden them with the end. Last Resort was here for them, a place where they could go to fulfill their last wishes and be surrounded by people who were just like them. She had activities planned everyday based on what her current residents wanted to do. Anything from movie marathons to rock climbing, their final dreams were given to them for as long as they were physically able to participate, then they were modified to be less demanding, but still catered to what they were interested in.

Sam had lost both of her parents to cancer within two years of each other. They had some extra money, but that didn't help stop the disease; however, it did give her the start-up money for the Last Resort. She bought an old ranch near the coast in northern California, a short drive north from San Francisco, and set about renovating the old farmhouse and outbuildings to living quarters, which were set up for all her guests' needs, from the time they were able to walk through the front door, to when they were wheeled out, no longer breathing.

Once Elizabeth was attended to, Sam left the small building knowing the cleaning crew would be in later to get it ready for the next guest. That was another sad truth. There was always going to be another person ready to replace the one who'd just died. They had a waiting list. Sam was trying to figure out how to add more cabins without disrupting the current guests or losing the family feel of the place.

Her mind flitted from one task to another, cataloging what she was going to have to do and when, trying to keep her heart from crying out. Deep down in her gut, she knew how she was supposed to spend her life, helping people, but this didn't mean their deaths didn't affect her. It was hard not to get attached to the people who came to her, to her resort, but she couldn't help herself.

They were lonely. They were sick. They were dying.

Like all humans, they just wanted someone who was there for them, to care for them in the end, to make them feel like they mattered. Whether they were young or old, not one story was any more tragic than the other, because in the end, they were all heartbreaking.

Walking through the grounds, she purposely steered clear of the garden. She couldn't go there at the moment. She also made sure she took the long way back to her office, hoping not to run into anyone. All she wanted was a good thirty minutes alone when she could cry and grieve for Elizabeth before carrying on with the rest of her day. That was all she could allow herself, any more and it would destroy her. She'd learned the hard way she couldn't grieve as she really wanted to for each and every one of them. She wasn't strong enough.

Sneaking in the backdoor of her office, she sat down in her chair and spun it around to look out the big window, which faced the Pacific Ocean. She could barely see it; the marine layer was still hanging around, but Sam knew it was there. She closed her eyes and thought of Elizabeth's spirit finally free from the pain and sickness, flying and laughing over the ocean, dipping her fingers in the cold water as she frolicked with the whales.

She opened up and let the grief come, which came in waves. Over and over it silently raged through her body until she was spent, leaning back in her chair with swollen and dry eyes, staring at the ceiling. Taking a deep breath, she turned her chair around to get to work and froze. A man stood in her doorway, watching her.

120 DAYS...

DAY 2

ETHAN-

WELL, I'M ALL SETTLED IN. YOU SHOULD SEE THIS PLACE. IT'S BEAUTIFUL. IN REALITY, YOU'RE SURROUNDED BY DEATH HERE, YET EVERYONE IS HAPPY AND VERY HELPFUL. 'WE'RE NOT DEAD YET' IS THE MOTTO.

FROM THE FRONT PORCH OF MY CABIN, I CAN JUST MAKE OUT THE OCEAN. I KNOW I'M GOING TO BE SPENDING A LOT OF TIME IN THE FRESH AIR AROUND HERE, MAYBE EVEN GO HIKING SINCE I CAN'T REALLY RUN ANYMORE.

IS IT STRANGE THAT I FEEL MORE ALIVE NOW, KNOWING I'M GOING TO BE DEAD SOON, THAN EVER BEFORE?

EVAN

"I'm sorry, they said I could come in. If you want, I can come back later." Ethan fidgeted from one foot to the other at the door, trying to appear non-threating.

The lady behind the desk stood up. "No, no, it's no problem. How can I help you?"

"Sorry," he smiled shyly at her, trying to remember not to be the hard as nails businessman, and held out his hand. "I'm Ethan McGregor, your newest employee."

"Oh, yes, Ethan." She took his hand in hers and said, "I'm Samantha Truman, the owner. I'm sorry, it's already been a busy morning and I forgot you were starting today. Did they already have you fill out your paperwork?"

"Yes, ma'am, all done and turned in."

Sam shook her head at him and the corners of her mouth tipped up. "Please, you don't need to call me ma'am."

He shrugged. "Sorry, that's how I was raised." Part of him was shocked at how easily he'd slipped back into the manners his parents had taught him.

"And that's the third time you've apologized since we started talking, a lesser woman would totally take advantage of you."

Not sure where she was coming from, or going with that statement, Ethan decided nodding was the best course of action. The last thing he wanted was his normal arrogant self to come through. He needed to gain her trust if he was going to learn how she scammed the dying out of their money.

Looking at her, he could see why Evan wrote so fondly of her. He wouldn't describe her as beautiful, but she was cute, and even with her red-rimmed eyes, he could see her personality coming through, like Evan said it would. No-nonsense, get to the point, help other people to the point of getting sick herself. Ethan had always loved puzzles and he knew he was going to love putting the pieces of Ms. Truman together. The odds of her being one of those rare people who gave without ever thinking of taking were slim. He'd known plenty before his parents had died. Or she had to be a first class liar, an expert in deception, like the majority of the people he knew after their deaths. It was no longer about just finding out what she was up to; it was a mission for him. There'd be hell to pay if she took advantage of his brother.

"Here, I'll show you around while we talk." She left

her office and his longer legs easily kept up with her fast pace. "This is the main ranch house. All the offices and on-site staff rooms are here, along with ten rooms for the guests who prefer being near people, or have special needs. Meaning, they need to be tended to on a more regular basis."

They walked around the main building and she pointed to her right—the building that was attached to the main house by a breezeway. "That's the kitchen and dining room. Each guest can either dine with everyone, or alone in their room. We even set up special picnics or events, which are scheduled or requested. Behind that are the stables, which we turned into a garage and where we keep the vehicles and golf carts."

"Then over there"—she pointed to her left—"is our game room, rec room, fun area. Most will hang out there at one point or another throughout the day, depending on how they are feeling. We have ten cabins back there, all within easy walking distance. Or if they are in wheelchairs, we have paved sidewalks made to blend into the landscape and treated so they don't have to worry about slipping when it rains and guests are still able to get around. I'm in the original house, which you can see on that ridge over there."

He listened carefully to her as she spoke about the resort. He'd already learned all this from their website, but he was hoping for more insight into her. "How do you decide what activities you are going to do?"

"It really all depends on the guests we have. I like to call it a menu. They can pick and choose what they want to do. We also have scheduled daily events they can come to if they wish. The maximum number of guests we can have at any time is twenty. It seems like a lot of work for so few, but it makes them happy, and even if only one person shows up, we like to make sure they have as much fun as they can, that each one is special and they deserve to be treated that way." She looked at him. "When someone comes here, the doctors have told them there's no hope, and they only have a handful of weeks left to live. The average number of days someone has to live before they arrive is forty. The average number of days they spend here before they die is one hundred and twenty. We feel, *we know*, that in the right environment, with the right attitude, people can extend how long they live, and have an amazing quality of life, even when they've been given a death sentence. We make sure they live what is left of their life to the best of their ability. Think about it, on average, we give someone eighty extra days of life. To me, that's amazing. To them, it's everything."

Her impassioned talk hit him in gut. He immediately thought of his brother and his last days here. Clearing his throat he said, "And this." He pointed to a wall, which was about four-feet high and flowed around a garden.

"That's our Legacy Wall." Her voice shook, but she stepped forward. "As soon as a new guest arrives, I have them create a handprint, one they can decorate however they want. As you can see, some only have their name, others have added their disease and some have taken the time to paint them. Once they are . . . gone, their handprint goes up along the wall."

"How long is the wall?" He tried to see around the plants to get an idea of the size for himself.

She paused for a beat. "Too long."

He couldn't stop himself. He walked over to the wall. "How do you decide who goes where?"

"We started here." She pointed to the first handprint near the ground. "That's Kenneth Johnson.

120 DAYS...

He was the first guest we lost after we opened. The colon cancer took him at the age of sixty-one. He'd been here for seventy-seven days. They follow around the wall, then when they get to here,"—she walked to the other side of the gate opening—"we go up one level and they wrap back around to the beginning, and so on."

"Wow, you have four full rows." He tried to wrap his head around the fact that so many people had died at the resort. They'd taken care of them, and maybe milked them out of their lifesavings while they were at it, he speculated.

"We've started on the inside." She walked through the gate and showed him the additional two rows.

"So many people."

"Too many."

He found the last handprint and looked at it. It had today's date on it. Looking back over his shoulder, he saw her take a deep breath and look down as she scuffed her shoe in the dirt. Walking a few feet, he didn't have to go far to find Evan's handprint. Crouching down, he placed his hand in his brother's. Evan's had always been a little smaller, but he was surprised how much wider his own fingers were compared to Evan's. The sickness had already taken so much from him before he'd even arrived. His brother created this before he died. Ethan wasn't sure how he was going to have the strength to get through his time at the resort. His heart ached for what he'd lost, and coming face to face with so many handprints, he wasn't the only one.

The stones behind him were kicked and he knew she approached him. Letting his hand drop, he bowed his head and hoped for strength.

"We recently lost Evan McGregor, is he a relative of

yours?" she asked quietly.

"Yes. My brother."

She placed her hand briefly on his shoulder. "I'm so sorry. He was a very good man."

He didn't want her touching him, giving him comfort. His reason for being there was to find out if she was taking advantage of the dying. "Yes, he was. He was the best." He had to keep focused on his brother, and giving her that little bit of information was his way of ultimately making her less suspicious of him.

Taking a step back, she scowled at him and her body tensed. "Why are you here? Why did you apply for a job? I don't understand. I don't recall anything on your application stating you had a relative who'd died here." Confusion and anger filled her voice.

He stood up and ran his fingers through his hair. He'd already prepared his answer, knowing these questions would be coming at some point. Wanting to get them out of the way, he tipped his hand early. "When Evan was diagnosed with the cancer, he didn't want me to drop everything to take care of him, again. I'm seven years older than him and when our parents died, when I was nineteen, I put my education on hold so I could get a job and raised him."

"He was very lucky, a lot of people wouldn't do that." Her body relaxed a little bit, but she still seemed on guard.

Deciding to give her a little bit more, he continued. "All we had was each other." He shrugged. "It was the only thing I could do. Anyway, he didn't want me to remember him sick and dying. He wanted me to remember everything else. Well, as you know, he died recently. After I was notified, I had an appointment with his lawyer, who gave me Evan's journal. I started

120 DAYS...

reading it. The way he talked about this place . . ." He turned to look at her. "Really, it's remarkable what you do for them. Something pulled me here. I applied here, got the job, and here I am."

"There's more to it than that." Her head tilted to one side and her eyes narrowed as if she was trying to get into his mind and figure him out. "What about the job you had before coming here? I'm trying to remember." She tapped her finger to her lip. "Didn't you have your own company?"

Ethan held his ground. He didn't want her to know she was right, and there was more to it. "My brother didn't want me around in his last days. I need to be able to give back. I need to be able to be there for someone else since I wasn't there for him. Yes, I do own a company, and because of that, I'm able to take off as much time as I need to try and help someone else."

She nodded and relaxed some more. A smile spread across her face and she pointed to his shoulder. "It would seem someone's happy you're here."

Ethan looked at his shoulder where a large butterfly had landed. It stood there, its wings slowly opening and closing, flashing its colors. He had no idea where the eyes were, but he was pretty sure they were staring at each other.

"My mother told me before she died, whenever I saw a rainbow or a butterfly, it was her thinking of me. We see a lot of them here in the garden surrounded by so many handprints. Looks like Evan is thinking of you."

Ethan was lost in the moment, wondering if what she said was true. The child who used to be filled with wonder, hoped it was, but the cynical man he grew into told him she talked a good talk. It was all part of the scam. He wasn't going to let his defenses down.

His purpose was to expose her to the world so she couldn't take anyone else's money.

The butterfly fluttered its wings and took off, leaving him alone with her and at odds with himself.

Chapter 3

DAY 4

ETHAN-

SKYDIVING, WHO WOULD HAVE THOUGHT, ESPECIALLY SINCE I MADE DAMN SURE I DIDN'T JOIN THE AIRBORNE DIVISION OF THE ARMY ALL THOSE YEARS AGO. BUT I FINALLY DID A JUMP AND I CAN CROSS THAT OFF MY BUCKET LIST. I WILL TELL YOU THAT I DON'T THINK I'LL EVER NEED TO DO THAT AGAIN, UNLIKE PATTY. MAN, SHE LOVED IT. TODAY, WE BOTH JUMPED FOR THE FIRST TIME AND HAD TOTALLY DIFFERENT REACTIONS, THAT'S FOR SURE. WHILE THIS WILL BE MY LAST, I'M WILLING TO BET MONEY SHE COMES BACK, EVERY DAY IF THEY'LL LET HER.

I WISH YOU COULD MEET HER. THERE'S SOMETHING ABOUT HER THAT REMINDS ME OF MOM.

EVAN

120 DAYS...

"All right, come on, folks, let's move it! Time to jump out of a plane," Patty said as she adjusted the straps on her harness and looked over at Ethan. "What's the matter, Bucky? Scared?"

Sam looked over at the new guy, Ethan, and tried not to laugh, instead settling for a smirk. He did look a little green around the gills. Patty was in her mid-forties and still full of sass, even though a large-mass tumor in her stomach was slowly starving her, making her extremely thin.

"What?" Ethan asked. "No, I'm fine. But tell me again, why am I doing this?" His brow furrowed when he looked over at Patty.

"Because if those of us who are at death's door can go up to eleven-thousand feet and step out of a plane, a healthy man like you should be able do it too. Don't wait."

"So you aren't scared, at all?" he asked.

"Nope, jumping out of planes was something I always wanted to do, but never found the courage or time to. The first week I was at Sam's place, she took us up here to jump, and I've been back every week since then. I love it. Besides, what's the worst that can happen? My chute doesn't open? I die? Well, I'm weeks, maybe days away from dying as it is. This"—she pointed to sky—" . . . this I've got."

Ethan nodded. "It seems like I've got a lot to learn."

Sam turned away to make sure the other guest, Bruce Blucker's, harness was secured properly. It was his first time up as well. He loved everything to do with fitness; even though he was in his eighties, he could run circles around the staff half his age. It seemed the lung cancer wasn't slowing him down and he wanted to try it.

Sam took a deep breath and thought about Ethan.

His skill set wasn't something they needed at the ranch. He seemed like he'd be better suited for an office, but he was a quick learner and had the drive to put 100 percent behind what he was doing. He didn't seem like the type who would take a leave of absence from his company to come up here and get his hands dirty. This wasn't the first time she'd wondered if his brother's passing changed something at the core of his being.

As they all piled into the plane to take them up, she went through her mental checklist, making sure everyone's safety equipment was operational. Yes, what Patty said was correct; they were all days or weeks away from death, but she didn't want their death to come earlier by an accident. She wanted them to have every single second they could.

"Are you going to make it?" Stopping next to Ethan, she looked at him and noticed he looked a little pale.

"This? Oh, yeah. No problem, I'm fine." He gave her a thumbs up.

"It's not too late to back out, you know." She nodded to the man strapped to Ethan's back. She'd made sure he had the best, most competent instructor to tandem jump with him.

"No." He shook his head. "If they can do it, so can I."

She raised an eyebrow at him. "This isn't a competition."

"That's not how I meant it." He sighed. "Patty had a good point. I'm not going to pass this opportunity up. I have to be honest, I may never do it again, but I can say, at least once, I jumped out of a plane."

"Fine, you're up next." She slapped him on the shoulder, walked to the door of the plane and jumped out.

120 DAYS...

As she freefell, the wind flew past her face making it difficult to breathe. It was always the part she hated, never feeling like she could breathe. Every single time she jumped, it still took her by surprise, and she had to fight the natural urge to panic and hyperventilate in order to get the oxygen her body wanted. Once she pulled the ripcord and her body was jerked into position, she settled in to enjoy the slow ride down. Pulling on one side of the chute and then the other, creating big lazy circles, this was the part she enjoyed. It was so quiet, she couldn't hear any of the hustle and bustle that went on down below. It was her time: no responsibilities, no questions, no duties, no death, just falling gently back to earth.

Too soon, the ground was coming up to meet her. She bent her knees and walked her way down. She looked around to see who had landed and made sure they were okay before gathering her chute and watching her newest employee land. *Not bad for his first time*, she thought, as he was able to stay on his feet with the help of the instructor.

Once he disconnected, she walked over to him and smiled. "Good job. The first jump is always the hardest. You end up either loving it or hating it. Although, I'm guessing you aren't chomping at the bit to get back up in a plane."

"Yeah . . ."

She laughed. "Well, if it makes you feel better, it's not my favorite thing to do."

He tilted his head to the side. "Then why do you?"

"Because I found out really quick, even though some people are dying, and this is something they want to do, doesn't mean they still don't get scared the first time they do it. They can't all be Patty." She shrugged. "The easiest way to show them it's going to be okay is to jump with them myself. To be honest, I hate the freefall, but after the chute is open, the peace is perfect. You take the good with the bad."

"So, am I going to have to jump every time?" He looked at her out of the corner of his eye.

Sam smiled at him. "No, not at all. Having someone on the ground to help out would be great. I'm usually never the first one to jump, and sometimes, our guests need a little bit of help after they land. If you could take that over for me, then I can stay on the plane and make sure the rest of them are good to jump."

"Now *that* is something I can do." His shoulders sagged with relief.

"Then we have a plan." She casually patted him on the back and was surprised at how the feel of his muscles tensing under his shirt sent butterflies dancing in her stomach. Normally, it wasn't something she thought about. Human touch was a big part of what went on at the resort. People wanted to feel connected, wanted the love, wanted to know someone cared enough and wasn't scared to touch them because they were dying. She always tried to show them they mattered.

"We have a plan."

They both smiled at each other.

DAY 5

ETHAN—

WOW, FINALLY GOT TO SIT DOWN AND TALK WITH SAM. SHE'S AMAZING. YOU CAN TELL SHE LOVES THIS PLACE, AND US. SHE GIVES IT HER ALL, PUTS EVERYTHING INTO HER PROGRAM. YOU'D BE SURPRISED BY HOW MANY THINGS THERE ARE TO DO AROUND

120 DAYS...

HERE. EVERY SINGLE DAY, THERE'S SOMETHING NEW. EVEN WHEN I GET TO THE POINT WHERE I WON'T BE ABLE TO GET AROUND AS WELL, THERE ARE STILL GOING TO BE THINGS FOR ME TO DO, OR HELL, EVEN IF I WANT A CHOCOLATE CREAM PIE AT TWO IN THE MORNING, THEY'LL GET IT FOR ME, AND NEVER MAKE ME FEEL LIKE I'M PUTTING THEM OUT, OR ASKING TOO MUCH. I CAN'T PUT INTO WORDS HOW GREAT THAT IS.

AND WHEN YOU HEAR THE REASON WHY SHE DOES THIS, WELL, ALL I CAN SAY, BRO, IS IT MAKES IT ALL THE BETTER. THERE NEEDS TO BE MORE PEOPLE LIKE HER IN THIS WORLD.

EVAN

After everyone unloaded from the van and disbursed to their rooms or cabins, Sam drove the van around to the garage near the kitchen and parked it. She sat there for a moment before climbing out and going to the vehicle log, making a note that they were due for an oil change. She'd somehow have to schedule it in, and they really should get the tires rotated. Bending down, she checked the tires closer. It was going to be the last rotation before she had to get new ones.

Opening up her task app on her phone, she added them to her list and started to walk out when Ethan came through the door.

"Hey," he said. "I was wondering if you needed help with anything. I used to work in a garage after high school."

"Funny you should mention that. The van is due for an oil change, and if you could take care of it, it would save me some time and money. Then all I'll have to organize is the tire rotation."

"I can take it into town for you and have that done."

"Great. Can you make sure you get it done this week? We use the van a lot and end up racking up miles quickly." She stepped over to the shelves of different vehicle fluids and checked to make sure they had enough on hand.

"No problem. So . . . ummm . . ." He rubbed his hand over the back of his neck. "Can I ask you a question?"

"Of course." She kept checking the shelves.

"Why do you do this? I've been watching you for the past couple of days. You're on the move from when you wake up to when you go to sleep. You're always taking care of everything on the ranch and everybody. What drives you to work so hard?"

Stopping what she was doing, she turned and faced him, giving him her full attention. "They deserve it. I know some people think I'm wasting money, or throwing it away on people who are going to die sooner rather than later, but the extra days they have mean everything to them. One more sunrise, one more sunset." She went over and grabbed a couple of waters out of the small refrigerator before walking to the door and held it open. "Come on, I want to show you something."

Instead of walking back to the main house, she took a path leading up the small hill behind the garage. It wasn't a difficult or long hike before they reached the top. It was one she'd taken many times over the years. She walked over to a bench under a tree and pointed to it.

120 DAYS...

> *A mother and a father taken too soon.*
> *They fought long.*
> *They fought hard.*
> *Cancer may have destroyed their bodies,*
> *But it did not destroy their spirit or their love.*

"My parents, Bill and Bonnie Truman," Sam said as the wind gently blew her hair. "We had money, but all the money in the world couldn't buy cures for the cancers that ravaged their bodies. My dad was diagnosed first with stage IV colon cancer." After all this time, she could say the words, but it still didn't seem possible. "He went through chemo and radiation before having surgery. He ended up getting a bad infection and was in and out of the hospital for a couple of months. We thought he was going to die a few times before we found out he was allergic to the sutures they'd used." Still, the image of him lying in the hospital bed looking so thin and his skin appearing grey haunted her. "When they went back in and removed them, he was fine. He started rebuilding his strength, getting better. Then they found the spot on his lung, and removed it. When he was first diagnosed, they said he'd be lucky to make it to five years. He proved them wrong"—she teared up but held them back—"all because of his attitude. He said he wasn't going to be ashes in an urn sitting on the fireplace mantle. He was going to fight it, he had too much to live for. And he did. I'm not saying he didn't have down days, but for every down day he had, there were a dozen or more positive days. He's one of the best men I've ever known and I was lucky enough to call him Dad."

She walked back toward where they'd come from and stood looking out over the ranch. "My dad was doing better, great test results, recovered from his surgeries, we thought we were out of the woods, then my mom had a heart attack. That was when they found her cancer, lung cancer, stage IV."

"I'm so sorry. To have both of your parents have advanced stages of cancer like that . . ."

"Sadly, it happens more often than it should, especially with lung cancer. Anyway, it was large and in both lungs. There was no way they could do surgery or radiation. The doctors said if the chemo worked, she'd make it a year, if not, three months." Her lips trembled as she tried to smile. "She took the same attitude as my dad. She fought it and blew their estimations out of the water." She turned to look at him. "You see, attitude has so much to do with life. That's what I'm doing here." Her voice became stronger. "With the money they left me, I bought this place and fixed it up, and now I help people in the same position as they were. I help them live a few extra days, have a few extra sunrises and sunsets. Give them everything they could possibly need to make their last days here as wonderful as they possibly can be."

"What about you though? You work so hard for them, and I'm not knocking that, but what about you? You need to take care of yourself."

"I do, don't you understand? The more I give, the happier I am, the more fulfilled I am. I don't need for anything. This is what I want to do. This resort has become my reason for living." She walked to the tree. "I planted this tree the very first day I took possession of this land. I hauled the sapling up here by myself, dug the hole, emptied my parents' ashes in the hole and planted a tree for them. They are always together and it sits up here, watching over my property. Watching over all the other people who come here with cancer or any other terminal disease."

"What about family? Don't those people down there have family?"

He almost sounded angry. Sam assumed it was because he was trying not to show that what she was saying affected him. "Some of them do, but some, like your brother, wanted to make a clean break. They don't want to be a burden to their families, or to have their loved ones watch them die. They want them to remember them as they were, not as they died. They say their good-byes and come up here. Some don't have anyone and some actually have their families come up here for visits."

"I can't believe so many people would come up here to die, without any family around."

"You still can't understand how your brother wouldn't allow you to take care of him."

"No. I don't understand it at all." His fists clenched at his side.

She hoped she was helping him transition. "Maybe after you've been here for a little bit longer, you will, maybe you won't. Everyone handles their disease differently. A lot of soul searching is done to decide what they can or can't deal with. Some give up and die quickly. Others fight."

"I'm glad he wanted to fight, to have extra time here, even though the doctors said there was no hope, but why couldn't we do that together? Why did he have to shut me out?" His brow furrowed and a vein popped out on his temple.

"You know he ended up living an extra thirty-nine days by coming up here than what the doctors said. You read his journal. You know he was as happy and as comfortable as he could be. We have staff and doctors, who know exactly what he needed. As the big brother, you were used to taking care of him, looking out for him, and this time, he decided to do it all on his own, and not consult you."

He spun on her. "What? You think I'm all pissed off that my pride got hurt because he didn't depend on me? Well, maybe it is, but dammit, I could have done all of this for him, and more. Who knew him better than I did? Hell, we could have gone to baseball games like we used to do when we were kids, recreate all those memories, made new ones. *I* could have jumped out of a plane with him, not some stranger."

"That's it, that's exactly it. You knew him best. And yes, you could have done all of that for him, but then you also would have seen him at the end, when he couldn't take care of himself, when half the time he forgot what day it was, if he even noticed the sun was shining. When he was at his weakest."

"He was *my* brother, *my* responsibility."

She stepped closer to him and put her hand on his shoulder and her voice quieted, hoping to make him hear what she had to say. "And he felt you'd done all you could do. He was going to die. That was a fact. Nothing was going to change that. There was no reason to put more responsibility on you. He was trying to make it easier on you."

Ethan looked at her with his hand clenched at his sides and tears threatening to overflow his eyes. "Dammit, he was my brother . . ." His voice broke. "I've lost my only brother."

She'd never been able to let someone grieve and not comfort them. Stepping toward him, she gathered him up in her arms and let his grief flow over her, hoping somehow, someway, she took some of the pain from him. This was so unusual, they'd never had a family member spend so much time up here after their loved one had died. She couldn't put her finger on what it was, but there was something about him that pulled at her. Knowing this wasn't the time to analyze, she simply held him as he was able to finally voice the words she figured he'd kept locked up inside for too long.

Chapter 4

DAY 8

ETHAN-

SAM TOLD ME IT WAS BOUND TO HAPPEN, BUT I DIDN'T BELIEVE HER. I THOUGHT I HAD COME TO TERMS WITH DEATH, BUT TODAY ONE OF THE OTHER GUESTS DIED. I DIDN'T KNOW HIM WELL. HE WAS ALREADY PRETTY BAD WHEN I GOT HERE.

WE HAD A CELEBRATION FOR HIM THIS MORNING. WHEN I WALKED BACK TO MY CABIN, I SAW HIS HANDPRINT ON THE LEGACY WALL AND I SAT DOWN, RIGHT THERE IN THE MIDDLE OF THE PATH AND CRIED LIKE A BABY.

I HID FROM EVERYONE FOR THE REST OF THE DAY.

EVAN

120 DAYS...

Sam's story was still fresh in Ethan's mind the next morning. At that point, he didn't know which was worse, losing both of his parents in one night, without a chance to say good-bye, or Samantha watching both of hers slowly die from cancer. He had to give her credit; she was strong dealing with death every day.

Ethan hated the fact that he'd broken down in front of Sam. He knew it would make her trust him, but he felt too exposed for doing it. And as much as he hated to admit it, he did feel better for getting it all off his chest. For the next couple days, he tried to avoid her as much as possible. Thankfully, they had busy days with a new guest arriving and getting ready for Dolores's birthday party. Why, he wasn't exactly sure; it wasn't like it would make a difference in her life. He didn't know how they managed it, but Noah Matthews, the lead singer for Last Stand, was coming to her party.

Ethan remembered listening to a lot of Last Stand while working in the garage when they first hit it big. They'd been a popular rock band for years and had just recently retired. He remembered Noah and his wife had been in the news not too long ago. There was an international manhunt for a psychopath who was after her. After the sick bastard was found dead, the two of them settled down north of Boston.

He had just finished blowing up the last balloon and raising the net they were resting in. At the correct time, he'd pull the rope and they would fall on the dancers. Dolores had never gone to prom. So for her birthday, they were recreating the event, complete with Noah as the prom king to her queen. Dolores had non-Hodgkin B-cell lymphoma, specifically Primary Pancreatic Lymphoma, a disease so rare only 0.3 percent of people who have the disease have that specific type of it. She came to the lodge after she'd learned it had metastasized. Everyone, her family and those at the resort, knew there wasn't much time left.

Looking around, he saw the decorated tables and streamers hanging from the ceiling. He had no idea what his prom looked like. He'd been one of those 'too cool for school functions' teenagers and he didn't go to his. There was no way he'd be caught dead there. He rolled his eyes, wondering at his choice of words because there he was, somewhere he'd never thought he'd be—prom. Everyone was coming in tuxes and formal dresses, and *everyone* was required to be there. There'd be no way for him to get out of it.

Checking his watch, he knew he had just enough time to get back to his room, change and make it back for the start of the party. He already knew there'd be no way he could be fashionably late and leave early. He was hoping there would be some way he could stick to the shadows and not have to interact with anyone.

He still didn't understand why she did this. Sure, she'd told him about her parents, but could they really have been that well-off that she'd be able to buy this property and remodel it? And what about the upkeep? Surely she had to get the money from somewhere. Evan had left her, along with other charities, some of his money, but Evan had known Ethan wouldn't have needed it or wanted it, so he didn't have an issue with it. He wondered if she was taking money from everyone, how much she could end up with, and what she did with it all. Remembering all those handprints along the wall, she wouldn't need much money from each of them to never have to worry about money again. He was going to find out, one way or another, and not get close to anyone in the process.

120 DAYS...

DAY 9

ETHAN—

TODAY IS A NEW DAY.

ANOTHER SUNRISE.

ANOTHER BEGINNING.

YESTERDAY IS GONE. TODAY WILL BE BETTER.

TODAY, I AM NOT GOING TO DIE.

EVAN

Music blasted through the speakers in the rec center, and almost everyone was on the dance floor singing their hearts out to "YMCA." Ethan stood in the background wondering what he could do next so he wouldn't get suckered into dancing, especially to disco. His rock-and-roll heart shuddered at the thought.

The crowd parted and he saw Dolores dancing with Noah Matthews, acting like crazy teenagers. He did have to smile as he remembered the look on her face when they had pulled her up on stage and announced she was prom queen. And what would prom be without a king? Over the speakers, a male voice started singing "Happy Birthday." Everyone could practically see her start to vibrate with excitement, and when Noah stepped on stage with her, a crown already on his head, she almost collapsed.

He hated to admit it, but it did warm his heart. There was no denying the fact that she was happy, and this was a dream come true for her. Who was he to berate the fact that Samantha wanted to do something good for these people? There had to be some other reason than helping people who were at the end of their life. He knew he had to get close to her. Keeping his distance was only going to make him have to stick around there longer, and he could only stay so long. He needed to get back to his work. Back to where he could make money, the one thing he really knew.

The music slowed and the lights dimmed. He saw her lean body gracefully glide across the floor, moving this way and that to avoid the other dancers as she went over to the bar and took the glass of wine Tracy, one of the kitchen staff, had ready for her. In her midnight blue long dress, she looked like a dream come true herself. Before he knew what he was doing, his feet moved in her direction. When he was ten feet away, her eyes swung toward him and she didn't look away, holding his gaze until he stopped in front of her. Silently, he held out his hand, his heart racing in his chest. As her cool hand slid into his, he could have sworn he heard his brother laugh. Shaking his head to clear it, he tucked her hand into the crook of his arm and escorted her to the dancefloor, past people who could still move to those who were confined to wheelchairs.

Spinning her around, he pulled her back and into his arms and she easily followed his lead, matching him step for step. As a teenager, he would have never danced with a girl, but as an adult, he knew all women loved a man who could dance and sweep them off their feet, and he used the knowledge to his advantage. Part of him didn't want to have to strategize or doubt her tonight; tonight he only wanted her in his arms.

He had to admit, she felt good in his arms. It had been too long since he'd been with a woman, having a dying brother kind of put a damper on things, even if he had disappeared and wouldn't let him help.

120 DAYS...

"Why do you go to all of this trouble? Dolores would have been happy with the prom alone, but to get Noah here, that couldn't have been easy to do."

"Because it's what I do. I make the impossible happen for them." She sighed. "Dolores told me how she'd always loved Last Stand and would listen to their music all the time, it was also no secret she had a crush on Noah. After she was diagnosed, she went through all the treatments, radiation, chemo, surgery. Obviously, there were a lot of days where she felt terrible, and she'd listen to them, every day, every hour. That band and Noah were part of the reason she kept going, even though the doctors said the odds of the treatments working were almost non-existent, she kept fighting."

"You think by doing this you're giving her more time?"

"I don't think it, I know it." She looked over at Dolores. "Look at her, she's so happy. She hasn't been this free or able to move this well in weeks. It's breathed new life into her. Sure, she'll be sore tomorrow, but she'll be oh, so happy; so very, very happy. That makes everything worthwhile."

"How long do you think you can keep this up? You make sure everyone else is taken care of before you take anything for yourself."

"I'll keep this up as long as I'm allowed to. They fight every day. I'll fight harder for them to make sure each day is a treasure for them."

"Who fights for you?"

"I don't need anyone to fight for me."

"We all need someone." The more he thought about it, how she did this on her own, the more it confused him. It would be a lot of work to scam people out of their money, much less by yourself. Everything he'd

• 44 •

seen her do made his protective instincts awaken.

"Says the man who pushes everyone away."

He caught himself before he missed a step. "What makes you say that?"

"Besides the loner vibe coming off you in waves? Maybe it has something to do with how you've been acting the past couple of days since you actually mourned your brother in front of me. Or it might have something to do with the fact that Evan and I spent a lot of time talking."

He looked away from her, over her shoulder, not focusing on anything, his heart sinking, wondering what his brother would have said about him. Part of him knew Evan had always looked up to him, but the other part wondered what he truly felt about him and his lifestyle. It was so different from how they'd grown up. He wondered if the ache in his heart was for the fact that his brother thought he'd pushed him away. Or that his brother had told the woman he allowed to care for him while he was dying that he didn't want anyone in his life.

"People change."

"Yes, they do, Ethan, but sometimes the price to make that happen is just too high."

She slipped from his arms and walked away. He stood in the middle of the dance floor for a moment before turning and leaving the building. No one would miss him and, quite frankly, he couldn't stay there any longer. He hoped by leaving the dance, he could get a few minutes reprieve from all the happiness that was just covering up the pain, which was always just below the surface.

Chapter 5

DAY 15

ETHAN,

YOU WON'T BELIEVE THIS! SAM SET UP A PRIVATE TOUR OF THE SEATTLE SEAHAWKS' FACILITY. IT WAS A LONGER TRIP THAN THEY USUALLY TAKE, BUT SHE KNEW HOW MUCH IT WOULD MEAN TO ME. I WAS ABLE TO GO INTO THE LOCKER ROOM AND DOWN ON THE FIELD. SOME OF THE PLAYERS WERE EVEN THERE. IT WAS SO AWESOME.

I KNOW I SAID I DIDN'T WANT YOU TO SEE ME DYING, BUT I WISH YOU COULD HAVE BEEN THERE.

EVAN

Ethan looked around the rec hall and thought wreck hall would be a better name. Who would have thought a bunch of people living the last days or weeks of their lives would party so hard, or so late? Grabbing a trash bag, he started going around from table to table tossing plates and other garbage away.

When the door opened, he turned and saw Dolores come in. She still wore a huge grin. He nodded at her.

"Oh, I didn't expect anyone would be here yet. I just wanted to have one last look before everything was taken down." She shrugged. "Relive the moment, if you don't mind."

"Of course I don't." He wasn't sure what to say to her so he continued to clean up as she talked.

"It was perfect last night, wasn't it? I still can't believe I met Noah Matthews, *the* Noah Matthews." She spun in a circle with her arms out. "And we danced to everything, even a slow dance together. He was the king to my queen. I want to remember this night for as long as I have left."

Her happy sighs filled the silence. He moved around the room, filling up another garbage bag. When he came around to the stereo, he pushed the button and Last Stand's music filled the room. When Dolores clapped and laughed, he turned and smiled at her. To look at her at that moment, nobody would know her doctors didn't give her much time to live.

Ethan remembered reading Dolores' file after he started. Last Resort wanted all of their employees to know every guest's story. She had been a dancer on Broadway before she retired to Washington State and opened her own dance studio. Then she became sick, but her muscles still remembered, even though most of the time her body was too weak to do the steps she knew by heart. Today she danced like she was on stage in front of thousands of adoring fans, who'd come just to see her. Dancing her solo, she moved around the room, dipping, spinning and kicking gracefully. She used her whole body, and let the music move her.

Ethan leaned back against the wall and watched her move. Evan had always been an athlete, and Ethan wondered if he'd been able to hike during his stay like he'd wanted to, which trails he might have taken. Did he ever throw the ball around with anyone? Did he push his body as much as he could for as long as possible?

So engrossed was he in his thoughts, he didn't notice when she tripped the first time but something must have registered because he pushed away from the wall and narrowed his eyes at her. This time he did notice when her left knee buckled. Everything moved in slow motion as he ran toward her, his heart racing, wondering if he'd be able to catch her in time if she fell.

Skidding to a stop, he was able to grab her and turn so she landed on him instead of the floor. He hardly noticed the pain as it radiated through this body from the hard landing, his attention focused solely on Dolores and the way her eyes were rolling back in her head.

"Dolores . . . come on, honey . . . Dolores . . ." He gently shook her. Not taking his eyes off her, he pulled his phone from his pocket. Quickly dialing Sam, he rocked back and forth with Dolores's head in his lap hoping she'd wake up. "Come on . . . answer . . ." The phone rang on the other end.

"Hey, Ethan," Sam said.

"Sam, we're in the rec hall. Dolores collapsed."

"Is she awake?"

"No. I caught her before she fell, so she didn't hit her head."

"Good. I'm on my way."

"Hurry." He disconnected the phone and turned

his attention back to Dolores. "You have to wake up. You haven't told me what you and Noah talked about yet."

It seemed like an hour but was probably only five minutes before Sam came flying into the rec hall with one of the nurses right behind her. Ethan took a deep breath and pressed his shaking hands to the floor, leaning back on them, glad he wasn't alone anymore. He focused on both women as they worked on Dolores, moving her off his lap and getting her vital signs.

Finally, Sam looked at him. "Thank you for being here for her." She gave him a sad smile. "We've seen this before. Sometimes when we've been able to do something spectacular for someone, they get a little too excited and end up having to rest for a few days. She'll be fine, I'm sure she didn't get any rest last night, and as you can see, she was up and going early."

Ethan cleared his throat. "She was dancing to the music. It was beautiful. I should have stopped her. It was too much."

"No, you were right to let her do what she loves. Every day she goes through her stretches, maybe a few steps here and there, but she hasn't felt the music in her blood in order to dance. This was what she needed. Don't beat yourself up. Besides, she's sassy. If she wanted to dance, there was no way you were going to stop her."

"Yeah . . . well–"

"Ethan, you can't try and protect them from everything. You have to allow them to do what they want, when they want. They don't have much time left. They want to live every single moment of it, really as all of us should without having the doctors put a time limit on it."

"But—"

"We'll talk soon. Right now, we need to get Dolores to her cabin and get her settled." She nodded toward the tables. "Why don't you finish up in here? We'll have time later."

"Yeah, sure." Ethan stood and walked away from them, rage flowing through him. He wanted to punch something. Cancer sucked; all terminal diseases sucked. No one should have to go through this. Grabbing a couple of garbage bags, he went out the back door and down to the dumpster, tossing them in with more force than necessary. He tilted his head back and looked to the bright blue sky, rolling his shoulders, hoping to release some of the tension they held.

He wanted to go back home, to his home, back to the business of making money. The last thing he wanted was to get attached to the people at the ranch, adding more pain to his already grieving soul. For the last ten years or so, he'd purposely lived alone, not spending much time with his brother, allowing him to go on his way, and do his own thing, become his own man. But being truly alone, he didn't know what to do with himself. While he had a heap of money in the bank, he was completely and totally alone, working for next to nothing at a ranch where everyone was dying.

One-hundred-and-twenty days wasn't that long in the scheme of things, but to someone who'd only been given about thirty-five days to live, it was three lifetimes. He wasn't supposed to care. He wasn't supposed to get close. In and out—find out what kind of scam she was pulling, and leave, exposing her so she wouldn't be taking advantage of other unsuspecting dying people.

Walking over to a large rock, he sat down on it and looked out over the buildings and the Legacy Garden.

120 DAYS...

So what if she was running a scam, maybe skimming off the top for her own purposes? He'd been there long enough to know every single guest was well taken care of and no expense was spared, making sure everything they could possibly want was given to them. While the average was one-hundred-and-twenty days, some people only lasted forty, while he knew a few others lasted well over two-hundred days. She never kicked them out, all she did was allow them to stay, and live, in the positive environment she created. Was that so bad?

His mind moved from one thought to another. From Evan, to Sam and Dolores, to Last Resort, to his house and business, then around again and again until finally, he couldn't take it anymore and wanted the physical outlet. Maybe if he worked hard enough, his body would allow his brain to shut off for a while. With long strides, he walked back into the rec hall and began cleaning with a vengeance. Too soon, it was back to normal and guests started wandering in.

The last thing he wanted to do was be around people. Going out the back door again, he weaved his way around to his room. Changing into shorts and running shoes, he strapped his iPhone to his arm and shoved the ear buds in his ears. Cranking Metallica up, he took the trail that went straight up the hill and tried to run as fast as he could away from the feelings overwhelming him.

Ethan stood in the shower with the water going cold, pounding on his head and running down his body. The run hadn't done anything to calm his thoughts. Angry, he flipped the handle to off, grabbed a towel and started drying himself vigorously. The image of Dolores falling down played over and over in his head. Evan and his parents wouldn't leave his thoughts.

Once he was dressed, he looked around his small room. Ethan's mind was still jumbled. He knew there'd be no way he'd be able to stay in this room all night. He'd feel like a caged tiger. His eyes fell on his car keys and he realized what he needed to do. Drive. Get away for a while.

Jumping in his car, he raced down the mountain, not sure if he was running away from or to something. The late afternoon sun hid behind the storm clouds which were rapidly building like his emotions. He'd spent many years moving as far away from the wide-eyed happy child he used to be to the reserved man he had become.

His mind must have been on the past more than he'd realized. As he drove from the resort, he skirted the city, going around until, and as darkness fell, he realized he was driving down the street he grew up on. Finding a parking spot, he pulled over and cut the engine. Glancing up in his rearview mirror, he could make out the front porch of the house he'd lived in before everything changed. Before his parents were killed by a drunk driver. They never had a lot of money, but they had everything they needed, with a little extra for fun things for him and Evan, or to help someone who needed it. His parents were like that, always wanting to help people. They were coming back from visiting Miss Webber who went to their church, who had been sick.

He laid his forehead on the steering wheel. He hadn't been back to his old neighborhood in years. The last time he'd been here, he'd still been young and feeling nostalgic, wishing for something that could never be. Taking a deep breath, he straightened up and put his hand on the door to open it, pausing before actually pulling the handle. His losses gripped him. The agony of being alone in this world a heavy burden on his shoulders. Moving those shoulders to release the tension, he quickly opened the door, and with a sharp slam, closed it then walked across the street to the house where he became who he was.

As the first few cold drops of rain fell on him, he went back to a time when things were perfect. On rainy nights, it seemed they'd always gather together to have a family game night or watch a movie. Something about a storm bringing them all together made him long for those days. He stood there as the rain poured down harder and watched on as the lights went on inside the house, remembering what the living room looked like, with him and his brother goofing around, his parents laughing at them. Even as he got older, he still loved those nights; although, he played it off like he was too cool and they were forcing him to stay in, he'd really loved it.

His eyes glanced up to the window that used to be his bedroom. White walls covered with posters of whatever rock band he was into at the time, he'd always loved music and the bands were forever changing. A student desk in the corner of the room where he'd do his homework or try to figure out what he was going to do after high school and community college. The small bed with a blue comforter where he'd fall asleep every night and never have to worry where the money for rent or food was going to come from. Where he didn't have to worry about his little brother's safety. They were both safe there.

The breath in his chest hitched as he remembered the night the police showed up at their door with the news his parents had been killed. Hours earlier, he'd paid no attention to his mom cooking soup, even when she put a bowl of it down in front of him while he worked hard to finish up his homework. There was a hot piece of ass he'd been hoping to take out later, but he knew he had to finish before he could leave. He still remembered his anger when his father had come home and said he was going to have to stay home to watch Evan, the way his father had gently reminded him that it was their duty to help other people, and how taking a few hours out of their evening wasn't going to make a huge difference either way.

Little did he know, it would change everything.

The tears mixed with the rain as it ran down his cheeks. Ethan remembered the loss, the fear, the guilt, and not knowing what he needed to do. Both his parents were only children, so there were no aunts and uncles to ask for help. He didn't know what arrangements to make or even how to pay for anything. By the time the small amount of life insurance they'd had came through, they'd already lost the house, and the little bit of security the two brothers had left.

Out on the streets and not knowing what to do, Ethan quit college and found a job at a local garage that would work around Evan's school schedule and had a room for rent above it. It wasn't in the best neighborhood so the owner of the garage was happy to have someone above it keeping watch, and he knocked a couple of bucks off the rent, which helped.

The first six months was a blur, working all day then helping Evan with homework, and trying to feed them—cooking wasn't a talent of his. They both had nightmares which kept them up at night. Slowly, they got into a rhythm and started working together. Part of Ethan hated how quickly his little brother had to grow up and the other was glad he'd stepped up. There was so much he had to do and think of to keep a roof over their heads and food in their bellies, not to mention, keeping them safe in a neighborhood where people would take you out for looking at them the wrong way.

One night when Evan was seventeen and out on a date with a girl, Ethan laid there on the lumpy couch, which doubled as his bed, staring at the grease stains above the stove ten feet away, and knew he didn't want to live the rest of his life this way. Day to day. Paycheck to paycheck. His mind started going back over things he'd seen and heard around the neighborhood, things that played to his strengths. Swinging his legs around, he quickly sat up and slid his fingers through his long hair, pushing it back out of his eyes, starting to see clearly for the first time in years.

A few hours before, Evan had told me he was joining the Army. Dad had served and had always been patriotic, instilling in his children a sense of duty and pride for what so many men and woman had sacrificed so they could live free. The thought of joining had briefly passed through Ethan's head, but he knew better. He didn't take orders well. In the end, things worked out as they should have. He would have been in the Army when his parents were killed. Ethan had tried to raise Evan as his parents would have wanted, and apparently, he had since Evan planned to enlist as soon as he graduated from high school.

Evan had told him he would be sending money back to him because he wouldn't need it, and he felt he owned it to Ethan since he'd had to put his life on hold to raise him. Ethan's first thought was to put it in savings for the kid, so when he got out he'd have a nest egg, but he had another idea. He'd pulled open a kitchen drawer, taken out a pen and paper, and started making notes, creating a new budget, a budget that was going to change everything.

It was strange being in that small apartment all by himself after Evan had left, and in a moment of weakness, he'd made the trip back to the house they grew up in and stood in almost the same spot he was standing now, years later. The only difference was the rain, but his emotions were no less calm. He remembered the loneliness coursing through his veins like a virus, and wondering if it would ever go away. Picking up extra hours at the garage helped bring in the additional money he'd needed. Any free hours he had were spent doing research around the edges of the neighborhood, looking at properties and tracking what was selling and for how much. Watching the trends, he was almost ready to take his first gamble. His hands shook at the thought. It was either going to be the best thing he'd ever done, or the worst, but he had to do something. He wasn't going to live the rest of his life above a garage working for someone else.

That was how it all began. His gamble had paid off more than he could've imagined. The trend continued over and over until he purposely moved as far away as he could from that lonely young man in that small apartment above the garage, who'd wondered daily how he was going to pay for Evan's new school clothes, to his own multi-million dollar home. Somewhere along the line, he'd lost the smiling, happy boy he used to be and grew into the hard, distant man he'd become in business and his personal life.

He remembered Evan coming back on leave and being in disbelief of how Ethan was living. They had a good time the first few times he'd visited, and then slowly, over time, they grew apart. They lived such different lives, with Evan being all about the service and Ethan being all about the next sale. Even the phone calls dropped off.

Before Ethan knew it, they were both living their

own lives with barely any contact between them. Until Evan showed up in his office to tell him he was dying.

The weight built up and his knees could no longer hold him up. The pain as they hit the wet sidewalk only added to the emptiness he felt. His head fell forward and his shoulders sagged under the weight of all the lonely, wasted years replaying repeatedly in his head. He wanted to go back and do everything over again, starting from that night at the kitchen table of this very house. He wanted his parents back. He wanted his brother back, but all he had was an aching hole in his heart where they used to live. His hands balled into fists on his saturated jeans, fingernails digging into the palms of his hands. With the tears still falling, he slammed his fists onto the hard concrete, his chest heaving from trying as hard as he could not to scream. He focused his attention on the rain, which was washing away the blood from his hands.

Turning them over, he noticed for the first time how much they were like his dad's. His gentle giant of a father. He'd loved God, his country and his church, always there to give a helping hand. Evan had been like him, which was why he went into the service; he'd wanted to help people. Where did that leave him? Kneeling there in front of his childhood home, he could finally see how far he'd come from what his parents had hoped he'd become. He knew they'd still love him, nothing could have ever changed that, but he wondered what they would have thought of the man he grew up to be. Deep down he knew, they wouldn't like the coldness, the distance.

Blinking, he looked up into the rain at the clouds, looking toward Heaven, wondering if the three of them were together looking down at him and what they were thinking. "I'm sorry," he whispered. "I don't know what to do."

With no one to answer him, he slowly stood and looked at the house one last time. He hoped the family who lived there was happy. He could have bought the place years ago, but he couldn't bear to do it. Part of him never wanted to go back, or set foot inside that door ever again. The other part wanted to run up the steps, throw open the door and call for Mom like he used to as a kid.

He closed his eyes and took a deep breath before turning around and walking back to his car, not looking back. Once he was behind the wheel, he started the engine and cranked up the heat, hoping it would help his body stop shaking from the cold. Putting the car in gear, he headed back out of town and up north, back to Last Resort. The old saying went through his head. *You could never go home again.* And in a sense, it was true. But he knew, this time, he needed to. He needed to remember; remember who he was, what he'd become, and try to figure out where he wanted to go and how his intrigue with Samantha fit into everything.

Sam tried to fool herself as to why she'd stayed in the main house watching the rain on the road coming into Last Resort. They hadn't had rain in a while and it was nice to sit there and enjoy it with a fire burning close by. All the guests were huddled up in their rooms or enjoying games in the rec hall. For once, she didn't have a thousand things to do hanging over her head.

Dolores had slept most of the day, and besides being a little sore, she was ready to get back into the swing of things and had joined the other guests. There was a fierce battle of Monopoly going on that Sam wanted no part of. She was happy to sit there and

120 DAYS...

watch the storm progress. In reality, she was worried about Ethan. This was her resort. She knew everything that went on. She knew when Ethan had gone for a run, when he'd came back, and when he'd left again without a word to anyone.

There was no denying it; she was worried about him. Seeing Dolores collapse had gotten to him more than he wanted to admit. Sam was pretty sure he hadn't fully dealt with his brother's death and that hadn't helped anything. She was beginning to wonder if this really was the best place for him, or maybe it would be best if she let him go to find his own way, not to be surrounded by death every day.

Since she had some time for herself, she finally admitted that every day she specifically searched him out, wanting to spend time with him. She'd had a hard time falling asleep the previous night. His scent still clung to her from their dance together. He wasn't the first man she'd danced with. They held dances every few months and she'd always danced with guests or staff, but Ethan was different. There was no denying his good looks and long lean body. It was the fact that she fit so perfectly in his arms, and how good they felt around her, which concerned her. She hated knowing she was losing the battle and it would only be so long before she fell for him. Getting involved with a staff member wouldn't be good either, even one who was only going to be staying until he felt he'd repaid his debt.

Her thoughts were still going around and around when headlights cut across the night sky. He was home. Jumping up, she ran out to meet him, compelled to find out if he was okay. Pulling the door open, she looked at his face. Normally his expression was hard. But not now. The man before her was broken. Without thinking, she pulled Ethan out and wrapped her arms around him, hoping to infuse him with some of her strength and hope.

Awkwardness suffused her while his arms hung by his side. Finally, his arms came around her waist and rightness settled in her. Cold rain seeping into her clothes, she pulled away and grabbed his hand. "Come on." Quickly, she ducked into his car, shut the engine off and slammed the door. He followed behind her without objection as she jogged down the path to her house.

Once inside, she dropped his hand and went over to the fireplace and knelt, striking a match to the wood which was already there. Within a couple of minutes, the fire was blazing. She watched as he slowly walked over to her. Taking his hand again, Sam pulled him down next her. Once she was sure he was settled, she stood up and walked to the linen closet to grab a couple of towels, draping them around his shoulders first before pulling one around herself.

Going into the kitchen, Sam flipped the switch on the coffee pot and breathed deeply as the aroma filled the space. Taking a couple of cups from the cabinet, she went to the pantry and decided the night called for some cookies. Chocolate chip were her weakness and she always baked them. They never went to waste around her. Placing some on a plate, she poured the coffee and arranged everything on a tray, and headed back into the living room. Still staring into the fire, Ethan trembled, his skin freezing. She'd felt him shaking when she'd hugged him and figured he was soaked to the bone and needed to warm up, from the inside out. She let him sit there and drink his coffee, absently eating the cookies she pushed toward him, waiting for him to arrive at the point where he wanted to talk.

She didn't have to wait long.

120 DAYS...

"When they say you can't go home again, they sure were right." His low voice filled the room.

"Is that where you went?" She gripped her coffee cup wanting nothing more than to reach out to soothe him.

"Yeah . . . Seeing Dolores collapse was too much. It got me thinking about Evan and how I wasn't able to be there for him." He shrugged. "One thing led to another and I had to get out of here. I ended up back at the house. The one we lived in before my parents died. I hadn't been back there in years. In some ways, it hadn't changed; in others, it was completely different."

Evan had already told her about his past and what had happened to his parents, and how Ethan had raised him, but somehow it was completely different hearing the story from his perspective. Her heart had gone out to the little boy Evan had been, so young and losing his parents, and it went out to Ethan, who had just started living his adult life when responsibility had been thrust upon him. Losing a parent was never easy, Lord knows she knew, but somehow, it seemed all the more tragic for them. Especially when years later they had both grown so far apart. And since Evan had died, there would be no going back. They'd never have the chance to reconcile and become brothers again.

As his voice trailed off, she couldn't take it anymore. She put her arm around his shoulders, resting her head on the one closest to her. Feeling a tremor go through him, she knew she couldn't waste any more time; he needed to get warm. Giving him a quick squeeze, she stood, and went to the downstairs bathroom where she turned the shower on as hot as it would go. Running upstairs, she went to the spare room where she kept racks of clothes, which had been donated to the resort. The guests typically lost so much weight during their stay that what they'd showed up in never fit for too long and they needed new clothes to wear. Grabbing some she thought would fit him, she dumped them, along with extra towels, in the bathroom before going back out to him.

"Ethan . . ." She stood in the doorway waiting for him to turn to her. When he did, she continued. "You need to get into some dry clothes. I've started a hot shower for you and left you something to change into while yours dry. Just leave them outside the door before you get into the shower and I'll put them in the dryer for you."

Standing slowly, like a man much older than his years, he walked toward her, pausing when he was next to her and putting his hand on her shoulder. "Thank you."

"It's no problem."

He looked down into her eyes. "Is anyone ever there for you?"

Her heart clenched painfully. "That's not what tonight is about."

"Samantha, if there's one thing I've learned is that eventually, everyone needs someone. You take on everyone else's problems. Someone should be there for you."

She shifted, uncomfortable under his watchful gaze. She was sure he didn't miss much. What she never told anyone was the fact that she'd resigned herself to being alone for however long she was allowed to walk on this earth. Running the resort was all-consuming. It would be difficult to have a normal relationship with anyone. Besides, the last thing she ever wanted was to start relying on Ethan, no matter how attracted she was to him. "Some people are put here to help others. I do as much as I can."

"You could do more if you'd let people in to help *you* once in a while." He patted her shoulder and walked away, gently closing the door behind him.

Sam leaned up against the wall, her head tipping back to rest on it. Ethan didn't realize she'd already let him in further than anyone else. Her stomach knotted, after all of these years someone meant more to her than a friend. She took a deep breath to calm her nerves and hoped she was strong enough to find out what was happening between the two of them.

Ethan woke up with a pounding head and tried to remember what had happened the night before. Six months ago, he'd have to wonder if there was some woman next to him who he'd have to find some way to get rid of before she started seeing hearts and flowers whenever she looked at him. He was, however, sure he was alone. His thoughts turned to the pain from the night before, and Sam. She seemed to be the first thing on his mind every morning. He'd never met anyone as strong, or as stubborn as she was. She gave this place her all, but the longer he was around her, the more he realized she always held a little bit of herself back. He wondered if it was a defense mechanism or something else that kept everyone apart from her. He frowned considering her past, losing both of her parents to cancer, and now running Last Resort, surrounded by death. Knowing each and every person was going to die sooner rather than later, it made sense not to want to get too close to them. Then there was the staff. She'd need to keep separate from them as well, because at some point, they were all going to move on. Not everyone could spend every day for years watching people die.

Glancing over, he saw the clothes she let him borrow from the night before and he frowned. Whose clothes were they? He didn't think she had a boyfriend; frankly, he didn't know when she'd have the time to see anyone. She also didn't seem like the type to screw around for fun. Maybe he'd have to do some more digging. Swinging his legs around to get up out of bed, he stopped himself. Why was he wondering about her? Sure, he came here to dig into her past, figure out how she was scamming people, but it was almost like he was starting to care what happened to her. He rubbed his hands across his face feeling the growth of stubble across the palms of his hands. This place must be getting to him, making him go all soft.

The alarm on his phone went off. Turning it off, he stalked out of the room. It was time to get back to business. Figure out what was going on and get out. He needed to get back to what he was used to, what he knew.

Chapter 6

DAY 17

ETHAN-

I HAVE TO ADMIT IT IS SO BIZARRE HERE. NOW, DON'T GET ALL WORRIED THINKING SOMETHING EVIL IS GOING ON. IT'S THE FACT THAT WE'RE ALL DYING AND YET I DON'T KNOW IF I'VE EVER BEEN CLOSER TO ANYONE SINCE WE WERE LIVING TOGETHER, OR WHEN MOM AND DAD WERE ALIVE. THERE'S THIS BOND THAT BRINGS US ALL TOGETHER AND CLOSER. IT'S SAD IT HAS TO TAKE SOMETHING LIKE THIS TO BRING PEOPLE TOGETHER.

EVAN

"Ethan! Ethan, wait up!" Dolores called from the garden.

He stopped and turned toward her. "What are you doing up? Shouldn't you be resting?"

120 DAYS...

"Shit, I'm dying, not dead. Sam made me rest yesterday. I'm as good as I'm going to be and not about to miss this gorgeous morning." She closed her eyes and took a deep breath. "Smell that? Everything always smells so clean after a good rainstorm. It's like all the bad stuff is washed away, you know?"

"The rain can't wash it all away." He thought back to last night when he was standing outside of his old home in the rain, wishing for everything that went wrong to be washed away and go back to how things used to be.

Dolores moved closer and put her hand on his arm. "The rain is like tears, Ethan. It's a cleansing, a release. Even if you don't realize it, they both help." Squeezing his arm, she gave him a small smile and walked away.

Shaking his head, he started walking toward the main house again. After everything that happened the previous day, he couldn't remember what was on the schedule. Going into the meeting room, he stopped when he saw most of the employees around the table. "Am I late?" He looked down at his watch.

"No," Sam said from the doorway. "You're right on time." Crossing over to the head of the table, she opened up a folder and tapped it. "Today is going to be our first rehearsal for Shakespeare in the park. We have a few guests who've always wanted to act and a few others who are willing to try. The performance is this Saturday, so we are going to be heading down every day from now until then. Since we never know how any guest is going to feel on any given day, we are also going so we can aide them in any way they may need and make sure they fulfill their dream." She handed the sheets out to everyone. "I've assigned one staff member to each guest. We've already talked to the troupe who is performing and worked out parts."

Ethan looked down at his paper. He was paired up with Bobby, a young kid, only about twenty, who had Tri-lateral Retinoblastoma, a rare terminal cancer which targeted the eyes. He tried to remember what he had read in his file, something about being diagnosed with cancer when he was eighteen months old and they hadn't given him eight months to live. His mother, Elizabeth, or Sissy as her family had called her, had already passed away six years earlier from ovarian cancer. He couldn't fathom what it would be like as a parent to fight for your child's life from such an early age. Then to go through your own battle with it when he was still dealing with his. He did the math in his head. Bobby had only been fourteen when his mother died.

Looking up, he saw Sam staring at him. He wondered if his poker face was still as good at it used to be. Seeing her brow furrow as their eyes locked, he knew she couldn't see past what he wanted her to—at least for the time being. Unfortunately, she'd seen him weak twice now. He didn't want to make it a third.

"Good," Sam said. "It's almost time to go. Ethan and I will each be driving a van. Let's collect our partners and get this show on the road." She smiled at her joke and walked over to him. "Here." She waved a set of keys in front of him. "Since I know where we are going, why don't you let me lead the way?"

"Sure."

They stood looking at each other, not knowing what to say for a minute before Sam turned and walked away. There was something about her, something healing and beautiful. He found himself being drawn to her like a moth to flame, which didn't sit well. When she didn't look back at him, he wasn't sure how he felt about it. In the past, women were always falling at his feet, chasing him, but Sam, she walked in the other direction. He began to wonder if the real reason he was still here was because of her. So far, his research hadn't pulled up anything wrong with the resort, and no one would push themselves as hard as she did if she were only in it for the money. Sighing, he followed her out the door and walked to the second van, which was waiting for him.

"Hey there, Bucky!" Patty said and slapped him on the back. "Decided that doing some theater in the park is a little more fun than jumping out of a plane?"

Raising an eyebrow, he nodded. "So much more fun," he said dryly. "Are you going to relax your daredevil ways and come with us?"

"Damn, Skippy, I am. They're even giving me a couple of lines." Her voice shook with excitement and she waved a script in front of his face. "I've been studying the play. I don't want to miss my mark."

"Which play are they doing?"

"Romeo and Juliet." She patted the rose she had tucked behind her ear. "See, I'm *all* ready for it!"

Ethan gave her a small smile. "Looks like we're getting ready to leave. You'd better get a seat." He walked around the van, inspecting the tires before doing the same on the other vehicle. Needing something to keep him occupied and not having to interact with anyone was what he needed. He didn't know all of Shakespeare's work, but that one, full of hope and romance, death, poison, knives and suicide . . . the last thing he wanted was more death added on top of everything else he was dealing with. He shook his head at himself. What was he thinking? He was working at Last Resort, where people went to die. There was no escaping it.

He made sure Bobby was settled in—although, he'd been raised in such a way he could get around just as well as anyone else—and then Ethan finally climbed into his seat and started the van. Putting it in gear, he started the trip down into the city listening to the cheerful chatter going on behind him.

Sam sat on the ground in the park with her back resting against a tree, her tablet on her lap and cell phone in one hand, while she tried to keep an eye on everyone and run her business. The developers were trying to get her land again. It seemed like every couple of years, they'd try to pull something, or offer some outrageous amount to get her to sell. Last time, she'd ended up having to get the police involved since they'd been sabotaging her vehicles and buildings, trying to put her out of business and needing to sell. She didn't want that to happen again. But with the mystery of the abandoned gold mine somewhere on her property, she knew it was never going to go away. She shook her head. Didn't they realize as the owner, she already spent a lot of time and money looking for it? If there was a gold mine, a lot of her worries would be gone. She'd never have to stress about paying bills and the resort could run for as long as it needed without emptying her bank accounts. She sighed, thinking it would be wonderful if they could find a cure for all cancer so her resort would never be needed again. But that was wishful thinking, and not going to happen any time soon, so she had to get back to work.

The weather looked like it was going to be pleasant for the next few days, which was good. They had the rehearsals, and then the show, not to mention a campfire cookout planned for the following night. Quickly taking care of a couple of emails, she noticed how Ethan stayed in the background, never actively involved in anything. Sam also noticed time and again, if anyone needed help, he was right there.

She was under the impression from what Evan had said that Ethan no longer cared about anyone else but himself, and money. He liked to make it, and invest it in developments. Cocking her head to the side, she narrowed her eyes at him, wondering once more why he had applied for the job in the first place. Her first instinct was always to believe what people told her. Most of the time it all worked out, but there were the times people were trying to scam her, and she ended up in shock someone would do that to her.

Tapping her finger on her bottom lip, she considered doing some digging on Mr. Ethan McGregor. Seeing Patty walk across the stage like a queen, she knew she had to. If he was here to find out if she was ripe for the picking and would try to get the land from her, by any means possible, she had to know.

Her eyes darted around. She felt guilty for doing it, but there were so many people who needed the resort and she wasn't going to have it fall into the wrong hands. Pulling up the information Ethan had supplied her with when he'd signed his contract, she skimmed the documents for his general details, her eyes landing on the next of kin section, which was blank. Once she found his company information, she put that into a search engine and quickly looked to see what type of developments they typically dealt in. She was relieved when she didn't recognize the properties he'd bought and sold, and that they were mostly in the city, in areas which were up and coming, not rural developments.

Her finger hovered over the About section of their website, wondering what else it might tell her about Ethan. Before she could talk herself out of it, Sam tapped it and blinked a few times as his image filled the screen. Holy moly, he cleaned up nicely. Who would have thought this man could wear a suit like it was a second skin? A second, very sexy skin.

Closing her eyes, she let out the breath she had been holding. She really didn't want him to be the bad guy. While he might not be the knight in shining armor, the fact that he seemed to tip the scales toward the good side made her feel better.

Ethan had stayed backstage, making sure the guests all knew where they had to go and had everything they needed. It also gave him an opportunity to watch Samantha while she didn't know he was. He had to admit that, even here, in the park on a beautiful day, she was there working for the resort instead of just enjoying the day. He found it ironic that someone who based the resort on living life to the fullest actually was the one working the hardest and had the least amount of time for fun.

Watching as the gentle wind blew her hair around and she absently tucked it behind one ear, he was again amazed at the person she was. The scales were tipping in the direction of her being one of those rare people who'd do everything in her power to help someone else. Just like his parents, but it had been too long since he'd been around people like her, he still wasn't 100 percent sold on her innocence.

After all of the weeks at the resort, he knew she was always up before the sun and went to bed long after it had set. The only time she ever left the resort was on business. This was her whole life. Something pulled at him to go to her, make her see that she needed to take her own advice. Maybe make her see him as more than just an employee.

120 DAYS...

"Don't let the boss catch you napping. She'll dock your pay."

Sam jumped at the smooth voice of the man she'd been investigating as he stood above her. "Ha-ha. Luckily for me, I know she'll give me a break."

"Do you mind?" He pointed next to her without taking his eyes from hers.

"No, not at all." Feeling her cheeks flame with color, she looked down and tried not to gasp as his picture stared back at her. Flipping the tablet over, she hoped he hadn't seen it and glanced at him out of the corner of her eye. He didn't seem smug, like he'd caught her checking him out, but she couldn't be sure and knew her face was getting even redder.

"How's everyone doing back stage?" she asked.

"Great. They're all having a ball trying on costumes and running around with swords."

She heard him chuckle at her gasp and narrowed her eyes at him.

"Not real swords of course. Don't worry, they're fine. Although, they are talking about staging a revolt and making us stop for ice cream before heading back to the resort."

"Well," she chuckled softly, "I think that can be arranged, without the swordplay of course."

He smiled at her. "Of course." Tilting his head to the side, he studied her. "I bet your favorite flavor is vanilla."

"Why do you think that?"

"Because it's a staple, a traditional flavor. Think about it, everyone knows exactly what they are getting with vanilla. It's like the comfort flavor of ice cream."

He smiled at her. "So am I wrong?"

The last thing she wanted to do was to let him know he was right. While she did love other flavors, she could always rely on vanilla, and most of the time picked that flavor. "You'll just have to wait and see."

"I'm sure you won't disappoint." He moved to face her. "Can I ask you a question?"

Looking into his eyes, which changed colors based on the emotions he was feeling, she felt her heart hiccup. Not trusting her voice, she simply nodded.

"We've talked about why you do this, but I was wondering, what do you do for fun? I don't think you've had a night off since I started, what, three weeks ago?"

"This is my life." She shrugged. "I don't need a night off. If you love what you do, you never think about the hours, just the feeling of a job well done."

"Sure, I understand that, completely, I do. But who's to say you don't need to recharge your batteries. You know, fill up your reserve tanks so you can bring something new to what you love."

She raised her eyebrow at him, hoping to bait him. "Or you could look at it as I have everything I need at the resort, so why look elsewhere?"

Leaning in closer to her, he smiled with a gleam in his eye. "Because to fully enjoy life, you need new experiences; otherwise, you stagnate."

She loved to banter, but she could practically feel the heat from his body as he kept getting closer to her and it was starting to distract her. "You don't always have to be on the move for new experiences, after all, still waters run deep." Slowly, she nodded.

"But the depth of one's devotion should not be measured by the amount they sacrifice." He reached over and tucked a strand of her hair behind her ear.

Her stomach fluttered at his soft touch and she licked her lips and saw his eyes darken. She wasn't going to back down. "To work at what you love is never a sacrifice."

His face was no longer teasing, but serious. His brow furrowed and he frowned. "To love without the passion of living is no life."

She thought her heart was going to pound out of her chest. "The passion we bring to our lives is what we make of it," she whispered.

"There should always be room for more, more of everything, but especially passion." His voice shook with emotion.

"I . . . I think I have enough passion in my life." An image of the two of them, wrapped in each other's arms, kissing passionately, flew through her brain.

"Do you?" He leaned in closer to where there was only a few inches separating them, his voice so soft she had to strain to hear it. "Samantha . . . I've watched you. You're like an exotic flower that only blooms once every hundred years." He traced her jaw with a fingertip. "You wait and wait for the petals to open, and when they do, you revel in her beauty, letting her sweet scent envelop you, and wait for the richness of her colors to blind you. You, Samantha, are on the verge of blooming. Are you going to hide away, or are you going to embrace it?"

Her skin tightened as her dizzy brain tried to figure out where he was coming from. "I . . . I don't understand."

"I've never met anyone like you." He picked up her hand, laced his fingers through hers and looked down at them together. "Since I came here, I've been slowly waking up. You've made me wake up. See things I haven't wanted to see in a long time. Made me take a good, long, hard look at myself. For too many years I'd lost track of who I am. Just like you, I'd buried myself in work, but now it's time to start living. I'm saying maybe we should do this together."

She was trying to hide the fact that she was shaking. He was getting too close, making her feel things she'd never thought possible, and she wanted it to stop. Wiggling her fingers, she tried to free her hand from his. "I'm happy for you, Ethan. Really, this is great. Live your life."

"Why don't you live?" he asked roughly.

"What do you mean?" She became still and frowned. "Of course I live. Every damn day."

"No, I think you exist." His voice turned hard. "You take care of everyone else but yourself. You won't let anyone get close to you. Oh, sure, everyone loves you and will do anything you ask, but you only ask for the resort or the guests. You never ask for yourself. What does Samantha want?"

They sat there in silence, eyes locked, neither one of them able to break contact.

"Tell me." He growled and grabbed her upper arms. "Tell me what you want."

"I don't—"

"Stop!" He hauled her up and across his lap, crushing his velvety soft lips to hers. It had been too long since a man had kissed her like there was no tomorrow.

She wanted to fight him. She didn't want this. He was making her feel too much. Since he'd first walked into her office, she'd known there was something different about him; she'd been drawn to him, even if she hadn't admitted it to herself. She always seemed to be looking for him. He'd tended to her, like the delicate flower he'd talked about until she was ready to blossom for only him, and there was no stopping it. Instinctively, she grabbed onto his shoulders, her fingers digging in as she tried to figure out if she wanted to pull away or melt into his kiss, knowing there really was no decision to be made.

When his tongue teased her lips, she couldn't hold out any longer and her lips parted on a sigh. He wasted no time deepening the kiss, his arm snaking around her waist to pull her closer to him. Their bodies pressed together, they forgot where they were until the sound of applause filled the afternoon.

Scooting off his lap, Sam would have tipped over if he hadn't held on to her. Not looking at him, she squirmed out of his grip and quickly stood up, brushing the dirt off her butt before looking up into the happy faces of her guests, still clapping at the two of them. She didn't think she'd ever been more mortified in her life. Every single guest, including the actors in the play, had seen her lose herself to Ethan, in public.

Fighting the urge to dunk her head in the cooler, she decided to get everyone ready to leave. "Okay, everyone, show's over. Let's pack it up and head back."

"We're still stopping for ice cream, right?" Patty smirked at her.

"Yes . . . yes, of course." She had forgotten about the ice cream.

"Excellent. I wouldn't want you to be the only one who got a sweet treat today." Patty laughed, turned and walked back to the stage.

Sam bent down and picked up her things without looking at Ethan, trying to hide how much he affected her, and how embarrassed she was. "I'll meet you at the vans." She needed some distance to figure out what she was going to do. There was no denying the fact that she was attracted to him, but she still wasn't 100 percent sure he didn't have an alternative motive for being at her resort.

"Wait—"

"We'll talk later. Make sure everyone is ready, please." She walked away before he could say anything else. She didn't know what had gotten into her. The guests had completely slipped her mind, and they were the ones who needed her, not her traitorous body, which was still humming from the feel of his against hers. She kept telling herself this over and over with each step.

Ethan shook his head and chuckled to himself when Sam pulled into the first property he'd ever bought. They stopped in front of the ice-cream parlor, which was one of the original stores that were a part of the small strip mall he had turned around for a nice profit.

He wasn't surprised when she was the first one through the door ensuring the employees would know she was paying for everyone, all the while still keeping an eye on her guests and making sure no one was left behind. He made sure he was the last one in the ice-cream parlor, hoping he'd be able to talk to her, as soon as possible. He was going to make sure she wasn't wriggling off the hook. She'd melted into him so sweetly and he wanted another taste of her.

When she only glanced at him briefly out of the corner of her eye, he knew getting her to open up again wasn't going to be easy. A grin spread across his face when she ordered a vanilla cone. Leaning down, he whispered in her ear. "Ahhh, it would seem I was right. Vanilla is your favorite." He didn't move when her head whipped around and her eyes locked with his.

Sam didn't say anything to him. All she did was narrow her eyes before she spoke up. "Excuse me, can I change that to raspberry?"

"Sure thing, miss."

"That doesn't count," he said.

"Sure it does. I only ordered vanilla because that's the thought you put into my head. If I hadn't been distracted, I would have looked at their selection and chosen something else." She tipped her chin up, daring him to challenge her.

Grinning down at her, he couldn't help but ask, "And why were you distracted?"

Sam raised an eyebrow at him. "Well, let's see . . ." She started ticking items off on her fingers. "I run a guest resort for the terminally ill. We've been in the city for hours, away from said resort, and now everyone wanted to stop for ice cream. I need to make sure we are back at a specified time since some of the guests need to take medication. I need to make sure everyone is settled in and everything is set up for tomorrow. Then once that is done, I need to go over the financial statements for last month. Then maybe I can curl up and read for fifteen minutes before I have to go bed. And that, Mr. McGregor, is if I haven't forgotten anything or if there isn't a new emergency waiting for me when we get back."

"You did forget one thing," he baited her.

"Really, and what is that?" She crossed her arms across her chest and moved away from him, resting against the counter.

Following her retreat, he leaned in and rested a hand on the counter next to her hip. "The kiss we shared."

"Oh, that." She waved her hand to the side.

"Yes, *that*, Ms. Truman." He slowly moved in closer, his voice getting quieter with each word, not breaking eye contact. "That completely amazing, 'touched your soul' kiss we shared in the park." He closed his eyes and breathed in her scent as he nuzzled her neck. "The kiss I can't get out of my head." He sighed against the curve of her shoulder. "The kiss I can't wait to repeat."

She shivered. He didn't pull away as he waited for her next move.

"I can't . . ." she spoke so quietly he had to strain to hear her, even though her lips were only an inch from his ear.

"Yes, we can." He tried to put all the conviction he had behind those three little words. There was something about her that pulled at him. Made him want to be the man he was meant to be before his parents were killed and everything changed. "Don't shut me out. Let me be there for you."

When her head tipped toward his, he hoped his words and actions were getting through to her. He may not know what was going to happen, where he was going to end up, but at that moment, he wanted to be with her, to help her. He didn't want to believe she was scamming people, but he was also going to make sure if she was, she'd never see what was coming and he'd take her down.

"I can't deal with this right now." Her soft voice shook in his ear.

"Ma'am?" A young voice called from across the counter. "Your ice cream . . ."

"Yes, sorry."

As soon as she pulled away from him, he felt the loss of her. He knew it was time to retreat and reevaluate his plan. The odds of her running a scam were so low, and the odds of him being attracted to her were sky-high. When she walked over to the cash register, he turned and walked back out to the vehicles to make sure everything was ready as soon as they were all finished with their treats.

For a man who had spent so many years alone, not worrying about anyone else, he was going out of his way to make sure others were happy. He climbed up in the van's driver's seat and sat there in complete silence. Typically, the vans were filled with talk and laughter, everyone making the most of what little time they had left. The quiet was so different. With no chatter to take his mind off everything, he didn't like how his thoughts started racing about Evan, the resort, and what he wanted for his future. That was something he hadn't considered in years. His plan had always been to make as much money as possible and never get involved with anyone. It seemed everything was changing. He still checked his email every day, but he wasn't tracking the trends anymore, or actively pursuing any developments. Granted, he couldn't spend all the money he had, even if he tried, but that didn't make the thrill of the chase any less.

His breath hitched. Could that be it? Samantha was so different from any other woman he'd been around. Maybe something as simple as the fact that she wasn't falling at his feet to be his girlfriend was what was making her so attractive. Maybe after he had her, all these feelings he was having would go away.

With that thought in mind, he had to decide if he was going to continue on the track he was on, or if he was going to step back and let things stand.

Chapter 7

DAY 18

ETHAN—

TONIGHT WAS CAMPFIRE NIGHT. WE ALL SAT AROUND AND TOLD STORIES THAT MEANT SOMETHING TO US. I TOLD THE STORY ABOUT THE TIME OUR PARENTS TOOK US CAMPING, OR TRIED TO ANYWAY. AFTER ONE NIGHT, WE ENDED UP IN A ROOM AT THE CLOSEST MOTEL. MOM SAID SHE WASN'T MADE TO SLEEP ON THE GROUND WITH THE BUGS. REMEMBER HOW FROM THEN ON, EVERY TIME WE STAYED AT A MOTEL, WE CALLED IT CAMPING?

EVAN

The next day, Sam was too busy to think about the kiss from the day before or what it meant. She was in the main kitchen making sure they had everything they needed for the campfire. Every few weeks, depending on what was going on and the amount of guests they had, they would plan a campfire where everyone would sit around and tell stories that held significance to them, about growing up, family or the people who meant something to them. They could talk about whatever was on their mind that day, what they wanted to share. She made sure each story was recorded and preserved for the future. She never knew which relatives would want something from their loved one after they'd passed. Sam kept these precious stories safe for the future.

She liked to think it wasn't only for the family members. It was also for the future of the human race. In the past, people would write letters to each other, something that documented what people were feeling or what experiences they had. With technology came the lack of personalization and historical facts. Maybe one day, these stories would tell a future generation what life was like.

Arranging everything on the trays, she placed them on the cart and went to her office to check on the waiting list. It was a sad fact that the list was always changing. Either people wanted to come, or they didn't make it long enough to stay. Once she'd updated her information, she closed down her computer for the night and went to set everything up around the fire.

It hadn't been hard to stay away from Ethan. She'd been so busy; but last night, while she laid in bed alone staring up at the ceiling, she longed for another kiss. Strange how something so simple, that some people did every day, and often, meant so much to her. Before her parents had gotten so sick, she'd been in a relationship, one which hadn't been strong enough to support her and understand her need to be there for her parents. Afterwards, the grief had been too much and then she'd started Last Resort. There hadn't been any time for romance, and in the long run, that worked for her.

If she was being honest with herself, she knew Ethan wasn't going to stay at the ranch forever. Why would he? He had his business to run and Last Chance was vastly different from where he spent all of his time, not to mention the difference in the types of people. She knew it would be better if she forgot any romantic fantasies she may have started to imagine between them.

Walking back into the kitchen, she frowned when her cart, which held everything for the campfire, was missing. Looking around, she told herself she wasn't going crazy; she had left it right there. She glanced out the window and saw Ethan taking the cart up to the site, his broad shoulders filling the light jacket he had on. It was going to be a chilly night, which worked out perfectly. She hated to admit it, but she'd gotten used to Ethan doing a little something for her each and every day. He was taking it seriously, the fact that he thought she needed someone to make her life easier. It didn't make getting used to the knowledge he'd be leaving her any easier, though. Making sure she didn't forget anything, she closed the door behind her and enjoyed the crisp air as she walked up the path to the campfire.

The fire had already been lit and a pile of wood lay nearby, the smoky smell already permeating the air as the flames flickered as dusk fell. The guests started arriving and soon enough, everyone had a seat. She wasn't sure how it happened, but Ethan was sitting next to her, a serious expression on his face as he nodded to her. They still hadn't spoken a word.

She tried to block out his presence next to her, but

it was impossible. His scent was all around her and the heat from his body reached out toward hers, teasing her to move closer. It took all her strength to ignore his pull.

They always spent time cooking hot dogs over the open flame, and of course, s'mores. Depending on the guest's talents, sometimes they'd sing, other times they might tell ghost stories, but there would always be laughter before things turned serious and they started videotaping the personal stories.

"One of the hardest things I've ever done," said Patty, "was telling my daughter I had cancer, and when things got too bad, I was coming here. See I couldn't have kids. We adopted Erika when she was a baby and she was by far, the best thing that ever happened to me. She was the constant in my life. Her father and I split when she was two, so it was just the two of us against the world. Music and books had always been deep in my soul and I wanted to make sure she had the same love as I did for my two passions, and she did. We always had music on and I'd encourage her to sing. She has an amazing voice. She's my angel. There's an old Helen Reddy song, "You and Me Against the World," that was us. We traveled the world together, both in books and in real life. We'd always try to find the best Chinese restaurant wherever we went." She laughed. "And some of them, oh my, they were so terrible. But this one place, The Makaha, we found that one when we went to Boston, I'm still thinking about that food." She paused for a moment. "Now, don't get me wrong, I miss the rest of my family something fierce, my sister, Barb, and her husband, Sten, but I know they're helping my baby girl. I was able to say everything I needed to them, how much I loved them and would always be with them. My daughter has her own personal guardian angel looking over her once I'm gone. There's no way anyone is going to hurt my baby girl, not if I have anything to say about it."

Sam took a tissue out of her pocket and wiped at her eyes. Patty had told the same story at every campfire she'd been to since she arrived. She missed her daughter so badly and wanted to hang on to that love for as long as possible.

Thomas McClain, or Tommy to his friends here, was next. He had colon cancer and was fading fast. This was going to be his last campfire. "Kids, the best and worst thing that could ever happen to you. The best, that's the easy stuff, to love them unconditionally, that easy. The worst part, the hard part is knowing you're going to fail them. Some way, somehow you're not going to be good enough for them. All I could do is try the best I could." He shook his head and laughed humorlessly. "You know my kid, he got me sober. When I think back to what I put him through when he was so young, it kills me. When I was drinking so bad, I'd black out on him, but that kid, Derrick, is stronger than I ever was. I used to take him on gigs. I remember he loved them. Sat there like a good boy, all quiet so as to not cause trouble for me, and he really listened. You know, I'd like to think that's what makes him such a great narrator, by listening through life he can make the voices from the books come alive when he records them. I'd like to think I'm the reason he's pursuing his dreams, so that even when I'm gone, a bit of me still remains."

"Up to this point I have never let the Hodgkin's disease slow me down," Edward Willbanks said. "Being in the Navy, especially in Vietnam, I always worked hard and played hard. Those damn doctor's didn't give me much of a chance, but I showed them. Coming up on ten years since I was first diagnosed.

120 DAYS...

My wife and two girls are so important to me. No matter how hard or long I worked before I was diagnosed, to how crappy I felt after the chemo treatments, I always made time for my girls. But after they told me about the Hodgkin's, I knew I had to fight. Tabitha was only six, and I wanted to make more memories with them. In a way, I fought so hard because of them, because of my love of them."

"Most people don't realize I should have died before I was three," Bobby said. "The doctors said I wouldn't make it, but my parents, especially my mom, wouldn't allow that to happen. They did everything they could, tried every treatment, and here I am, still alive. My eyes are gone, but my mom never thought I was handicapped because I couldn't see. She made sure I had what every other child had. Even glasses. I was in grade school and the school nurse had no idea I was blind. I was just like everyone else. She sent a note home saying I needed an eye exam, and then I decided I wanted to wear glasses, even though I didn't need them, and she got them for me. Somehow, I got through my mom's death from cancer when I was fourteen. My dad and I were close by that point, and I had my aunt and uncle. Soon after, I went back to Duke for more treatments, the cancer was back. But again, they worked their magic and I was fine. Until about six months ago. I knew what it was, and the doctor's confirmed it, but this time, it was too far gone. My aunt planned my twentieth birthday party early, invited friends and family, who came. I took the time to make sure I said good-bye to each of them. I know what happened with my mom, what everyone had done for me all my life. This time, I couldn't ask them to watch me die. Have the people who mean so much to me, my dad, aunt and uncle, watch a child die, so I came here, knowing the next time I *see* them, I'll really be able to."

"I was very lucky," said Dolores. "Grew up in Bayside New York, the neighborhood was full of second-generation immigrants, and you know what that means? I was exposed to all these different cultures. I loved it. I thrived in that environment. I met the love of my life when I was still in high school and we were married fifteen days after I turned eighteen. My pride and joy? Bar none, my four kids. My job, my dancing might have been my passion, but my kids, and grandkids, well, that is what makes everything worth it; all the long hours, sacrifices, those are easy when you have the love of your children. I tried to instill in them how important family is and to respect everyone, even if they were from a different culture and to work hard. My legacy lives on with them."

"I have to say, Sam, you've got a great place here," Bruce said. "You've made it possible for this old man to go on living, just like I would at home. I'm able to play basketball here. In fact,"—he nodded toward Ethan—"I'm pretty sure I've kicked that whippersnapper in a few games. You've taken me down into the surrounding towns so I can find my antique treasures to restore, and you've proudly put them around the resort. I know I'm from an older generation, but for us, it's all about working hard, being responsible, doing the right thing, being there for your family and praying. I might be old and dying of cancer, but you let me do all of that, and I'm rightfully grateful, ma'am."

Sam always made sure her pockets were full of tissues for these nights, and that night was no different. When Ethan put his arm around her and pulled her close to him, she wanted to crawl up on his lap and let all of her defenses down, cry like a baby for all the pain they were in, but she wouldn't allow

120 DAYS...

herself to be weak.

"You all know my story. I make sure I share it with each and everyone one of you because it matters, my parents mattered, and you matter. Every night before I go to bed, I pray as hard as I can that they will find a cure for cancer and I'm not needed anymore. Growing up as an only child is both a blessing and a curse. It did make me more independent, since there wasn't a sibling to rely on, but it was also lonely. On the other hand, I had my parent's full attention. I never had to compete for it. The three of us were always together in this crazy thing we call life." Sam gave a small laugh. "My parents passed down to me more than just genetics. They also taught me right from wrong, to be a good person, to drive, really there's so much more. I could go on, but instead, I'll leave you with a funny story. My dad taught me how to drive because my mom knew he was going to end up being better at it than her. So, there was this huge hill leading out of where we lived. I always loved to ride down that hill on my bike. I love the wind in my hair. Anyway, we pulled around the corner and he turned to me and said, 'I'm going to do this so you never do, and don't tell your mother.' He punched the accelerator and he caught air in the car going over that hill. I'm pretty sure we looked at each other when we were airborne and grinned, but I could be remembering wrong; it was a while ago. Then we came back down with a bounce and he continued to drive me wherever we were going. I can honestly say, I never jumped that hill. I didn't need to since my dad did it for me. That's what family is all about, taking that hill for the other person." Sam looked over at Ethan.

"You know," Ethan began, "I'm all alone in this world now, just like Sam. But I have to admit, she amazes me." He kept his arm around her as he spoke.

"What she's built here, it's more than what the average person would think it was. You all spoke of it in one way or another with your stories, how important family is. Well, Sam, is alone in this world and wanted to do something to help others. In essence, she's created her own family here with each of you. So while you all may have decided to die away from your family, it must be comforting to know this new family you're a part of is there for you, just as much as the other one you grew up with."

Sam had a lot of experience holding back the tears, only letting a little out in front of other people. Her dad had always said, 'Tears never helped anything,' and she wanted to be strong for everyone. But hearing Ethan's words, she couldn't hold them in. Tears streamed down her face. He understood, he completely understood what she was doing here and how important it was.

When Ethan finished his story, there was silence. Everyone had a chance to speak. There wasn't going to be any more stories that night. Sam looked around at everyone and tried hard not to think about the fact that the next time they had the campfire not everyone who was seated around the fire would be here. This was always the hardest for her, thinking of the future and these wonderful people who would no longer be with them. She tried to focus on the fact she was helping them. They were living the last of their days the best way they could, enjoying experiences they never thought they'd be able to. She knew that should count for something.

Slowly, guests started leaving, the staff helping the ones who needed it. Before long, it was only Sam and Ethan left. With her legs propped up on the log she was sitting on, she rested her chin on her knees and wrapped her arms around her legs, staring into the dying fire. These nights always made her nostalgic for her younger years.

"Why don't you go home? I'll make sure the fire is out and everything is back in the kitchen," Ethan said, stretching his legs out in front of him.

"It'll go quicker if we work together." She started to move to get up, but his hand on her shoulder stopped her. Sam looked back over it at him.

"Samantha, please, let me do this one little thing for you."

"You do things for me all the time."

"Yes, you let me help, as an employee. This is something I want to do for you, as a friend."

"Is that what we are?" It took everything she had to keep her voice level.

"You've made an unbelievable difference in my life. I'd like to think I'm a better man for meeting you. I know I still have a long way to go. You have to understand this is all so new to me. For the first time since Evan was seventeen, I don't know what comes next."

"That's the thing, Ethan, none of us ever really know what comes next. You can fool yourself into thinking you do, or can control it, but everything can change in a moment, and nothing will ever be the same." She stood up and kept her back to him. "You know, maybe I will take you up on the offer to finish cleaning up. I'll see you tomorrow."

"Sam, wait . . ."

Without turning, she spoke, "No Ethan, it's been a long day. Please, just let me go."

She didn't hear him come up behind her and jumped when he sighed right behind her. "I will . . . for now." He rubbed her upper arms, and gently tugged her back to him and kissed the top of her head. "Sleep well."

Because she wanted to sink into him and soak up his strength, she purposely pulled away. "You too." She put one foot in front of the other and walked away from him. The further she moved away, the worse she felt. Blinking back tears, she looked up at the full moon shining down on her. She wondered what life had planned for her. How come when she finally had everything figured out, Ethan came into her life, encouraging her to dream of things she could never have?

Chapter 8

DAY 19

ETHAN—

EVERYONE'S STORIES WEIGHED HEAVILY ON MY MIND LAST NIGHT AND I DIDN'T GET MUCH SLEEP. EVERYONE TALKED ABOUT FAMILY, AND I THOUGHT OF YOU. I WISH THINGS COULD HAVE BEEN DIFFERENT. THAT MOM AND DAD WEREN'T KILLED THAT NIGHT. DO YOU EVER WONDER WHAT COULD HAVE BEEN?

I FEEL ITCHY IN MY SKIN TODAY. I'VE KEPT UP WITH MY RUNS AND WORKOUTS, GRANTED, I'M TAKING IT SLOWER THAN I USED TO SINCE THE LAST THING I NEED IS TO HURT MYSELF. BUT TODAY I PUSHED MYSELF. I NEEDED TO BE PHYSICALLY EXHAUSTED SO I COULD SLEEP.

EVAN

Ethan spent the night tossing and turning thinking about Sam and their conversation. Throwing the covers off him, he sighed in defeat. It was the first time a woman affected him. Even in high school he hadn't second guessed himself, but Sam brought that out in him. Stepping into the shower, he let the cold water beat over his head, hoping it would clear the cobwebs, which seemed to be multiplying by the minute.

The schedule said he was off for the day, so he stalked toward one of the unused outbuildings he knew Sam had been talking about turning into a gym, some place for the guests to stretch and move. He was hoping he'd be able to work so hard, he'd drop into bed and not open his eyes until the following morning.

He should have known better than to yank the door open with such force, but he hadn't been thinking about it until dust and who knew what else swirled around and blew into his face. "Dammit," he sputtered as he quickly closed his eyes and tried not to breathe in. He spun around when he heard laughter.

"Ha, boy. Might want to slow down there. You don't always need to go barging in." Phil, one of the nurses continued to laugh as he walked by.

"Yeah, thanks." Ethan waved after him. "I'll try to remember that."

That time he was able to ignore the other man as he walked into the large shed and looked around at the old equipment, which was surprisingly somewhat organized. He walked over to the first piece and noticed it would have been used when this was a working ranch. Getting down on his hands and knees, he looked under it trying to figure out exactly what it was and if it looked as good underneath. His mechanics mind whirled with the possibilities on what he could do with the different pieces of equipment, and their different usages. Even if it was just something she could just put somewhere so guests could use it as a place to sit and relax, something different, which tied the new and old purpose of the land together.

Pulling his phone out, he started taking notes on the different equipment and what he would need to either fix it, or get it ready to see if Sam wanted to sell it off for a profit. There was also a lot of crap that could just be thrown out. Having a good idea on what was in the barn, he went over to the garage searching for garbage cans and cleaning supplies. Dumping everything he needed into a can, he put it on a cart and started back toward the shed.

"What's your hurry?" the raspy voice of Edward Willbanks said from the porch of his room. "Racing around so you miss the little things does more harm than good."

Because of the Hodgkin's disease and emphysema, Edward moved slowly. It was a joke he used all the time because before the disease, he was always running around between work and family, never taking the time to sit back and enjoy the day.

Ethan slowed down. "I've got something I need to accomplish today. Sometimes I need the physical labor to calm the mind."

Nodding, Edward smiled at him. "I wonder why you need the physical labor." He held a hand up to stop Ethan from speaking. "Now, son, don't get your pants in a wad. We've all been there; sometimes that's all you can do. Go on now, try to calm your mind."

"Yeah, thanks . . ." Ethan turned and continued walking to the shed. The last thing he wanted was everyone analyzing why he was there and what he was doing. Of course, that brought Sam back into his mind and how soul deep, he felt he was changing. He wondered where she fit into everything.

120 DAYS...

Hours later, Ethan stepped outside and squinted up at the location of the sun, which was higher in the sky than he thought it should have been. Rolling his shoulders, he tried to release the tension which had built up in them. The trash pile right outside the door was getting so large he was going to have to start moving it somewhere else if he wasn't going to end up trapped in there.

"Here," a soft voice called from behind him. "Phil said you were working over here and could probably use some water and maybe something to eat by now."

"Thanks, Tracy," Ethan said to the young cook. "You didn't have to come all the way out here to deliver it to me."

"It's no problem. I've finished making lunch." She looked around at the junk. "Exactly what *are* you doing?"

"Sam wants to turn this place into a gym for the guests. I decided today would be a good day to start on it."

"Isn't it your day off?" Tracy narrowed her eyes at him.

"Yes, but I didn't have anything else to do, so I figured I might as well start on it."

"That's all fine and dandy, but you don't want to miss out on life while you're so focused on work. You should use your day off to do something you want to do."

"But this is what I wanted to do."

She looked at him for a moment, tilting her head to the side studying him. "Are you sure?" She didn't wait for him to answer, but turned around and left him standing there, the condensation from the water bottle dripping down his hand while he thought about what she'd said, what everyone had been saying to him.

Was this really what he wanted to be doing? Why was he working so hard, so focused on this project that he felt like if he didn't get it done that day, it would never be done.

No, he thought, *this isn't what I want to be doing today. What I really want is an answer on why Sam brushed me off last night, why she wouldn't take the time to talk to me.*

Ripping the cap off the water, he chugged it down before tossing it in the garbage can. Using the back of his hand, he wiped off his mouth as he stalked toward the main house where Sam could usually be found that time of day. He didn't care if it was during business hours. He wanted answers and wasn't going to settle for anything less than her honesty.

He barged into her office without knocking and quickly turned and slammed the door shut when she wasn't in there. The kitchen was also empty, along with the dining and living rooms. He stood for a moment trying to think of where she could be when he heard soft voices coming from what they called the nurse's command center. Snapping his fingers, he started off in that direction knowing someone there would know where she was.

"Where's Sam?" he demanded when the staff, who were meeting in there, turned to look at him with wide eyes.

"Right here, Ethan. I'm sorry, I'm not sure what you need, but I don't have time right now." She brushed past him, walked down the hall and out the door without a backward glance.

His legs didn't respond right away. It took him a minute before he started to follow her. There was no way she'd brushed him off, again, for the second time

120 DAYS...

in less than twenty-four hours. His blood started to boil. Where did she get off treating him like that? He'd spent all morning trying to make her dream a better place yet she couldn't spare a few moments to talk to him.

Pushing the door open, he didn't care if it slammed shut behind him. His eyes were focused on the backside of the woman he wanted answers from. It didn't take him long to catch up to her and when he did, he raced around to stop in front of her. "Listen here, lady—"

"No, you listen, Ethan. I don't know what the hell your problem is today, but you need to go back to wherever you've been most of the day. I don't have time to deal with you."

"You're going to make the time. We've got too much to—"

"Stop, just stop, Ethan." Her voice wavered and tears filled her eyes. "Please stop."

"Samantha, what is it? What's wrong?"

"It's Patty. She only has hours left . . ."

He felt like someone had kicked him in the gut. He stared at her as he tried to catch his breath. "No, she was fine yesterday morning."

She shook her head. "Sometimes that happens. They are fine one minute, the next, they collapse and aren't going to make it."

"What can I do?" This wasn't the first death to have happened since he'd been there, but he'd gotten to know Patty. She also arrived here the same day as Evan, so her looming death felt different.

"There's nothing you can do." She turned from him and started to walk to Patty's cabin.

"Please," he whispered. "Let me go with you."

Sam stopped and looked back at him over her shoulder. "Are you sure? This isn't going to be easy?"

"I feel like I have to."

Nodding, she held her hand out to him. As her cold hand slipped into his, he was thankful she was going to be with him during this. He'd never seen someone die before; he had a sinking suspicion in the pit of his stomach that he wasn't ever going to forget the moment.

Wariness seeped heavily into Sam's being. It had been a long day. Soon after leaving Ethan the night before, she'd received the phone call about Patty. They all knew it was coming, but it still took her by surprise.

Patty was still coherent when she arrived, but it hadn't lasted long. After that, she'd slipped in and out of consciousness, sometimes her body convulsing from the pain, other times she'd lay so still they had to check the machines to see if she had passed.

When Ethan had said he wanted to help her, she wasn't sure if it was going to be a good idea to have him there. She knew the connection between Patty, Ethan and Evan. Death was never easy, and Patty's would be hard for him, but she was surprised at how well he was doing. She noticed he always seemed to pick things up quickly, and that night was no exception. He was there getting anything anyone needed, lending his quiet support.

He was the first one there with cool water for Sam, so she could bathe Patty's face if she was hot, and the first to offer a blanket, which had been warmed, if Patty started to shake from the cold. She had to admit, he was helpful, especially since she was so exhausted.

Sadly, Sam had been through so many of these. She

120 DAYS...

knew when it was almost time. Leaning in close, she whispered in Patty's ear. "It's time, lovely lady. Let go and spread those wings. It's time for you to fly." She kissed her cheek. "Godspeed."

Ethan came up behind her and placed his hand on Sam's shoulder, gently rubbing it and leaned down to be closer to Patty. "Hey, you think they'll have skydiving in Heaven?" His chuckle came out sounding off. "Can you . . . can you say hi to Evan for me?" He took a deep breath and squeezed her shoulder harder.

It didn't take long before Patty took her last breath. Ethan stayed with Sam while she waited for the coroner to come. When they walked out into the cold night air, it seemed natural they both should head up to her house together, hand in hand.

Chapter 9

DAY 21

ETHAN-

SOME OF US WERE TALKING TODAY AND WE ALL REALIZED NONE OF US HAVE GOTTEN FALLING DOWN DRUNK SINCE RIGHT AFTER WE WERE DIAGNOSED, SOME HAVEN'T EVEN WAY BEFORE THAT. SAM'S HOOKING US UP WITH SOME GOOD STUFF, AND HAS EVEN ORGANIZED DESIGNATED DRIVERS FOR THOSE IN THE WHEELCHAIRS. WE'RE GOING TO TIE ONE ON TONIGHT.

WISH ME LUCK.

EVAN

"To Patty." Sam lifted her glass of scotch high and clinked it to Ethan's.

"To Patty." He took a long, thoughtful drink. "Did

you know I talked to Patty?" Ethan slurred as he waved his glass of scotch toward Sam. "I did. She knew my brother.... Yeah... he died too..."

Sam's head tilted to the side and she closed one eye to look at him, her vision blurring due to the amount of alcohol she'd consumed. "One-hundred-and-fifteen days, that's how long she was here, just under average. She would have hated that, being considered anything average."

"It's not going to be the same, going to the field, to jump out of a plane." He looked up. "I'm going to expect to hear her laugh as she gets closer to the ground. Did you know she was always laughing? Every single jump, she was so happy."

"She was." Sam couldn't hold back anymore and the tears started flowing as she paid her respects to Patty. "Sorry . . . I always . . . do this . . ." She hiccupped. "Cry, thirty minutes, no more, no less. Get it out, move on."

"How can you do that?"

"Practice." She swayed. "I can't do more. It breaks me too much."

His brow furrowed as he tried to sync up his swaying to hers. "Then why?"

"Because . . . they deserve more . . . more than pity . . . more than dying in some clinical setting . . . more than . . . so much more."

"Doesn't it hurt all the time?"

"Oh, it kills me. Every. Single. Time. Every. Day."

"How long can you do this?"

"As long as I'm allowed to."

"Huh?"

She tried to point to the ceiling. "It's not in my hands how long. He has a plan. I try to do my best."

"Come here." He snaked his arm around her and pulled her close to him. "You're too far away."

"It is a big couch." She nodded.

"Too big." He nuzzled her ear. "Why won't you let me taste your lips? You fill my mind. I can't get you out."

"Who's stopping you?"

"Was someone stopping me?" he asked.

"I think you were."

"Well, why would I do that?" He tried to tilt his head and ended up falling back against the couch. "Here." Attempting to lean forward to put his drink on the table, he couldn't reach it, so he settled for setting it down on the floor. "Now yours." It took a couple of tries before he got a good grip on the glass and set it next to his. "There. Now, where was I?"

"Not kissing me?"

"Wait, what? You don't want me to kiss you?"

"No, I do, but you weren't."

"Oh, I should fix that."

"You should."

They stared at each other, Sam didn't know if her body was responding to him, or if it was the amount of alcohol she'd consumed that made her body feel alive as it was pressed up against his.

He leaned down and his lips softly slid back and forth against hers. She turned a little bit more to get closer and wrapped her arms around him, enjoying the feeling of his hands moving over her back. "Don't stop," she whispered.

"I wasn't going to." Pulling her closer to him, he leaned back, laying down on the couch with her on top of him.

120 DAYS...

She moaned when he deepened the kiss, relaxing into him. At that point, she wasn't sure if she had any bones. When she was with him, she felt like she was home. There was nowhere else she wanted to be.

His hand slipped around to her hip and she couldn't control herself. It was the one tickle spot she couldn't turn off. Giggling, she wiggled and they both ended up rolling off the couch, landing hard on the floor.

Glancing up at him through her hair, she laughed harder at the pained expression on his face. "Sorry . . . so sorry . . . ticklish . . ."

"Yeah." He rubbed the side of his head where he'd hit it on the ground. "I kind I've found that out."

She tried to stop laughing but couldn't. When she saw his lips twitch, she laughed harder. They relaxed, laughing until they both ended up falling asleep, together, where they had tumbled to.

Chapter 10

DAY 22

ETHAN—

WHY? WHY DID I GET SO DRUNK? YEAH, I DON'T RECOMMEND IT. YOU'RE OLDER THAN ME, AND I SURE COULDN'T HANDLE IT LIKE I USED TO. EVERYTHING HURTS. YOU'LL END UP OUT OF COMMISSION FOR A WEEK. FOR ONCE, LISTEN TO ME. DON'T DO IT.

EVAN

Ethan groaned and his hands flew to his head right away. He rolled over and curled up in a ball on the hard floor. The last thing he wanted to do was move again, or make a sound. As fast as his sluggish brain would work, he tried to figure out where he was and why his whole body hurt so badly. Slowly, it all came back. He had been working out in the shed and getting angrier with every passing minute. When he went to

120 DAYS...

confront Sam, he'd found out about Patty. The one part of his body that hadn't been hurting clutched in pain, his heart.

He kind of understood what his brother had been talking about now, about not wanting him around when he died. The end was never pretty. While Patty went relatively quickly, most did not, and some hung on for a long time, needing more and more care.

As more of the evening came back to him, he realized he was at Sam's house. He moved his hand around trying to find her. The last thing he remembered was kissing her and falling off the couch. He wished he could remember more, but since he was still on the floor fully clothed, he had to assume nothing else happened.

Squinting his eyes open, Ethan knew it was going to hurt when the bright morning light hit them. He wasn't wrong. Cursing, he tried to work through the pain so he could get a better look around. The only thing he could hear, besides the ringing in his ears, was silence. Either she was sleeping comfortably in her bed or she wasn't next to him.

He rolled over and moved his knees under him. Ever so slowly, Ethan pulled his weight up, and crawled over to the couch, resting against it. In the past, he never had more than a couple of drinks at a time—he never wanted to lose control, or his edge in any situation. The previous night, he'd thrown all of his rules out the door, and was paying for it.

His tongue felt two sizes too big and fused to the roof of his mouth. He whimpered deep in his throat when he saw a huge glass of water with a bottle of aspirin next to it. Moving as quickly as he could, he pitched for the coffee table and grabbed onto the glass as if he'd been in the desert for the past week. He drank deeply, stopping only to pop a few pills into his mouth before draining the rest down.

Sighing, he sank back and sat on the floor for a few minutes and let everything start to work. Glancing around him, he noticed the clock on the wall. "Shit," he said and swiftly jumped up, before racing out of the house and back to his room. He was late for work. Hurriedly, he showered and dressed, trying to remember what events were scheduled for the day.

"Hey, Country Club, you're late," Phil said with a laugh. "Shake a leg, you've got a long list of things to do before your tee time."

"Ha-ha." Ethan waved him off and searched for Sam. He wanted to make sure she was fine and apologize for being late. Even after his parents died and he was learning how to raise a kid and work, he'd never been late.

Everywhere he checked, he had just missed her. He finally caught up to her in the Legacy Garden. "Sam, how are you feeling? I'm sorry I'm late."

She turned hard eyes toward him. "I'm fine. Yes, you are late. Some of us still managed to show up on time, even after the events of the night before."

"Well, maybe you should have woken me." He narrowed his eyes at her and crossed his arms over his chest.

"I did." She mimicked his stance. "You, on the other hand, told me to leave you alone, so I did. You're a big boy. You can handle your own responsibilities." She turned to walk toward the gardening shed.

"Listen, I'm sorry, I don't drink. I've never felt this shitty before and I overslept. So sue me, I'm sure I'm not the first and I won't be last."

Halting, she stepped up to him, and poked her finger in his chest. "Yeah, you're not the first, but you're here for who knows how long while you figure your life out. Once you're done, you're gone. I should have known better than to rely on you for anything."

He grabbed her finger to stop her from poking at him and didn't let go. "Listen here, lady, when I make a commitment, I stand by it. Sure I'm only here for a bit, but while I'm here, I give it my all."

"You didn't give it your all this morning."

"There were extenuating circumstances." He threw up his hands in frustration.

"Funny thing, I had those same other *circumstances* this morning too, yet I managed to make it here on time."

"Samantha," he said quietly. "Cut me some slack, I've never seen anyone die before, let alone someone who came here the same date as my brother. It was a difficult night."

Her shoulders slumped and she looked down. "I know it was. It was hard for me too. They all are. But that doesn't matter, what does is getting up and being here for the guests who are still living." When she looked back up at him, her eyes were brimming with tears. "Think about it, Ethan, don't you think they'd love to feel how bad you are today instead of the pain they live in? That's what gets me out of bed every morning, no matter how shitty I feel, or how late I was up tending to another guest."

She turned and disappeared into the shed, leaving him alone with his thoughts. She retuned shortly with something heavy wrapped in a cloth. "Here." She handed it to him. "This is Patty's handprint. Please add it to the wall." Without another word, she turned and left him again.

Taking a deep breath, he pulled back the cloth to expose her small handprint. There were a few other guests who had died between Evan and Patty, but they'd be pretty close to each other on the wall. It made him wonder how many other people had come here as strangers, but ended up with a new friend. Sometimes, even though someone is only in your life for a few days, or weeks, they left a lasting impression on you. He'd always remember Patty and what she did for his brother, and how he was able to be there for her in the end.

Swallowing past the lump in his throat, he looked up and watched Sam's figure getting smaller as she walked down the path toward the main house. She always seemed to be walking away from him. He wondered what would happen if she stopped and actually let him catch up to her. He knew no matter what happened in the future, she had already left such an impression on him that he'd never be the same. He shook his head, he was so different now from the man who first came here, so sure she was running a scam to get their money when they died. Ironically, he felt as if he had buried that person, and he was finally becoming the man he was destined to be.

He went into the shed, collected the cement and the tools he would need, then headed into the garden to add her handprint to the wall. Kneeling at the next open spot, he looked down and could see his brother's handprint along with so many others. So many people were dealing with cancer, so many had lost the battle. He'd heard the stories from some of the guests, who didn't have anyone, or their families didn't want to deal with it and they were pushed aside with very little help. There was a fee to stay there, but not everyone could afford it. If they couldn't, Samantha would still make sure they were welcomed and treated just like everyone else. He couldn't imagine what it would be like, to be someone, who was alone in this world with no one to take care of them, having this heavy sickness hanging over their heads. Maybe not having enough money for medicine, food or even a place to live. To be able to come to Last Resort and not only have all of those things, but also love and laughter with a little bit of adventure if they wanted some would be a miracle to those guests.

Looking around the garden, he was amazed at how many butterflies flew around. He remembered what Sam had told him on the first day about the butterflies. Slowly, Ethan stood up and looked around. The garden was filled with them. There were hundreds. He contemplated if they were all guests, who had previously died and were up there to welcome Patty as one of them. His hand hesitated at his pocket, he wanted to pull his phone out to take a picture of it, but then he stopped himself. The moment felt bigger than him, bigger than any picture could be.

He turned his back on the butterflies and set about carefully hanging up her print, making sure it was straight. "I hope you know how much you helped me." He placed his hand on hers for a moment before he stood and collected his tools to put them away. Restlessness thrummed through him. He looked out into the distance and toward the hill to Sam's tree. No sooner had he headed in the direction and climbed the hill, when his unease calmed. He turned around and looked down over the property, his developer mind making calculations and trying to decide on the best possibilities for the use of the land. There had to be a way to get more out of it. He moved a few feet to the left and wondered if this was even the best piece of property for the resort, maybe something else would be better.

He'd done his research before coming out to the ranch. He knew the value of the land and all of the other investors who had been looking into it. Some of them not using the best methods in order to get her to sell. She was sitting on a gold mine, literally. There were stories of an abandoned mine around these hills, most likely on her property. Which was the main reason why the other developers wanted it, that and to build a new housing development. He had to hand it to them. It would be the best use of both. They'd be able to mine for gold, while also planning a master community. They could end up making at least double, if not triple their money with very little effort. Of course, if the gold was really there, who knew what those numbers really could be.

Maybe he could work that to his advantage. He pulled his phone out and quickly started making notes and doing some research. If this resort was going to become the place Samantha had always dreamed of, she was going to need his help. By that point, he was already in trouble with her, might as well see what happened when he brought up his ideas. Sometimes, you needed to clear the air one way or another.

Chapter 11

DAY 24

ETHAN-

YOU KNOW, I'D BEGUN TO THINK OF SAM AS SOME KIND OF WONDER WOMAN. SHE IS ALWAYS ON THE GO, HELPING EVERYONE. BUT TODAY I LOOKED AT HER, AND SHE ACTUALLY LOOKED TIRED. I WANTED TO HELP HER, BUT SHE WOULDN'T LET ME. I DON'T THINK SHE EVER LETS ANYONE HELP. I WISH SOMEONE WOULD TAKE CARE OF HER.

EVAN

Sam wasn't about to admit it to anyone, but she was exhausted and felt terrible. All she wanted to do was go home, turn on some music and maybe read for a few minutes, before she finally passed out and slept for, hopefully, ten hours. When she walked into her home, the first thing she was greeted with was the empty scotch bottles from the night before. She couldn't believe they had drank so much, no wonder they both felt so terrible. All day she'd been thinking about why Patty's death had affected her more than the others, and the only thing she could think of was the fact that she was connected to Evan, and therefore connected to Ethan.

Taking the bottles to the recycling bin, she continued to straighten up, knowing as soon as she stopped, she'd drop, and she hadn't had dinner yet. Opening the fridge, she stood, looking blankly at its contents, not knowing what she wanted to eat. She mentally kicked herself for not stopping by the main house kitchen and grabbing some of what the guests were having for dinner before heading to her house.

When there was a knock on her backdoor, she jumped and her heart sank. She couldn't deal with another death so soon after Patty, her mind not realizing that someone would have called her first, which was quicker than coming up to her house if something was wrong. Seeing the shadow of a man, and knowing it was Ethan didn't make her relax either.

"Can I come in?" he asked.

"I'm pretty tired, Ethan." She sighed.

"Which is exactly why I brought dinner." He held up a bag in one hand. "And there's dessert in here too. I think some kind of double chocolate fudge mousse cake or something decadent like that."

She crossed her arms over her chest. "You're fighting dirty."

"Hell yeah, I'll do whatever I need to, in order to spend some more time with you and show you how sorry I am for this morning." He held up his other hand, which held a large bouquet of flowers. "See, I tried to find something that matched your beauty, but none did. These were the best I could do."

A smile twitched at her lips. "And now you're charming me. What else do you want?"

"Nothing, I just want to spend some time with you . . . please?"

"Okay, but no repeat of last night." She held the door open for him as he walked in.

"Of course. Honestly, I don't think I want to look at any booze for the next decade or so." He stopped in front of her and looked down. "But I do need to know, does that include the kissing part too?"

All day she had wondered if she had dreamed the kiss; it appeared she hadn't. Lord help her, but she wanted more. "Yes, it does include the kissing part." She couldn't help it, she smirked at him when his face fell. "For now."

"As long as there is hope . . ." He quickly leaned down and kissed the top of her head before going over to the counter and putting the bags down. "Here." He handed her the bouquet. "You put those in water and I'll take care of everything else."

When he turned his back, she buried her face in the flowers and inhaled deeply, touched he'd brought them for her.

Once she'd arranged her flowers, Sam crossed over to the sink, and placed them on the windowsill above it. She'd be able to see them from her back porch while she relaxed on her swing. When she turned around, Ethan had the table all set, and the aroma of the food permeated the area and made her mouth water. Holding herself back from running to the table and shoveling the food in, she crossed to the refrigerator and pulled out a pitcher of lemon flavored water, pouring them each a glass. She knew better than to offer a glass of wine after their drinking session.

He pulled out a chair for her. "Please, sit."

"Thank you."

They didn't talk much through the dinner and it didn't feel uncomfortable to be sitting there eating in silence together. Sam didn't feel the need to fill the gaps in the conversation with nonsense. By the time dessert came around, she was full, but there was no way she was going to pass it up. She needed to move before she could eat another bite. "If you don't mind, let me clean this up and then we can finish on the porch. I always like to sit out there this time of evening. The trees are starting to change. Just wait, another couple of weeks and it's going to be spectacular here."

"I think it's already pretty spectacular from where I'm standing," he said in a low voice.

She turned and saw him looking at her. Shaking her head, she brushed him off. "There you go again, trying to sweet talk me."

"It's the truth." He moved closer to her and she backed up until she was trapped between Ethan and the counter. "I don't think I've ever met anyone as beautiful as you."

"Come on, I'm not going to fall for that. I know all about you. You're worth more money than I can count. I know you've had all the beautiful, single, and sometimes married women throwing themselves at you."

"Yes I have, but none can compare to you." He cut her off when she tried to interrupt. "Hush now. There is the beauty everyone sees first, then that which is inside." He tapped her chest, above her heart. "It's what's inside you that makes your outer beauty pale in comparison. You give so much of yourself to others and never ask for anything for yourself. What you do here." He gestured wide with his arm. "It's nothing more than a miracle to these people. Don't you understand that? Not many people would ever even think to do what you do. And yet here you are, again and again, allowing people to come here, and help them make the most of their last days while you hold their hand. To someone who has nothing, that would mean everything. To someone who doesn't want to burden their family, it *means* everything. More people should know about you and this place."

With tears in her eyes, she shook her head. "I can't take any more people. I don't have the resources."

"But you do! Don't you think people would be jumping on board to support you here if more people knew about it? And then there's the gold mine. If you could find that, you'd be set for life and you'd never need anything from anyone and you'd be able to help so many more people."

Her heart sank. The gold mine. Everyone who was ever interested in her property always went back to the legend of the mine. The fact that Ethan went there, started to break her heart. She thought this place meant more to him. "The mine is a myth. There is nothing." She tried to pull away from him.

"There's a lot of talk about it, some of it has to be true." He wouldn't let her go.

"No, Ethan, there is no gold, nothing. It's an old tale that people love to keep alive so the mystery of the gold rush stays alive." The exhaustion she felt in her bones seeped into her voice at the thought that he was only after her property.

"What do you know?"

She slapped the palm of her hand on his chest,

angry at him, that one of her biggest fears was coming true right before her eyes. "Don't you think when I bought this ranch I looked into everything that had to do with it, not to mention talked to everyone who had ever worked or lived on it? You know what that kind of money could do for my ranch, as you said, how many more people I could help. I've done all the surveys, hired the best people, actually walked every inch of this property. There's nothing, only people wanting to get their hands on it, and doing whatever they needed to do in order to get me to sell. Well, I'm not going to sell." She wiggled in his grip. "Now let me go. It's been a long day, and I want to be alone."

"No dammit, I'm tired of you walking away from me all the time. You're going to stay here and listen to everything I have to say. To talk to me for once without running. Don't make me beg, Samantha. You have to listen."

"Two minutes."

"I can tell you think I'm only after your property, and yes, I'm sure you've had a lot of investors here who tried to get their hands on it, one way or the other. But I'm not them. Can't you tell? Can't you see, you've changed me? Yes, I can look around and see what this property could be developed for, how much money it could make me. Sam, I have more than enough money. It isn't about that, but it's about you and Last Resort. There is more that can be done here. If you find the mine you won't have to worry about money, but that's not the only thing. I want to help. I may have come here trying to find out if you were scamming people out of their money, but I know you couldn't. It's not who you are. I want to do what I can to make this place everything you want it to be."

She wanted to believe his words but her exhaustion made it hard for to stay awake and not fall asleep standing up in his arms. She wanted to go bed and think about everything in the morning. "You know, you aren't the first person to come here thinking I was running a scam. I can't fault you for looking out for your brother. Now please let me go. I just want to go to bed."

"Why do I get the feeling you're brushing me off? Come on Sam, let me finish, I still have another minute. Listen to me."

"I don't have to, now let me go. You don't want me to have to say it again." Anger crept past her tired voice. Obviously, he didn't understand how much she's been through and how badly she needed rest.

"Or what? You're going to hurt me?" He puffed his chest up trying to intimate her. "Maybe you're scared of being this close to me."

"Oh, please. Ethan, I've taken many self-defense classes I can drop you on your ass quicker than you know. So let me go."

His eyes narrowed at her. "Well, if you aren't scared then maybe this is just an excuse for you to get your hands on me."

Sam closed her eyes, not believing what he'd just said and wished him away. "Sorry to burst your bubble, but it actually has been a long day and I'd like to be alone for a bit before I head off to bed."

"Answer one question, one only . . . for tonight, and I'll leave the rest for another." He tipped his head down so it rested on hers and whispered. "I still have thirty seconds or so."

She was so tired she felt as if she'd agree to anything just so he'd go away and leave her alone. Alone, that was what she was used to. The last thing she wanted was to get used to having someone around at the end of the day to talk with, especially someone who was going to be leaving soon. "Yes."

"I know because of the circumstances, it would be hard to do this in the usual way, but I'd like to find a way to date you, to get to know you better, but you'd have to not run away from me every time things got too serious." When she didn't say anything, he continued. "Samantha." He used his fingers to tip her chin up so she'd look at him. "It's obvious we both like each other. Even if I don't stay here as an employee, it doesn't mean we still can't be together. My office is only an hour from here. All I'm saying is if this is something we both want, we can make it work, but we both have to want it. So, do you?"

After all of these years up here, alone, along came Ethan McGregor to make her want a normal life like other women her age. If she was honest with herself, looked into the deepest, darkest corners of her heart, she knew it was what she'd always wanted. *Love*. The love of a man, a partner to share her life with. The ups and downs, everything. There were things he didn't know about her, things she would have to tell him, but there was time for that. But at that moment, she couldn't speak; the lump in her throat was too large. It was going to be one of the scariest things she'd ever done, but she wanted to. She simply nodded and laughed when his arms moved tightly around her, picking her up off the ground and swinging her around. In that moment, everything was perfect.

Chapter 12

DAY 27

ETHAN—

THERE'S SOMETHING ABOUT THIS PLACE. I SWEAR IT'S MAGIC OR SOMETHING. YOU KNOW WE WERE NEVER BIG INTO THE OUTDOORS, AND I HATED BASIC TRAINING WHEN THEY MADE US ROUGH IT. REMEMBER, THEY ALWAYS CALLED ME CITY BOY? BUT HERE, BEING AWAY FROM THE HUSTLE AND BUSTLE, IT'S SO PEACEFUL AND QUIET. WE ALL COME HERE WAITING TO DIE, KNOWING IT'S COMING. LIKE ME, MOST COUNT THE DAYS THEY ARE HERE. I'VE SEEN IT TIME AND TIME AGAIN WHEN SOMEONE MAKES IT PAST THE NUMBER OF DAYS THE DOCTORS GAVE THEM. IT'S ALMOST LIKE RENEWED HOPE. WHEN THEY WALKED THROUGH THE DOORS HERE, IT WAS RENEWED, THEN AGAIN, WHEN THEY BEAT THE DOCTOR'S PREDICTIONS, AND IF THEY MAKE IT PAST ONE HUNDRED AND TWENTY DAYS . . . ? SO FAR I'VE SEEN IT TWICE SINCE I'VE BEEN HERE. WE PARTIED LIKE CANCER-RIDDEN

120 DAYS...

ROCK STARS EACH TIME. WE'VE LEARNED NOT JUST TO CELEBRATE THE LITTLE THINGS IN LIFE, BUT TO REALLY APPRECIATE THE BIG ONES TOO.

EVAN

Ethan woke up with a smile on his face. It wasn't like he typically woke up in a bad mood, but he had to admit, the past six months hadn't been the best. Swinging both feet over the edge of the bed, he ran a hand over his chest. It had become a habit every morning to see if the ache from his brother's death was still there. While it was still present that morning, the pain wasn't as sharp.

Sitting for a minute, he listened to the hush of nature around him. There had been a gentle rain falling most of the night. He had left his window open and for the first time in a very long time, he'd slept like a child who had no worries hanging over his head.

Last Resort always had a plan for the days when rain would wash outside activities away. They'd make sure all the guests who wanted to go were safely moved to the rec center and they'd spend the day playing games and watching movies. There was always a huge amount of competition between everyone. They even made up teams and whichever team's members won the most games, picked out the movie they'd watch later.

The rec hall also had a huge fireplace and they'd have it burning all day to help keep the chill away and make the room cozy and inviting.

Since he ended up being one of the first to the rec center, he started moving the tables and chairs around to accommodate the different games. It may only have been his third time doing the task, but the first two left such an impression on him, he remembered exactly what to do, including the way certain guests liked things set up.

He paused for a moment and thought of Patty—she'd loved charades. They all did. The more outrageous you could be, the better. There was always a lot of laughter going on when they played that game. There was also a lot of good-natured yelling when people didn't guess the answer in time and the other team was able to steal.

He thought back to the time when he was young and his family would play games. Ethan supposed every adult longed for some aspect of their childhood, especially if they had a good one. Since his adult lifestyle was so different, it did seem like a completely different life to him. There was something in the water at the ranch, because the longer he was there, the more he longed for his childhood, the more he wanted to recreate it, somehow be able to tap back into it, but as an adult. And with a new family.

Looking around, as both employees and guests started to arrive, his stomach clenched as he saw their happy faces. The employees only stayed a short time, and the guests, unfortunately, would only be around for so long. To be fair, some of the employees stayed for a while, but at some point, they all ended up burned out by being around death all the time. The average retention was three years. Could he really be thinking of starting a 'family' up here with all of these people, who wouldn't be around for as long as he'd want them to be? Hadn't he learned anything from his family, when his parents were killed? Was it possible for him, like Sam, to go through the loss of someone you cared for over and over again? It wasn't the typical

120 DAYS...

amount of death someone dealt with in one's lifetime. It was purposely setting out to be around people who weren't going to make it to the next year. And not doing it a few times a year, but most likely a few times a month. Unless they found a cure, there'd be no end in sight.

"Hey, Ethan!" Edward waved at him. "Did ya finally catch what you were running after?"

Ethan's heart momentarily stuttered and he took in a sharp breath. "You could say that." He watched Sam walk in behind Edward and he could tell by the old man's chuckle that his poker face must have taken a vacation. "Good morning, Ms. Truman." Ethan nodded to her.

"Good morning, Mr. McGregor. It's a beautiful morning, isn't it?"

"I was thinking the same thing." He smiled at her.

"Well then, let's not waste anymore of it." She walked over to the stereo and put on some music. When "September" by Earth, Wind & Fire came on, several people started to dance, including Samantha, while they continued to set up games. Soon enough, people were seated around the tables or lounging on the couches, reading. They always started with the smaller games before doing the ones everyone could participate in. Ethan went around making sure everyone had something to drink and to snack on while settling good-natured arguments here and there.

There was a relaxed camaraderie on these days. It really did feel like one big family. On impulse, Ethan took his phone out and started to capture some pictures. He wished he had thought of this sooner; back at his place he had a nice camera. He always told himself he needed it for documentation with all of his investments, but in actuality, he loved to take photos.

Next time he was in town, he should pick it up and bring it back with him. Sam loved to video document her guests telling stories; they should also have stills. They could have a special section on the website and print copies and write on the back of them like they used to do before the digital age. Something for people to remember of those who came before them.

He wandered from table to table, talking and taking pictures. Adding notes into his phone about everyone, not just the guests, but the employees, who gave so much of themselves so these people could have meaning to their life at the end. Everyone deserved to have their story told.

He was also considering the building. While it was large enough for the amount of guests they currently had, if they were going to expand, they needed something larger. But he wanted, and he was sure Sam would agree with him, to keep the charm and old-ranch feel of the place. It couldn't be all new and shiny. The people who used this place weren't, and it needed to reflect them too.

Shaking his head he knew he had to stop before he completely re-developed this area. He tilted his head and stared at Sam, trying to get into her head, wondering what she would say if he brought his ideas to her. There was a good chance she'd be stubborn and say that while he had some good ideas, she couldn't afford it, and therefore, it would have to be planned out as money allowed, never letting him put any money into it. Or she'd say she'd never want this place to become an institution, because if that happened, it wouldn't benefit the guests anymore. He knew she wouldn't be worried about filling the place up; sadly, there were always enough guests to fill the room.

Sam clapped her hands together. "Anyone ready to play charades? Get in your teams, and guests decide

120 DAYS...

which employees goes on which team."

Soon enough everyone was grouped into their teams. Sam and Ethan were on two separate teams and were chosen to be the team captains. They sat in the middle of everyone next to each other. He smirked at her. "Are you ready to give up now?"

"Ha. Please. We're going to wipe the floor with you."

"You keep telling yourself that. Have you seen my team?" He gestured toward his group. "There's no way we could lose."

"I have a secret weapon, and you're totally going to lose."

"Care to place a little wager on that, Ms. Truman?"

Her eyes lit up. "Well, Mr. McGregor, I'd hate to see a grown man cry when he lost a bet."

"Good, then we're in agreement. What's your wager?"

Sam tapped her finger on her lips and squinted her eyes at him. "The person who loses has to do the next run into town for supplies."

He raised an eyebrow at her. "That's it? You must be scared of losing. Deal." He held his hand out for her to shake.

"Not so fast, buddy. That's just the first thing. The second is, whoever loses has to dress up like whatever the winner choses for them to wear. They have to be in costume all day while working."

Ethan narrowed his eyes at her and wondered exactly what her secret weapon was. Deciding to go with it, he held out his hand and they shook on it. He frowned when she started laughing. "What?"

"There's something you don't know about me."

"There's a lot. That's one thing I want to change."

Her face blushed red. "No, it's the fact I love Halloween. I was in theatre during high school. I love to dress up."

"So you're saying there is nothing that I could pick out for you that you'd be embarrassed to wear?"

"Nope." She smiled widely at him.

"Well, if that isn't a challenge, I don't know what is. Let's get this started so I can start searching for the perfect costume for you to wear when you lose."

"You do that, meanwhile, I've already got your costume picked out." She tapped the side of her head. "And it's a good one. Feel free to dwell on it while we're playing."

The game was fast paced and intense, both teams going back and forth. One was in the lead, and then the other one was up, never more than two ahead at any given time. With a wager on the line, it seemed both guests and employees took the competition to a whole new level. It had gotten so bad, they had to wait until they were tied again before deciding on only nine more turns so the game would end.

Coming down to the last game, they were tied once more. Ethan was up. What Sam didn't realize was he lived for the pressure. When millions of dollars were on the line, he had to be able to keep his head steady and focused. This game was no different. As soon as he looked at the title of the movie, a smile spread across his face. He knew exactly what he was going to do and she wouldn't know what hit her.

He let them know it was two words and ran to the closest table. Since they hadn't specified they couldn't use props, he quickly cleared it, then he ran to the kitchen where he grabbed a pie and placed it in the center of the table. He took the bowl of pretzels off another table and put sixteen of them in the pie then he walked over to Sam and picked her up, ignoring her squeal. Settling her down gently on the table, he climbed up and made sure the pie was between them. Ever so slowly, he leaned over the pie, and kissed her.

Pulling away from her, he looked at his team and gestured at Sam and the pie between them and slowly pointed to each of the sixteen 'candles' there. He knew his time was running out and he started to panic. Quickly, he leaned over and kissed her again, and looked back at them where that sat, shrugging and shaking their heads. His heart sank. There was no way Sam's team was going to miss this one. Last week they'd had a John Hughes movie marathon.

When her team was just as silent when it was their turn to guess, he narrowed his eyes and scanned the crowd, stopping when they landed on Edward. He sat, grinning at them. Breaking the silence, Ethan asked, "Okay, what gives?"

"I have no idea what you're talking about," said Edward, grinning so hard his cheeks must be hurting.

"How could no one have guessed *Sixteen Candles*? We just watched that movie. You all voted on it." Sam frowned.

"Seems like I'm a bit off my *game*." Ethan turned toward Sam. "We've been played. What I haven't figured out is why. Want to fill us in, Edward?"

"Sure, sure . . . see, if you ended up in a tie, neither one of you would win, and therefore, you'd both lose, and if you both lost, then you'd have to go to town together and wear the costumes *we* pick out for you."

Now Ethan was worried. What kind of costumes would they put them in? He looked over at Sam and noticed she was amused by the guest's antics, just as he was.

Chapter 13

DAY 30

ETHAN—

SAM AND I WENT INTO TOWN TODAY, JUST THE TWO OF US. YOU COULD TELL SHE DIDN'T LIKE 'GUESTS' HELPING HER OUT WITH THE SUPPLY RUN. SOMETHING ABOUT HOW WE'RE HERE TO RELAX AND NOT DO ANY CHORES. I SWEET-TALKED HER INTO TAKING ME. YOU'D BE PROUD. I TOLD HER, 'HOW COULD SPENDING TIME ALONE WITH A BEAUTIFUL WOMAN BE CONSIDERED A CHORE?' SHE DIDN'T BUY IT, BUT LET ME COME ALONG ANYWAY. IT WAS ACTUALLY NICE TO DO SOMETHING 'NORMAL' FOR A CHANGE.

IF THINGS WERE DIFFERENT . . . BUT SINCE THEY'RE NOT . . . BESIDES I THINK SHE'D BE BETTER FOR YOU. SHE'D KICK YOUR ASS AND MAKE YOU OPEN YOUR EYES AND ENJOY EVERY SINGLE MOMENT OF YOUR LIFE.

EVAN

120 DAYS...

The next day, Sam grabbed her list and the keys to the van. She looked up at the clouds forming above her as she walked to the barn and remembered the weather said there was another storm coming in. It was unusual to have so much rain in the fall. She hoped it meant they were going to be climbing out of their drought status. She wasn't surprised to find Ethan waiting for her when she reached the barn. They didn't say anything to each other as she approached, yet butterflies took flight in her stomach at the sight of him. She could get lost in his gaze for days and not notice the passing of time. When he held out his hand, she easily dropped the keys into his waiting palm, knowing he'd take care of her. It felt like more than a simple trip into town for supplies. If she had to label it, she would have to say it felt more like a date. She started toward the passenger door and was surprised when he beat her there. He gave her a small bow at his waist before opening the door.

"Thank you." Sam tucked a lock of hair behind her ear as she turned her face away and climbed in, too shy to look at him.

"You're very welcome." He closed the door, walked around the front and climbed in. Putting the keys in the ignition, the engine roared to life.

"Wow, I don't think the van has ever sounded this good. How much do I owe you, and when did you have time to give it a tune-up?"

He frowned at her and shook his head before putting the van in gear and backing out of the barn. "Please, I spent years working in a garage while raising Evan. The timing was off. It didn't take much to fix it. Time or money, besides, this is what you pay me for anyway."

"Well, thank you."

"Yeah, I think you need to find a new mechanic."

"But I've gone to this shop for years."

"That may be, but anyone could have fixed this easily with the right equipment. Between the two vans, if both of them weren't running perfectly, you'd be taking them back to him all the time, and he'd have a steady stream of income."

"But . . . but . . . but that's wrong."

"Honey, it happens all the time. Since you take them to someone local, they don't have a lot of business, so anything steady would be a blessing."

"But I bring other money into the local economy here, not just the garage. And dammit, the resort is for a good cause. I'm not up here milking dying people out of their money promising cures. They know exactly what they are doing when they come here, and how much time they have left." She pulled her phone out of her purse and started to scroll through it.

"What are you doing?"

She dropped her hands into her lap and looked at him with disbelief. "What do you think I'm going to do? I'm going to call the jerk and give him a piece of my mind."

Reaching over, he placed his hand over hers. "No, it's not worth it."

"What do you mean it's not worth it? I could be putting that money into something else for the guests instead of lining his pockets. And I could find another garage, or better yet, I could get some books and learn how to do some of this stuff myself! Yeah, that's what I should do."

"Samantha, really? When would you have time?"

"Don't you start with that tone. I could find the time." She narrowed her eyes and gave him a pointed look, hoping he got the picture not to mess with her about this.

"Sure you can." He nodded. "Maybe get a little less sleep a night. That'll be really good for you." He looked over and winked at her.

She raised her chin in the air and looked down her nose at him. "I'll have you know I get the perfect amount of sleep."

"Keep telling yourself that," he mocked her.

"I will. I've spent years figuring out exactly how much sleep I need. It's the only way I can get everything done I need to. Luckily for me, five-to-six hours is perfect."

"Exactly." He grinned at her like the cat who caught the mouse. "You're already at five-to-six hours of sleep. What are you going to cut out in order to become a master mechanic?"

She squinted her eyes at him. "No need to go all Mr. Sarcastic on me."

"Well, someone's got to do something; otherwise, you'll work yourself into the grave, and then where would the resort be? Have you thought of that?"

"Haven't you figured it out by now? This resort is what keeps me going. I don't know what I would have done after my parents died if this idea hadn't bloomed. And yes, I am going to die and I worry every damn day about what is going to happen to this land after I'm gone." She looked out the window and watched as the fields went by. On a whisper, she said, "The saddest thing would be for it to die with me."

His voice softened to match hers. "Do you have a plan in place?"

"Of course I do, but nothing is set in stone; besides,

this is a huge responsibility, and I don't know if there is anyone crazy enough to want to take on this kind of project." She shook her head. "No, all I can do is put everything into it and hope that whenever it the time comes, I've built this place up big enough, that it's a recognizable name and people will want to continue the work." Tilting her head from one side to the other, she looked at him out of the corner of her eye. "Ready to change the subject?"

"Depends, you still calling that mechanic?"

"I should." She folded her arms across her chest, still angry someone would do such a thing to anyone, let alone a person who was trying to help people.

"Let me take care of it." He continued before she could speak, "Please, let me do this for you. Seriously, I speak his language."

"What is that? *Man*?" Sam narrowed her eyes at him, afraid that was exactly what he meant.

He smirked at her. "Something like that. Actually, since I've worked in a garage, I can let him know, nicely, that I know what he's been doing, and he'd better not ever do it to you again, or to anyone else. Better?"

"Yes, that will work. For now." Sam leaned back in her seat and opened up the folder to double-check what they needed, and she relaxed to the music coming out of the speakers. She looked up when Ethan started to slow down and frowned. There was a sheriff's cruiser blocking the road.

When the van stopped, he walked over to the window Ethan had rolled down. "What can I do for you?"

"Where are you headed?"

"This is Samantha Truman from Last Resort," Ethan said. "We're going down into city for supplies."

120 DAYS...

"Ma'am." The deputy tipped his hat at her. "You're going to want to spend the night down there." He pointed up behind them. "Big storm, strange storm. It's coming down from the northeast. That's why it's still relatively sunny here and the ocean is calm." He pointed over the hood of the van toward the waves of the Pacific. "It's washing the roads out up there and it's heading down the canyons. You have enough time to get ahead of it and find a place a lot more comfortable than this van for the night, or longer."

"Are you sure we have enough time to get the rest of the way down without getting stranded?"

"We've been monitoring the road. We spoke with everyone who uses this road to get to their residences, and you were the only two who were unaccounted for. Everyone else is either staying in their homes or in town. If you made it to this point, we calculated you'd have enough time to make it past the last bridge before the water hits."

"But I need to get back to my resort. What if they need me?" Sam was willing to unbuckle her seatbelt and walk back up if she had to. She couldn't leave them alone up there.

The deputy's face became stern. "There is someone up there to make sure everything is fine. You're at a high enough elevation, there shouldn't be too much damage to your place. As soon as it is safe, you'll be one of the first allowed back up there."

"That's not good enough. Don't you understand what the resort is?" She couldn't keep her anger from her voice. She was always taught to respect authority, but she needed to get through to him how important it was. "There are guests up there who are very sick and need twenty-four hour care. I need to be there for them."

Ethan turned toward her and held her hands.

"Sam, you need to calm down. There's nothing you can do now. You may not be able to get up there, but no one else can come down either. All the staff are up there and they know just as well as you do what needs to be done. They can watch the place for you. It will be okay."

Squeezing his hands tightly, she didn't want to let go. She felt like he was the calm within this storm and if she was going to make it until they were able to return, she was going to have to rely on him to keep her grounded. "But what if it's a week before we can get back up there?" Unable to hold them back, tears ran down her cheeks. "So much can happen in a week."

"Shhh . . . it will be okay. Do you remember who I am? If anyone can get you back up there as soon as it's safe, it's me. Hell, if I have to, I'll rent a helicopter and we'll fly up there with whatever's needed. You can call and check in. Let's look at this as a kind of adventure we can have together and not about what's going on back at the resort."

"You're going to have to help me," she whispered. "I'm not sure I can do this on my own." She felt both weak in asking him and happy she was able to.

"Will you put yourself in my hands for the next twenty-four hours, or more if needed? I'll make sure you're completely distracted and have an amazing time."

"I'm not sure I'll be able to 100 percent forget."

He cupped her cheek with his hand. "And I wouldn't expect you to. I'll try my best, if you try yours."

"Looks like we may have a deal."

"Excellent." Ethan turned back toward the deputy. "Thank you for the information. Is there a specific number we can call for updates?"

"Here." He handed Ethan a card. "You can call this as often as you need to. Once it blows out of here, we'll start clearing the roads going to your resort first."

"Thank you so much," Sam said. "That really means a lot."

The sheriff tipped his hat at them again, backed away and waved them through. When they went over the bridge, Sam watched the water flowing quickly past. It was higher than normal and she wondered if there was more to come and if it would go over the bridge. If it was washed out, it could be longer before they were able to get back.

"Why don't you go over your list again? We'll be at the store soon."

Grateful for a distraction, she refocused her attention on the list, trying to block out what could be going on up at the resort while she was heading toward the city, on what still felt like a date.

The sun had been shining when they went into the warehouse style bulk store, but by the time they came out two hours later, it was pouring. Ethan had done a good job of distracting her while they were in the store, but seeing exactly how much rain was pouring down, Sam worried about the resort and the guests.

"Wait here," Ethan said. "I'll go get the van. This way maybe everything won't get sopping wet."

"Sure, we can try."

The parking lot was eerily quiet with everyone taking refuge in either their car or the store. Soon enough, Ethan pulled up, getting as close as he could to the small overhang she stood under. As soon as he was out and opening the doors, she started handing him boxes, surprised at how cold the rain was. Focusing on the task at hand, they quickly loaded everything and jumped back into the van. Shaking from the cold, Sam rubbed her arms.

Ethan started the engine and turned the heat on full blast. "Here." Ethan climbed out of his seat and rummaged around the box of supplies she kept in each van, pulled out a blanket and draped it around her shoulders. "This should help."

"But . . . I think . . . you're . . . wetter than . . . I am," she said, her teeth chattering.

"I always run hot." He winked at her. "I'll be fine."

"Why, yes . . . yes, you are." Her lips twitched.

"You must be starting to warm up."

"I am." She leaned forward and looked up at the sky. "What are we going to do?"

He hesitated. "We could always stay at my place until it clears up. I probably should check on it, I haven't been back in weeks."

Sam analyzed his hesitation. Was it because he didn't want to take her to his house? Or was he being a gentleman? She knew she had to make a quick decision and couldn't spend hours debating his meaning. "It does make the most sense, but how far away is it?"

"Actually, it's not far at all. So when the weather clears, we'll be able to get back up to the resort."

"Okay, yes. Take me home."

Ethan didn't know why her words meant so much to him. Was it because she used the word home? Or could it be because she was trusting him to take care

120 DAYS...

of her? Either way, it was something new to him. He felt like a teenager wanting to impress the girl he had a crush on, which was the truth.

First they stopped by the costume shop, since it had ended as a draw. They had no choice but to pick up what their teams had picked out for them. They were under strict orders not to peek. They were told where to go to collect the costumes, but they had to swear not to look at them until the day they were to wear them.

Hopping back into the van, Ethan hung the large plastic bags up in the back. "Gee, lucky they're protected. Wouldn't want them getting wet." He shook his head, trying to get some of the excess water off his hair.

"Hey! Trying to dry off over here." Sam looked over at the bags. "Maybe we should check to make sure they didn't get wet?"

"Samantha Truman, are you suggesting we should peek? After we swore we wouldn't?"

She folded her arms across her chest and stuck out her bottom lip slightly. "Fine."

Laughing, he turned the engine over and pulled out of the parking lot. Winding his way through the familiar streets, he pulled up to the keypad at the entrance to his garage. Punching in the numbers, he looked up at his three-story row house which had originally been two separate houses before he'd remodeled it. He remembered the pride he'd felt when it was completed and it was his. Back then, it was a way to show everyone how much money he had. No expense had been spared, and he'd wanted the best, and he'd wanted everyone driving or walking by his house to know it.

Now he was almost embarrassed by it. Spending so much money on something so frivolous when he could have spent half the money he did and it would still have been the nicest house on the block. He knew better than to overbuild for the area, but at the time he didn't care.

After parking, they walked up the steps into the house and into the living area. Looking around at the modern clean lines, he was faced with another aspect at how different his home was when compared to hers. Even if he took away the cost, they were vastly different. Remembering the time he'd spent there, he could say hers felt completely like a home, like everyone was welcome, just like the resort. It didn't matter who you were, she opened the door for you, invited you in, and accepted you. While he used to like his home, now it felt cold, like he had been before meeting Sam.

He rubbed the back of his neck. "So, yeah, this is where I live."

She turned and looked at him over her shoulder as she walked to the wall of windows which looked out toward the bay. "I hope so, otherwise, I'm assuming the cops should be showing up soon."

Chuckling, he crossed the room to join her. "The view is spectacular. That was part of the reason I bought this property."

"If I wasn't so worried about my guests, I'd still love this view. I'm sure it's nice to sit and watch the changing weather, not to mention the sunset."

"Oh, yeah. It is nice." He tried to remember the last time he'd sat and simply enjoyed something as breathtaking and beautiful as a sunset from his window, but couldn't. There was no time to sit and smell the roses when you were building an empire. "We'll have to plan for you to come back when it's clear so you can see for yourself."

120 DAYS...

"Sounds good. But we should probably bring everything inside so things can dry out, and we can put the food in the refrigerator. I'm going to call the resort and see how things are going up there."

"Feel better?" Ethan said after she got off the phone with Phil.

"Oh, so much better." She smiled. "They're all having a blast telling spooky stories. You know, the ones that all start with, 'It was a dark and stormy night...'"

"Great." Ethan rolled his eyes. "I hope no one has nightmares tonight."

"They're all going to try to bunk together in the main house and rec center. Easier than keeping track of everyone in the cabins. We always have rollaway beds in both places. We sometimes have sleepovers, and this way everyone can be comfortable."

"Well, since that's all taken care of, why don't you help me for a change, lazy bones."

"Ha!"

They worked together, laying everything out, or drying it off and putting it back in the van. Once that was done, Ethan was surprised when she asked him for a tour of his home and was genuinely interested in how the two houses had become one and what he'd changed. She wasn't that interested in his art collection, but since it was abstract, he wasn't surprised. When she stopped in front of one in the hallway leading to his home office, he looked at it and wondered aloud what she saw in it.

"Don't you see it?" She didn't look at him, just kept staring at the canvas.

"What am I looking for?" He tilted his head one way and then the other, trying to figure it out.

"There." She pointed to the canvas and moved her finger around, tracing in the air what she was seeing.

"Oh. Well, now, that's interesting."

"Back up and take the whole picture in, if you can, unfocus your eyes a bit. Do you see how many there are?"

"There are so many." He couldn't keep the awe out of his voice.

"Butterflies. All colors, all sizes."

"It reminds me . . ." He stopped, embarrassed to tell her what he thought.

"Reminds you of what?" She turned toward him. "You can tell me."

Looking away, he said, "In the garden, the day after Patty died, I was putting her handprint up when I saw hundreds of butterflies. It . . . it almost felt like they were there to greet her."

When she placed her hand on his arm, Ethan finally looked at her and noticed the serious expression on her face.

"They were. I've never said anything to anybody because I figured no one would believe me, but every time I'm in the garden after someone has died, I see so many butterflies. It takes my breath away. As far as I know, I'm the only one who has seen them."

"What do you make of that?" Ethan wondered if she was thinking the same thing. If the current owner was the only one who could see the butterflies, what did that mean for him? Was he right, that Sam was the one for him? He'd been leaning toward staying up there with her and being a part of the resort. The fact that they were showing themselves to him, could this mean he was a part of the larger picture?

"It could mean so many different things. Maybe others have seen them, but never said anything." She shook her head. "I don't know."

Ethan decided to let the subject drop and led her back to the living room. "Hey, are you hungry?" Ethan didn't wait for her to say anything and pointed outside the window. "Looks like we're going to have a break in the rain for a bit. I don't have any food here, but we could run out and get something. There are some really good restaurants around here."

"But I'm not dressed for anything. This was supposed to be a quick trip to town, remember?"

He waved her objections away. "No worries, there's this amazing casual place around the corner. We can stop there after we grab a few things from the store."

Sam frowned at him. "What do we need?"

"Honey, I don't think we're going to make it back up to the resort tonight." He tried to speak calmly so as not to panic her. "This way we have fresh coffee for the morning, and anything else we may need."

"But–"

"Samantha." He pointed to the window and where the clouds were still overhead, but not as dark as before. "This isn't letting up anytime soon. You've been checking the radar all day. This is just a break, and more rain is coming. All reports say it will be early tomorrow morning before it stops. Then we have to wait for all the water to make it down the mountain to make sure none of the bridges are washed out. We're looking at lunchtime if we're lucky." He rubbed her shoulders, trying to ease the tension out of them.

"Fine. Besides, if for some reason we can get back up there tonight, it's not like the coffee will go to waste. I've seen how much you drink." She gave him a small smile.

He tapped the tip of her nose softly and leaned in close. "You've got me all figured out, don't you?"

"And then some." She raised an eyebrow at him.

"If you know me so well, what am I going to do next," he asked in a whisper. Her cheeks turned pink and her breathing increased as he waited for her to answer.

"Kiss me." Her voice was barely audible.

He moved closer. "Your wish is my command." Smirking at her, he took full advantage of the moment when she opened her mouth to correct him and slid his tongue into her mouth. He knew she wasn't going to argue when her tongue started dancing with his and her arms came around his shoulders. Carefully, he backed her up and gently eased her onto the couch until she was laying down.

After a few gentle kisses, Ethan forced himself to pull away from Sam. The couch was not the ideal place for an intimate moment. He smiled when she whimpered. "Honey, we need to get something to eat."

She wrapped her arms tighter around him and tugged him back toward her. "Just a little while longer." She peppered his face with soft, quick kisses. "What harm could that do?"

"I think you know exactly what would happen."

"And your point is?"

Sighing, he tipped his head so his forehead rested on hers. "So much has changed for me. Hell, I've changed so much. I need for you to understand this means more to me than it would have six months ago." He pulled away from her and sat down on the floor with his elbows resting on his knees. "Do you know I've never had a woman come back to my place?" When she snorted, he looked over at her. "Not very ladylike there, Samantha." He sighed. "But it's true. I never wanted commitment. Having someone come back here would mean they held part of my heart, even if it was only caring for them as a friend. The only person who has ever set foot through that door, besides employees, is Evan . . . and now you."

"Wow."

"Yeah, wow." He turned to face her, capturing her ankle in his hand, and casually tracing the lines of her foot. "You need to understand what a big deal this is." He cocked his head to the slide. "And know, sometimes I'm going to slip up, go back to being the selfish bastard I was." He looked up and locked eyes with her. "But know this, I will do whatever it takes to prove to you I'm more than I once was. I'm asking for you to cut me some slack once in a while until I'm comfortable with becoming the man I should have been years ago."

She reached out to him with a shaking hand, cupping the side of his face. "Ethan, I think we've both learned there are no guarantees in life. Nothing is set in stone, and all we can do is try to be the best we can." Letting out a small laugh, she shook her head. "Sometimes I get the feeling you think I'm some kind of saint for what I'm doing. But I'm not, far from it. I mess up like everyone else. There are times I'm selfish, lazy, and sometimes, I'm in a nasty mood. In any relationship, all we can do is try our best. Try to think of the other person before ourselves. Try to do what is right. No one can be perfect all the time. Think how boring that would be. No Ethan, we are both far from perfect, but our imperfections together, become perfect."

Her words touched him. She understood, and wasn't that all anyone ever wanted, to be understood and accepted by another human being? "That sounds wonderful to me."

Smiling, she held out her hand to him and he placed his hand in hers. She stood up and pulled him to his feet. Wrapping her arms around his waist, she lay her head on his chest. "See . . . this . . . this is perfection."

"I can't argue there."

"Well, there's a first."

"Hush." He squeezed her. "I'm enjoying this."

"Me too . . ."

"But . . ."

Leaning away, she looked up at him. "How did you know there was a 'but'?"

"There's always a 'but.'"

"I was just thinking–"

"As you always are."

"Stop." She slapped his back. "I was thinking, we should get going because I'm starting to get hungry and that rain isn't going to stop forever."

"And we all know you can get a little . . ." He stopped and looked down at her before continuing. ". . . Just a little . . . ummm . . . *impatient* when you're hungry." When she didn't say anything, he continued. "What? It's not some big secret."

She smiled at him. "No, no, it's not. And sadly, I can't deny it. So yes, we'd better get going."

"Yes, ma'am. Your chariot awaits." He bowed to her. Laughing, they left and enjoyed the beauty and simplicity of being with each other.

Walking into the small restaurant, Sam felt out of place, and tugged at her faded, well-worn shirt. There was a difference between a ten-dollar casual shirt from a box store and a hundred-dollar causal shirt from an exclusive boutique. Looking around, no one, not even the wait staff, had anything this cheap on. She should have known better. Ethan was stinking rich, and while she had money, it all went into the resort. There was no way she was going to waste money on nice clothes when they were only going to be ruined because she worked in them.

She stood behind Ethan trying to hide from everyone, and hated the fact that she felt this way. While her parents had money, they never used it unless they had to. When she was in school, she never had enough to hang out with the rich kids, and had too much to be with the other students. Both circles made her feel inadequate. Her old insecurities came back to her.

Ethan reached back and grabbed her hand, pulling her gently along to the table. They were almost there when a voice stopped them.

"Why if it isn't Ethan McGregor," a booming voice called from the other side of the room. "Boy, come on over and say, 'Hi.'"

"This will only take a minute. Then we'll eat." He smiled down at her. "I promise."

"Peter, how are you? And Marissa, you look well." Ethan leaned down and kissed the cheek she tilted toward him.

"I'm fine, boy, just fine. We've missed you around here."

"Yes, well, you know, my brother's death hit me hard."

"Such a tragedy." Marissa shook her head. "Do you know I was laid up for a whole week with a cold last month? It was just terrible. There were so many committee meetings I couldn't attend. I don't know how they carried on without me."

Sam had been trying to hide behind Ethan. She didn't want to meet these people, and after how heartless Marissa was she was worried she was going to end up punching her for being so insensitive.

"Oh, come on, Riss," said Peter, "you can't compare the two. I'm sorry for your loss. It's never easy losing family."

"No, it isn't." Ethan's voice was level, showing no emotion. "I'd like you both to meet Samantha Truman. She runs Last Resort, north of the city. It's a place where people who have a terminal illness can go to live out their last days, fulfilling everything they ever dreamed of doing."

"Except living." Marissa waved her half-empty glass around. "Oh, come on. It's true. What do we call that place, darling? Waste of good land, that's what it is. Seriously, Ethan, you should talk her into selling. You'd both make a killing." She giggled. "It's like that Eagles song, you know the one, something about people going there, but never leaving. They all die there. It's such a joke. Whoever started something like that has to be seriously messed up in the head."

"Marissa!" Peter hissed. "Stop this instant."

"Oh, please, as if we haven't had this discussion before."

Sam felt like she'd been punched in the stomach. It never felt good to hear the bad things people thought of her, but to be told so casually was a shock. All that kept going through her brain was she needed to get out of there. She didn't care where she went. She tugged her hand out of Ethan's and turned, focusing on putting one foot in front of the other and walking toward the door. She had to make her escape, before

120 DAYS...

she did something that would get her in trouble or hurt the resort's reputation.

Once the cool fresh air hit her skin, she didn't know what she was going to do, or where she was going to go. Looking in all directions, she tried to remember exactly where Ethan had parked one of the cars he'd taken from his garage, but Marissa's words kept going around and round in her head. She knew what she did wasn't a joke, but to hear someone discount it as if it meant nothing, that the people who came to her meant nothing, hurt her down to her core.

Turning to the right, she started to walk, she had no idea where she was going, but she needed to get as far away as she could from those people.

"I can't believe you," Ethan said to Marissa. "I never knew you to be so cruel. Peter." He nodded toward the man who looked like he'd swallowed something rotten, and Ethan thought he may have. He always knew they were superficial people, but this short conversation was an eye-opener. He was going to have to reevaluate his business dealings with the man. And he suspected that's why Peter looked so sick. He knew he was going to be losing out on a lot of money.

Ethan turned, assuming he'd find Sam either sitting at their table or at the front of the restaurant. When she wasn't in either of those spots, his heart started beating double-time and he rushed to the door and out. Taking a few steps to the left looking for her before turning around, Ethan saw her turn a corner a few streets up. Running after her, he ignored the honking horns as he moved as fast as he could. Slipping as the rain started again, there was something inside of him, pushing him harder, telling him that if he didn't catch her now, he'd lose her forever. He was afraid if he lost her, he'd be the one who would end up lost forever.

"Samantha!" he yelled. "Stop. Wait up." With his lungs starting to burn, he kept running to her until he finally reached her. Grabbing her arm, he spun her around. "Stop. Please."

She looked up at him with huge eyes filled with tears he knew she'd be too stubborn to let flow. His heart broke seeing the sadness in them. "Oh, honey, no, don't listen to them." He took her face between his hands and forced her to look at him when she tried to turn away. "No, you know who you are, what you do. Don't let them win. We'll prove them wrong." He wrapped his arms around her and pulled her tightly into him as the gentle rain fell, his mind whirled, trying to think of the right thing to say to her. "Come on, let's go home."

"I do, I do want to go home." Her voice was muffled against his jacket. "*My* home."

His heart broke for her. He knew what it was like, wanting to run home, but not being able to. "I'm sorry, but we can't yet. I can take you to my home. It's not yours, but it's not bad either. We could play a game. I'll even let you win."

"Ha! There is no *letting* me win."

"See, there's my girl. Come on." He pulled away and tipped her chin up. "I'm serious, Sam, don't let them win. What you do is important. It means so much to so many people. You know this. Remember when you first had the idea for Last Resort. Remember when your first guest, Kenneth, arrived. Remember the days he spent with you. Remember how he died and every single guest after him. Think of the difference you made in *their* lives. You gave them

120 DAYS...

extra days, extra days to live. Samantha, everyone should know how amazing you are. Those people,"—he shook his head—"I'm sorry I ever knew them. They're the ones who need to wake up. Just like you made me wake up. What you do blows me away. *You* blow me away every day with your devotion to your guests, your cause. More people need to know how wonderful Last Resort is. I can tell you, that *their* opinion isn't what most people with half a brain would have."

Sam smiled sadly at him. "I know, Ethan. It still hurts, but I know what I do matters. You don't need to worry about me. I guess I'm a little emotional today."

"A little?" He tried to tease a smile out of her. "Because I'm pretty sure I've got proof somewhere you've been a tad bit over the top today." He burst out laughing when she glared at him. "When was the last time you spent a night away from the resort? Years, I'd be willing to bet. Let us have this night. Don't let them ruin it. Please, who knows when we'll get another one like it. When the two of us can get away together."

Her face was beautiful as her thoughts spun. He picked out confusion when her brows pulled together and shock that he knew her so well, as she blinked her huge eyes rapidly. Finally hope and resolution settled on her face when she smiled softly at him. "Let's go," he said. "I know exactly what we can do." He spun her around and pulled her back into him, dancing off down the street back to his car with her laughing at him. This he thought, was a perfect moment.

Sam lay back with her head on a pillow and couldn't remember the last time she'd laughed so much in one evening, especially considering they took the whole 'laughter is the best medicine' approach to heart up at the resort. Once they were back at Ethan's house, he made a huge production of setting up a picnic in the middle of the living room with the food they'd purchased from a second stop at the store. Lighting the candles around the room, she could tell they'd never been lit before. No doubt they were put there by some designer to make the place seem less cold.

They spent the rest of the evening talking, playing games, listening to music, and spending time together with no other obligations hanging over either one's head. She had to admit, it felt good. Deep down, she knew the resort could run without her. Maybe it was time for her to take some personal time, here and there. A night off, away, every once in a while.

"Here, have some more." He poured her another glass of wine.

"Why, Mr. McGregor, are you trying to get me drunk?"

"Hardly. I still remember what happened the last time we drank together . . . well, most of it anyway."

"It's what you don't remember that you should be scared of." When his eyes opened wide, she couldn't help but laugh. "Just kidding. You should have seen your face. Priceless."

"I'll show you priceless," he growled. Moving quickly, he rolled over, pinning her legs down with one of his. Grabbing both of her hands, he held them tightly in one hand while the other tickled her side.

"Stop . . . not . . . fair . . ." she said around fits of giggles.

His fingers paused. "You want to know what's priceless? Hearing you laugh."

Flexing his fingers at her side, she didn't laugh this time when he leaned in closer. His eyes were intense and so close to hers. The heat of his body washed over her and warmed her soul. It felt so right, his weight partially on hers. She wanted more.

Licking her lips, she lifted her head and captured his lips with hers. Slowly, her head fell back on the pillow, and his followed hers, never breaking contact. Moving, he let go of her hands. Once they were free, she used them to touch him. She wanted to feel all of him.

"Are you sure?" he asked softly in her ear.

"I've never been more sure of anything."

Gathering her up in his arms, he stood, his eyes locked on hers as he walked to his bedroom. Butterflies filled her stomach anticipating what would happen next.

Chapter 14

DAY 31

ETHAN-

YOU KNOW I THOUGHT GOING DOWN INTO THE CITY WOULD HAVE MADE ME REALIZE HOW MUCH I MISSED IT, BUT IT HAD THE EXACT OPPOSITE EFFECT ON ME. IT MADE ME REALIZE HOW MUCH LAST RESORT HAS HEALED ME. DON'T GET ME WRONG, I'M STILL DYING, BUT IN MY SOUL I'M AT PEACE. WHEN IT ALL COMES DOWN TO IT, I'M REALLY NOT THE CITY BOY THEY USED TO CALL ME. I THINK I LIKE THE QUIET BETTER.

YOU SHOULD STOP AND LISTEN ONCE IN A WHILE.

EVAN

The first thing Ethan noticed was the lack of quiet. For weeks now, it had been silent when he woke up, no city hum to greet him. He found it jarring, irritating him, and making him want to lash out. Usually he slept with the window cracked at the resort, the crisp morning air helping him wake up. But in the city, he kept the windows closed, all year around. No one wanted to smell exhaust fumes.

He felt the uncontrollable urge to go to the resort; he didn't belong here. It no longer felt like his home anymore. While it was familiar—he'd spent years here—it didn't have his heart. Last Resort did. Samantha did. Samantha . . .

Reaching over to the other side of the bed, he wanted to gather her up in his arms, but they came up empty. His eyes flew open. He couldn't tell if she was still there or not. He leapt up, pulled on his pants and raced out of the room, skidding to a halt when he saw her curled up on the couch, looking out the windows. The bright sun reflected off the water and, as promised, the bridge was visible. Breathing out a sigh of relief, he changed direction and went into the kitchen, filling up a coffee cup and enjoying the first morning taste of it before walking back out and sitting down next to her.

"You were right," she said.

"I usually am, but about what specifically?"

"Ha! Keep telling yourself that." She nudged her shoulder at him. "But you were right about being able to get back up to the resort around lunch time." She waved her phone at him. "Everything I've been able to check says that while there has been some damage, it wasn't too bad. The worst is the phones are out, along with a cell tower, so I haven't been able to talk to anyone up there yet."

"Well, that's great, but why don't you look happy?" He hoped she wasn't having second thoughts about their night together. He'd never had that kind of connection before, and he didn't want to lose it.

"I don't want you to get the wrong idea about last night. I'm sure you can figure it out. I typically don't go jumping into men's beds, but I also know there are no guarantees in life. I don't need any promises, empty or otherwise. I'm a big girl, and know everything can change in a moment. I need you to understand I'm going to take this for what it is and not ask you for anything."

He frowned at her, trying to understand what she was saying, or not saying. "Why are you talking like this?"

"Ethan, I'm not some young naïve girl. Look around here." She waved her arm. "This isn't me. There is nothing here that could fit into my resort. This is so far from what the resort stands for, but this is who you are, this goes with your job, where you make your money. I can't see you staying at the resort, and I'll never ask you to."

Standing up, he started pacing the room. Hadn't she heard anything he'd been saying over the last couple of weeks? She was confusing him and he needed to know why. "Sam, what's this all about? You know this means nothing to me. It's like the resort has seeped into my system so completely, it's changed me, made me a better person. I don't think there could ever be anything to make me leave." He stopped in front of her and dropped to his knees. "Don't you understand? *You* are what makes the resort. Without you, there's nothing. You both go together. It's not just the place that's in my system, *you* are who I don't want to leave. Do you understand what I'm saying to you?"

"But those people last night."

"Screw them. You didn't stick around to see the look on Peter's face. He knows his business dealings with me are done and he's scared. I've made him a lot of money over the years, and now he has to come up with something else to keep Marissa happy." He laced his fingers with hers. "Sam, I have more money than I know what to do with. Don't you understand what this could mean for the resort? Think of the wildest dreams you've ever had for the place. I can make them all happen for you. You'd never have to stress about running out of money, ever again. You'd be able to help so many more people. We could build something even more amazing, together." He looked at her with hope in his eyes. He was asking for more than just to be part of the resort with her. He tried to appeal to her first as a businessman, which was what he knew. All these feeling he had for her were so scary, he didn't know the right way to approach her, so he fell back on what he knew. Money.

She shook her head. "I can't take your money. That's not why I'm here." Wiggling her fingers, she tried to free her hands, but he wouldn't let go.

"Please, I know that. I think we've established I'm not an idiot. I didn't come from nothing to making all this money by being stupid. If it makes you feel better, we can become partners in the resort. Your knowledge and my money." He was panicking. He didn't want to lose her and was grasping at straws. He'd take being business partners to begin with before they moved on to their personal relationship.

"No, no, Ethan. I won't take your money." She held up a hand when he started to speak. "But, I will allow you to do certain improvements, which I have to approve of, on the property. You can get that look off your face, no you aren't going to run amok spending money. There are a few things I'd really love to have done and I don't want to wait ten years to be able to finish them all. And it will be a loan. We'll draw up the paperwork and I'll pay it back."

His first reaction was relief. She was receptive to

the idea of him staying and helping her. She didn't know how much it took for him to approach her with this and knowing everything was going to change between the two of them excited him. Then he narrowed his eyes at her. He should have known she'd be too stubborn to take the money right off the bat. He was losing his touch, he wanted both. But sometimes it was better to take what you could and try to rework the idea later. "Fine, but no interest." This time, he stopped her with a hand. "No arguments. We'll draw up what you want to do and a budget for each and I'll wire the money to your account. But there will be no interest. Please, do you really think I want to take money away from the guests?"

"No, no, you wouldn't." She looked down. "Thank you. This is going to make a huge difference."

"Anything for you. Anything." He lifted their hands and kissed the back of hers. "Now, let's get back up there, so we can put your worries to rest." It amazed him how far he'd come since he'd first believed she was somehow scamming people, trying to get their money, to ending up possibly giving her a million to do with whatever she wanted. He couldn't put a price tag on finding out who he was and finally realizing the type of man he was born to be.

Tension rode Ethan's shoulders the whole journey back up the mountain; the drive was far from easy. Thankfully, the weather had improved, but debris littered the road and some of the asphalt was washed out, so they had to carefully go around large rocks. He was grateful he'd taken so many years of defensive driving and racing classes. Looked like another one of his hobbies was going to end up paying off and helping

Samantha. The closer they were to the resort, the more tense he became. What if Sam's fears happened? What if one of the guests needed help and was unable to get any? What if one of the trees fell on a building? He was desperate to get there to make sure everything was okay.

Once they drove through the gates, a breath of relief whooshed out of his lungs. Everything looked good, so far. He took the road as quickly as he could and parked in front of the main house. Staff came out to greet them and help unload. He listened to everything they were saying to Sam. They had kept everyone in the rec center, together. Most of the guests thought of it as an adventure, while others didn't care one way or the other; they rolled with whatever was suggested.

He locked eyes with Sam and could see the tension, which had been around her eyes, was gone. She too was feeling better just being home and knowing everything was okay. Once everything was unloaded, Ethan parked the van in the barn, making sure nothing was leaking from the undercarriage. There were a couple of times it scraped on rocks during the drive. When he was satisfied everything looked good, he wondered what came next. He knew they'd both have things to do since they'd been gone for so long, but what would happen after that? He didn't want to spend any time away from her. After one night with her he didn't want to fall asleep without her in his arms.

Turning to walk out of the barn, Ethan saw her standing in the open doorway with the light coming in from behind her, he thought she looked like an angel and he wondered how he got so lucky. "Hey."

"Hey yourself." She kicked at the dirt with her shoe. "So . . ."

"So . . ."

"I was wondering, if maybe . . . Please don't feel like you have to say yes . . . I mean . . ."

He walked over to her and put his hands on her shoulders. "Samantha, just ask."

Closing her eyes, she took a deep breath. "If you want, you could spend some time over at my place."

Feeling a tremor run through her body, he knew she was asking for more than just him going over there for dinner and maybe spend some time together in the evenings. She was asking for more. He wanted more. "I'd love nothing more than to be with you, every day." He leaned down and kissed her softly.

Her dreamy eyes looked up at him and everything in his being fell into place. She was now his home and he'd no intention to ever leave it.

Chapter 15

DAY 37

ETHAN—

I FEEL GOOD, SO GOOD SOMETIMES IT'S HARD TO BELIEVE I'M DYING. I WAKE UP EVERY MORNING, THANKFUL FOR ANOTHER SUNRISE. I GO TO BED EVERY EVENING THANKFUL FOR THE SUNSET. IT'S THE LITTLE MOMENTS THAT MAKE EVERYTHING WORTHWHILE.

EVAN

Since they had all worked together to get everything cleaned up from the storm the day before, the scavenger hunt was still on. A couple of the employees had a fun time making up the clues for the rest of the staff and the guests. The guests said that both Sam and Ethan were disqualified from joining in and had to stay in their designated areas for the day.

120 DAYS...

Sam had strict written instructions that she was supposed to stay hidden in her office all day long. It also said that someone would deliver her food, and she could call down and have people bring her things, but she couldn't step foot outside. She had to make sure she was ready to go, in costume, at exactly six in the evening. That was it, no more, no less. Her fingers itched to open the zipper on the bag and see exactly what it was. She was told to give herself about an hour to get ready.

Shaking her head, she tried to get back to work, but she kept hearing the guests shuffling around, shouting out to each other about how far along they were. There was no denying they were having fun. She wondered what Ethan was doing and what his costume was.

Opening her files, she started organizing all the projects in order of importance. Ethan was almost done with the work-out room, so she could cross that one off the list. She tried to look everything over with an objective eye and see which ones would be the most beneficial to the resort.

When she had the surveyor come out to check the land for the supposed gold mine a few years back, she'd also had him map the land, where the best places to build would be. There was one piece of land, closer to the main road, which was the best for a large building, larger than the main house. If she could build that, she'd be able to help twenty more guests at a time. She could move the guests out of this building and use it all for staff purposes, which in turn would mean she'd also be able to hire more staff, which would then end up being more of a weekly expense.

Quickly, she started to figure out numbers, all with the thought that no guest would be able to pay for their stay. With the extra staff and care expenses, she'd run out of money in fifteen years, assuming there would be absolutely no income coming back into the resort, which wasn't going to happen. Some were able to pay for all of their care, others just a portion, though every little bit helped. They also had people who would donate to, or sponsored guests.

The question was should she play it conservative and maybe do something else with the money Ethan was going to loan her, or help more people, quickly. She crossed over to the big old chalkboard and started writing down the pros and cons for each. When she was done, she closed her eyes and shook her head; of course, she had equal numbers on both sides. Why did it seem everything was coming out even lately?

When her phone rang, she walked back over to her desk and answered. "Hello."

"Well, hello there, sexy lady. I've missed you today," Ethan said.

A grin formed on Sam's lips at the sound of his voice. "Me too. I've been going crazy being stuck in here all day. Where do they have you?"

"Let me put it to you this way, the gym will be all ready to go tomorrow. Complete with working showers, which is lucky for you, otherwise I might end up being smelly tonight."

"That's great!" She looked at the clock. It was only four. "They said it was going to take me an hour to get ready. I so want to peek and see what the costume is. Have you?"

"Nah, I can wait. But I did just finish up testing out the shower, so I've got nothing to do for an hour. They said it was going to take me an hour to get ready too. I can tell you that did make me a little nervous. I'm a guy, how can it take me an hour?"

"Oh! Now, I'm really curious . . . I wonder . . ."

"What?"

120 DAYS...

"Just trying to figure out a loop hole so we can look at the costumes without breaking the rules."

"You should have thought of that a couple of days ago. We've only an hour left to wait."

"I hate it when you make sense."

"Get used to it."

She snapped her fingers. "Speaking of making sense, maybe you can help me."

"Of course, what do you need?"

They spent the next hour going over the pros and cons she had listed for the improvements. When they hung up at five, she thought her spinning mind would never stop. He'd brought up a lot of good issues, both for and against, which was going to make it even harder to make a decision. But for the time being, she had to stop. It was time to get ready for the party. When there was a knock on the door, she went over and opened it up. Bethany smiled at her, which made her even more nervous than before. She was her right-hand woman who helped her run the office end of the business. She'd also help the guests with hair and makeup, either for fun or for a play they were doing. Since she'd been in theater during high school and college, she was the best one for the job.

"Move aside, missy, it's time to get ready. I've got work to do." She spun around to Sam. "You aren't in your costume yet? Girl, what am I going to do with you? Here." Bethany shoved the costume bag into her hands. "Get dressed. Now."

"Whatever." Sam grinned and walked into the small bathroom finally getting to unzip the bag. She laughed as her shaking fingers fumbled to pull the zipper down. A large, red, frilly, dress unfolded out of the bag. She cocked her head and frowned. "What in the hell—" She held up the tulle and shuddered, this was supposed to be fun, wearing a girly-girl dress wasn't what she considered fun.

"You do remember how to be a girl, right?" Bethany said from right outside the door. "Or do you need help?"

"I've got it. Hold your horses." Sam grumbled softly to herself as she took her clothes off and put the dress on. After struggling with the zipper for a couple of minutes, she gave up and asked for help.

"Ahhh . . . look at you. You know, you'd be absolutely gorgeous if you'd wipe that frown off your face."

"Yeah, yeah, yeah, just zip me up and zip your lips."

Bethany bent over laughing, "Oh, now, that's a good one. Oh my," She continued to laugh. "If you only knew! Man this is so much fun."

"I'm glad someone's having fun."

"There. All done. Turn around and look at yourself."

Sam turned and gasped. It looked like it was a blood red wedding dress. "What's going on here?"

"You'll have to wait and see! Now, come on, I've got to do your hair and makeup. You want to look good, don't you?"

"I have no idea, do I?" Sam wandered over to the chair Bethany held out for her and sat down, her stomach churning with nerves for what the guests had planned for them. She looked over and noticed everything laid out on her desk and blinked a few times. "Ummm . . . what *exactly* do you have planned for me? Because all of that"—she waved her hand—"looks deadly."

"Really?" Bethany put her hand on her hip and gave her a stern look. "You are female woman. I know you

120 DAYS...

know how to put on makeup and make your hair look all nice. That's all this is."

"No, all of that looks like torture devices specifically designed to make me look nothing like I really do."

"Have a little faith. It'll be fine; besides, it's only for one evening. Then you can go home and wash it all off."

"Promise?"

"Oh, hell, girl." Bethany held out her hand. "Pinky swear. How can someone who loves Halloween as much as you do hate putting on make-up?"

Sam pointed to the equipment on the desk. "That's not theatrical make up. That's girly make-up. *A lot* of girly make-up."

Bethany shook her head. "I wonder about you. Now hush, I have work to do."

Once that was out of the way, Sam tried to relax as her face was painted. She could feel the heaviness of it, and there was so much of it she was afraid it would crack if she tried to talk. Sitting there, she tried to focus more on what was being done to her than what was coming next, wondering what Ethan would be dressed up as.

"There! Yes, you look perfect."

"Says you," Sam mumbled, trying not to move her lips too much.

"Oh, come on, you can talk normally. Your face isn't going to fall off."

Sam tried to open and close her mouth a few times, surprised Bethany was right; her face didn't feel like it was cracking, or worse yet, falling off. "Hmmm . . . well, what do you know?"

"You should listen to me more often."

"Yes, ma'am."

"Don't you get sassy with me." She nodded toward the bathroom. "Go look at yourself."

Sam couldn't be sure, but she thought Bethany tried to hide the fact she was laughing at her. Taking a deep breath, Sam walked in and faced the mirror before she turned on the light. All she was able to do was stare at what she assumed was herself. It had to be, the person in the mirror mimicked everything she did, but it sure didn't look anything like her.

"Well, what do you think of my handiwork? Do you recognize it?"

Shaking her head, Sam didn't break eye contact with herself. She had to remind herself to breathe, and tell herself everything was going to be okay.

"Lydia, from *Beetlejuice*! You're Lydia! Isn't this a great costume? And if I do say so myself, I did an excellent job on the hair and makeup. You look just like her! Isn't this great? Now, come on, we've got to get you down to the rec center."

"Yeah... sure..." She felt like herself on the inside, but on the outside nothing was close to what she normally looked like.

Bethany grabbed her hand, pulled her out of the room, and kept the pressure on until they were at the side doors into the rec center. "Now, you go in and have a great time."

"Wait!" Sam wouldn't let her leave. "Where are you going?"

"Oh, I've got other plans for the night. You go ahead, and you'll be fine."

"What do you mean, 'I'll be fine?' I don't know what I'm doing here."

"All you need to do is walk through those doors and

enjoy the evening. Easy."

"Says you."

"Yes, says me, now shoo. Go relax and have some fun you didn't plan for a change." With that, Bethany disappeared.

There was nothing left for Sam to do but open the doors and go in. There was only a very low light coming from the rec room, so she couldn't tell what was inside. Taking a deep breathe, she squared her shoulders and flung the door open and stepped through into an eerie blue light and a lot of fog. It reminded her of the Halloween parties they usually had.

As soon as she stepped through, the blue light turned to red and the door directly across from her was flung open and someone stumbled through it. Sam squinted her eyes. There standing across from her was Beetlejuice, or as she suspected, Ethan. She couldn't help herself, she started laughing and walked over to him as someone started the stereo with the movie's theme music playing.

"Beetlejuice, Beetlejuice, Beetlejuice," she said.

"You know that means you've summoned me, and can't get rid of me."

"I do."

"Well, then, as long as we're clear." He held out his arm for her. "May I have this dance?"

He danced her around the room to the music coming out of the stereo system. As they passed by, she could see all the guests standing around in costumes from the movie. Everyone was laughing and having a good time.

"Was there even a scavenger hunt?" she asked him.

"Somehow I don't think so. It seems to be some

elaborate plan to get us to spend some more time together, and pay off our bet at the same time."

"Well, I really can't see anything wrong with this. Except maybe the fact that I have ten pounds of makeup on."

"If it makes you feel any better, so do I, and I must say, this isn't my typical shade." He smiled down at her.

"Yeah, and your hair... wow."

"What, you don't think this greyish-green is my color? They said it brought out the color of my eyes."

"You might want to see a different consultant next time."

The music slowed even more and Ethan pulled Sam closer to him. "I've got you in my arms. As far as I'm concerned, they could have done anything and I'd be happy as long as you are with me."

"I don't know why I was so nervous." She rested her head on his chest. "This feels so right."

They were allowed to dance for a little longer before the lights were turned up enough to see better and the chairs and couches were moved around, then the food and popcorn was brought out. The group all talked and ate as a large screen was pulled down and they watched the movie they were all dressed up as. People shouted out the lines they knew, especially if they were dressed up as that character. At the very end of the movie they all got back up again and started dancing to "Jump in the Line" by Harry Belafonte.

As Sam and Ethan walked back to her house hand in hand, she thought it was one of those magical evenings she was going to remember. After all, in the movie, Beetlejuice didn't get Lydia, but it would seem, in real life, he would.

Chapter 16

DAY 42

ETHAN—

DID YOU SEE THAT? DAY FORTY-TWO, BROTHER. THEY GAVE ME FOUR-TO-SIX WEEKS TO LIVE. NOW EVERY DAY FROM HERE ON OUT IS A BONUS. I REMEMBER MY FIRST DAY HERE, I WANTED TO MAKE IT TO FORTY-TWO, AND I DID. I STILL FEEL PRETTY GOOD AND I'M GOING TO DO EVERYTHING I CAN TO MAKE IT ONE HUNDRED-AND-TWENTY DAYS.

EVAN

Ethan knew this was a huge step for Sam. She was allowing him to meet their newest guest and get him all settled in. When she'd told him this morning what he was going to be doing, he'd acted like it was no big deal, but he knew better. She trusted him to do it by himself. Over the past couple of weeks, she'd been showing him more and more of the daily operations of the resort. The more he learned, the more amazed by her he became. He knew it was a lot of work, but to actually see everything, was something entirely different.

When he heard a car pull up, he walked out on the porch watching the tall bald man in a Green Bay Packers shirt unfold himself from the taxi. Ethan was there and ready, paying the driver and making sure the staff came over to collect the bags from the trunk, before reaching out to shake the man's hand. "Welcome, Mr. Lesky, to Last Resort, I'm Ethan."

"I'd say it's nice to be here, but you know." He shrugged. "And call me Kris. I'm dying. We don't need to be big on formalities."

Ethan smiled. "Kris it is. I can see you're a football fan." They headed toward the resort. Ethan also knew the tall, bald man in his early forties, was divorced and had two young daughters, Spring and Jules. He had battled brain cancer three other times before it came back even more aggressive. The surgeons weren't able to remove it all.

"Fan is too mild a word when it comes to my Packers. They're playing the San Francesco 49ers in a couple of weeks. I'm hoping to be able to make it to the game."

Stopping in front of one of the cabins, Ethan nodded to the man. "I'm sure we can make that happen. Sam, the owner, and myself, were talking about you and we made sure the television in your cabin gets all of the football games along with the rec center. You don't have to worry about missing any games this season."

"Perfect. I think this is the year the Packers win

another Superbowl."

"Don't let Sam hear you say that. She's a Bear's fan."

"Oh, really? Well, this should make for a very interesting season." Kris grinned and slapped Ethan on the back.

Later that evening, Sam sat cuddled up to Ethan on her porch swing, rocking back and forth, watching the sun go down. They had a blanket over their legs to ward against the crisp fall chill in the air.

"Did you have a chance to meet Kris Lesky today?" Ethan asked.

"Yes, yes, I did. Did you have to tell him I was such a Bears fan? I think that man had every single Packer's gear he brought with him on." She chuckled. "It was actually pretty funny. I made sure we got a picture of it. Although if they beat the Bears, I told him he may need to deal with you that day."

"I can do that. I guess he's more into football than we thought. He's been in a fantasy league for years. He was kind of bummed he wasn't going to finish out this year. He didn't want to commit to a spot and then not make it to the end of the season."

"I can understand that." Sam swung her foot gently back and forth, the wind rustling the leaves the only sound. "But he should still be able to play . . . I wonder . . ." The season had already begun, but they weren't that far into it. "Do you think we could come up with some kind of weekly fantasy game? I know there are other guests and staff who like football, and you know I do." She sat up. "Yeah, we could totally do this. It's Tuesday, perfect. We can get this up and running before the Thursday night game. We should have something for weekly winners, and then whoever wins the most for the season." She stood up, went into the kitchen and pulled out a pad of paper and pen, and then grabbed her tablet before coming back out and sitting back down next to Ethan. "Here." She handed him her tablet. "See if you can find any kind of weekly type football fantasy games we can use here." She tapped the pen to her lips. "Do you know enough about football to play?"

"Seriously?" He yanked on a lock of her hair. "I can't believe you're asking me about this. Of course."

"Really?" She sat up and turned to look at him. "You've never said anything about it before."

"Well, it's not something I need to bring up in any conversation, but yes, I like, and know a lot about, football. Just because we've been too busy working with the guests during the games this season doesn't mean I still haven't kept up on the scores."

She squinted her eyes at him, hoping it wasn't a team she didn't like. "Be careful how you answer, but who is your favorite team?"

Leaning back, he laced his fingers together and put them behind his head. "Wouldn't you like to know, Ms. Truman?"

"I would, which is why I asked. Now spill."

"What's it worth to you?"

"How about this." She leaned in close. "I won't hurt you, too much, even if you happen to pick a team I loathe."

"Well, well, well, a little blood-thirsty, are we?"

"When it comes to football, hell yeah. Now spill. Who's your favorite team?"

"Same as Evan, the Seahawks."

"Oh, whew." She relaxed and settled back into him.

"I was seriously worried you were going to say the Cowboys or something like that." She shuddered. "I'm not sure if I could get past that."

He laughed softly. "Well, I guess that's lucky for both of us then. But seriously, this is a great idea and it'll be fun for anyone who likes football. Maybe we can have some tailgate-style parties here on Sundays."

"Oh, yes! I love that idea. I don't know why we haven't done something like this before. This is going to be great. And the Packers are coming to town soon. We'll make sure we get Kris down on the field. I've already started putting out feelers, and it shouldn't be an issue."

"Let me know if you run into roadblocks. I may not like the 49ers, but I do have contacts and can get us access."

"Excellent. Now, let's figure out exactly how this is going to work every week for the rest of the season and playoffs."

Thursday night football was in full swing and everyone was enjoying themselves; in fact, they were all getting pretty loud. Ethan had made a trip down into town to make sure everyone had their favorite team's jersey to wear during the season. Everyone had made their picks and were alternating between the laptops stationed around the rec center and the big screen, which had the game on. The Chargers were playing the Saints and it was a close game.

He came up to Sam and wrapped his arm around her waist. When she leaned back into him, he took a moment to enjoy having her and this place in his life. His life was so different from a year earlier, and he could finally say, with complete conviction, he was happy with the direction his life was taking. He knew it wasn't going to be easy, but with Sam by his side, he felt like he could handle anything life could throw at him.

Half the room cheered when the Saints scored again, while the other half booed. Laughing, he had to hand it to her, she'd whipped this up quickly and everyone was enjoying themselves. As always, he wondered where her boundless energy and ideas came from. If you asked her, she'd only smile and tell you it was a gift.

"Did you see that?" Sam shook her ass in a dance. "That was my quarterback throwing to my tight end. You know I was worried when they traded the best tight end in the league, but I've got to admit, this new kid is pretty good. But isn't this great? Everyone is having so much fun! Seriously, I'm kicking myself for not thinking of this sooner. Oh, I know, it's going to change. There are going to be times when the majority of the guests won't like football, but still, it's something we can all do together. Who doesn't need an excuse to have a party? Now if da Bears could just kick some Packer ass this Sunday night, it'll be an awesome start to our little fantasy season." She turned to look at him when he didn't say anything. "Are you okay?"

"Oh, yeah, I'm great, just waiting to make sure you were done talking before I started. You're a little scary when you start talking about football."

"Oh, stop it. I am not." She bumped her hip into his.

"Next time you start talking about the eighty-five Bears as being one of the greatest teams ever, I'll be sure to record you. And when someone insulted Ditka, well, I feared for their life."

"Oh, now you're only trying to be funny. I'm not

that bad. I know it's only a game."

"Keep telling yourself that."

"Anyway." She narrowed her eyes at him. "We should do a half-time show. I think we'd be able to come up with something fun. We have the Thursday, Sunday and Monday night games where we wouldn't have to worry about interfering with the other games which are going on at the same time. Maybe doing three a week would be a lot. We should pick one night and do that game. Whichever one is going to be most anticipated. That way, as the season goes on and teams are fighting for playoff spots, it will be more intense."

"See, just a little scary there."

"Shut it. And we can come up with something for the people who want to play, but don't know much about the sport. We can give them lessons, you know, make it fun for them. Or maybe give them some other role in the festivities. Yeah, let me think on that. I don't want anyone to feel left out."

"Are you always like this? Or is it just because it's football?"

"Like what?"

"So excited, and your mind's weaving around, finding other ways to make the whole experience better."

"Oh, that. Well, I *am* excited about football, but basically, I'd be like this with any new idea. That's why we have so many different activities here because I can't only do the basics." She shrugged and looked sheepish. "I tend to go overboard. But look, everyone is having a great time."

"Yes, they are. Now, it's almost half time. We should make sure the hot dogs and hamburgers will be ready on time for the next round of eating."

120 DAYS...

"Now you're talking! Plus, I'm pretty sure I'm already beating Kris. I need to go talk some smack."

Ethan shook his head. "You're never going to change my mind. You *are* out for blood when it comes to this game."

She threw back her head and laughed. "Oh, honey, just wait until playoffs." She pointed to the screen. "You remember the last time the Bears went to the Superbowl, they played against the Saints, and we know who won that game. I should hate that team, but I want my fantasy team to win so badly, I picked their quarterback as mine. I tend to be a little competitive."

"I wouldn't say 'little.'" Ethan shook his head at her.

Sam laughed. "Me either. Let's get cooking, I've got more points to score in the second half."

Letting her pull him along, they walked outside to where the grills were set up. The smell of dogs and burgers filling the night air reminded him he hadn't had a chance to eat yet. There had been too much to do to make sure everything was ready for tonight.

"Look." She pointed up to the sky and the stars shining brightly. "Isn't it beautiful? Some people feel small when they look up at them all blinking up there. Me, it makes me feel special. There's never going to be another moment like this, ever. And that light we're seeing from those other stars? Their moment has already gone, but this." She looked into his eyes. "This moment here, with you, is right now. This moment is special. They all are."

He pulled her into his arms and his whole being felt complete when he held her. She was right. The moment was special. All of them with her were. He felt all of the pieces of his life click into place, and for the first time in a very long time, he was happy. They were spending more and more time together. Both of them not wanting to be away from the other. He'd never spent this much time with a woman before, and knew even if he had, none of them were Sam, so it wouldn't have been the same. In that moment, he belonged with her.

Chapter 17

DAY 45

ETHAN—

YOU KNOW WHAT I MISS? FOOTBALL. WELL, THERE'S A LOT OF THINGS, BUT TODAY I WAS REMEMBERING WHEN SAM TOOK US UP TO SEATTLE. AND IT BROUGHT BACK THE SOUND OF THE HELMETS AND PADS CRASHING TOGETHER, THE AIR TURNING CHILLY THE FURTHER WE GOT INTO THE SEASON, THE FOOD, THE BEER, GOOD FRIENDS GETTING TOGETHER TO CHEER ON THEIR TEAMS. YEAH, I MISS THAT. PROMISE ME THE NEXT TIME THE SEAHAWKS MAKE IT TO THE SUPERBOWL, YOU'LL GO. I ALWAYS WANTED TO GO, BUT MISSED OUT ON THE LAST TWO TIMES THEY WENT. I SHOULD HAVE GONE, I SHOULD HAVE MADE YOU COME WITH ME.

EVAN

120 DAYS...

The next couple of weeks were spent getting the cabins ready for the winter months, and Ethan and Sam were getting into a rhythm, living together in her home. They weren't going to waste a minute apart, both of them knowing how quickly things could change. They worked alongside each other by day, and by night, they spent time sharing their past, and tentatively talking about their future together.

Football season was really heating up, along with their fantasy football league, and that day was football Sunday. But not any Sunday. This was the Sunday the Packers played the 49ers. Ethan did his normal check of the van before they left. There were five of them going to the game. Kris of course, and Sam wouldn't miss it for anything. There were two other football fans who didn't care who was playing; they only wanted to go see a professional game played in person.

Ethan had pulled some strings and they were going to be able to go down onto the field before kickoff and would be in the owner's box for the game. He thought it would be best to keep the guests out of the elements since they never knew what the weather would be like that time of year. Hot, cold, rain, or any combination of the three. What Sam didn't realize was they were also going to be able to meet some of the players. He figured both Sam and Kris would be ecstatic. Kris more so since one of the teams was his favorite.

When Sam came out of the main building, Ethan had to do a double-take. She was wearing a Packers shirt.

"Not one word," she threatened as she walked by him and put a bag in the van.

"But—"

"I said, not one word." She narrowed her eyes at him and crossed her arms over her chest. "I'm serious."

Bruce and Dolores walked over and took their seats in the van without saying a word to Sam. Either they had already seen her and met with the same threats as Ethan, or they knew better. Kris came around the corner of the building slowly. It didn't take an expert to know he was fading. The tumor in his brain was growing too fast and he was starting to lose some motor skills.

Ethan came over and helped Kris into the van and waited for Sam to climb in next to him in the front seat before he headed down the hill. They were silent as they all listened to the pregame show on the radio and the updates from the other games going on around the league.

"I see you've finally got your head on straight there, Sam," Kris said from the second row of seats.

"I don't know what you're talking about." She didn't turn around.

His laugh was loud. "Of course you do. I knew I could make a Cheesehead out of you."

Sam raised an eyebrow and looked at him over her shoulder. "I'm pretty sure I could make a judge see it is only temporary insanity."

"You break out in hives yet?" he asked.

"No. Although I do feel dirty." She smiled at him.

"There we go." His smiled faded. "You didn't have to do this for me."

"Yes, yes, I did." She leaned over the seat and closer to him. "I'll let you in on a little secret. While I loathe the Packers, the 49ers are even worse. There are a few teams I'll root for, whoever is playing against them. This is one of those occasions where it's better to wear a Packers shirt than have the 49ers win."

120 DAYS...

"Are you telling me you already had that shirt before I got here?"

"Oh, yeah, I have all thirty-two team shirts, depending on who's playing when we make it to a game." She shrugged. "I like to be prepared."

"Now *that* is impressive. And by the way, you look good in green and gold."

"I look better in blue and orange. Now those shirts, I have a lot of."

The traffic became worse the closer they were to the stadium. Ethan had a special parking pass and they were able to park with the rest of the VIPs. He loved to see the wide-eyed shocked look on Sam's face. He didn't think people took her by surprise very often.

"What are we doing? What did you do?" She looked at Ethan.

"Just made a couple of phone calls. This is going to be a great game. Come on." He hopped out of the van and met one of the stadium employees, knowing they'd be following him. "This way." He walked a few feet over to a large golf cart and everyone took their seats.

Josie was their tour guide and made sure everything was pointed out to them. When they came through the tunnel and were out on the field, the air pulsated with everyone's excitement. Josie made sure they were on the visitor sidelines.

When Ethan heard Kris gasp, he whirled around and started walking toward him, afraid something was wrong, but everything was fine.

"No way," Kris whispered.

Ethan put his arm around the man's shoulders. "Way. We pull out all the stops at Last Resort."

Members of the Packers team came out of the

tunnel and headed straight for Kris. Ethan stepped back and took pictures as the team talked with one of their biggest fans. Kris's smile never left his face.

Too soon they were leaving, having to warm up. The group then made their way up to the owner's suite and Sam pulled him aside.

"What did you do?" she asked.

He couldn't stop the smile. "It's great, isn't it?"

"It is, but Ethan, the money . . ."

"Don't mention it." He placed a finger over her lips. "I wanted to do this. Come on, did you see the look on his face? This is a dream come true, and exactly what Last Resort is all about."

"It is. Thank you." She smiled at him. "But you know, when the Bears come to town, I expect the same treatment."

"Oh, well, I think I can make that happen."

"Perfect. Now I want to see this suite we're going to." He put his arm around her shoulders as they walked. "You know what would be perfect? If the Packers kicked some major ass here. Seems like we have something else in common. We hope the 49ers lose."

Sam stopped walking. "Wait. What are we going to do when the Cowboys play the 49ers? . . . Don't laugh at me. This is a serious question."

"Maybe we could boycott that game."

"Yes." She slowly nodded. "Yes, I think that could work. We should do that."

"Come on." He pulled her along. "Let's go root for the Packers."

"Yeah . . ." she said without enthusiasm. "Go, Pack, Go!" She raised her fist in the air.

120 DAYS...

The Packers effectively kicked some 49er ass. The ride back to the resort was upbeat as they all talked about the game and who had the best chance to make it to the Superbowl. Sam could see Kris in the backseat clutching a football, which had been used during the game, to his chest. All of the Packers had signed it for him and given it to him after the game. She had to admit, it was pretty cool they did that for him. Ethan said he didn't have any idea they were going to give him one of the game balls.

"You know, Sam," Kris began, "I think you might be the Packer's good luck charm."

"No."

Kris laughed. "I think you should wear that shirt every time they play. Come on, do it for me. Doesn't your website say something about making sure the guest's every wish is carried out?"

She turned in her seat and looked at him as the passing street lights lit up his grinning face. "There are some things in life that are just impossible. That's one of them."

"Come on, you've got to be a closet Packer fan. I was there. I saw you. You were excited and yelling for joy when the Packers scored."

"Of course I was. They were sticking it to the 49ers."

"Keep telling yourself that, keep telling yourself that." Kris nodded toward her.

Sam didn't let the smile reach her lips. The day had been perfect. Giving Kris a hard time was an extra bonus to the day, and she had already learned that about him. He loved to give it as much as he got it. There was no denying the fact that Kris wasn't going to be with them much longer and it brought her heart so much happiness knowing this one dream went beautifully for him.

Chapter 18

DAY 48

ETHAN

YOU KNOW WHAT SUCKS? A SUMMER COLD. YEAH, I'VE COME DOWN WITH SOMETHING. IT TAKES ME LONGER TO GET OVER THINGS THAN IT USED TO. THERE ARE SO MANY THINGS I WANT TO DO RIGHT NOW, BUT I DON'T WANT TO GET THE OTHER GUESTS SICK. SAM'S HELPED A LOT, FIGURING OUT THINGS I CAN DO WITH THE STAFF OR ALONE. SO HERE I AM, RESTING IN BED AS THE SUN IS SHINING AND IT'S THE PERFECT TEMPERATURE OUT, NOT TOO HOT, NOT TO COLD. MAYBE I SHOULD MOVE TO THE HAMMOCK. HEY, REMEMBER THE ONE DAD BOUGHT FOR MOM? SHE NEVER SAT DOWN LONG ENOUGH TO ENJOY IT, BUT WE DID, UNTIL WE WERE PLAYING ON IT AND YOU FLIPPED IT OVER AND LANDED ON THAT ROCK BUSTING YOUR HEAD OPEN. AHHH ... MEMORIES ...

EVAN

Ethan rolled over and fumbled for his phone when the alarm went off. He laid there for a moment trying to remember where he was and what day it was. He then realized what was bothering him. Usually Sam woke

120 DAYS...

him up with a cup of coffee a few minutes before his alarm went off. They'd fallen into a rhythm and were spending more and more time together, including nights. Reaching his hand out, he knew she wasn't in bed with him. His heart began to race, wondering here she could be. It wasn't like her. If one of the guests had taken a turn for the worse, she would have woken him up.

Once he swung his legs over the edge of the bed, Ethan saw the bathroom light coming through the door, which was ajar. "Sam, honey, are you okay?" He walked over to the door and slowly pushed it open. His heart went out to her as she looked up at him with huge tearful eyes. Crouching down next to her, he rubbed her back. "Is there anything I can get you? Crackers?"

He'd heard the saying about watching someone turn green before throwing up, but he'd never seen it, until that moment. He mumbled to her that everything was going to be okay as he helped to hold her hair back. Looking around, he found a wash cloth and left her briefly to soak it under some cold water. Placing it on the back of her neck, she shuddered, and goosebumps broke out along her arms before she sighed and seemed to relax.

"Why didn't you wake me?"

"Because it all happened so fast. One minute I was getting out of bed, all normal, and the next I knew, I was going to be sick. I didn't think. I just ran."

Ethan pulled another wash rag out of the cabinet and ran it under the water again. This time he gently washed her face off. "How are you feeling now?"

"I think better. Tired, drained, but that's to be expected, but overall better."

"Good, let's get you in bed."

"But I have so much to do today. We were going to work on the rec hall today, get it ready for Halloween. Plus, I was going to look at next week, and see if there was anything different we wanted to do."

"And you know I'm perfectly capable of doing all of that on my own. Besides, you of all people know you shouldn't be around the guests when you're sick. We need to make sure you're well before letting you back out into public." He easily picked her up and walked over to the bed, gently laying her down. "Now you get some rest." When she tried to sit up, he pushed her back down. "Samantha, listen to me. You work very hard around here, you never take a day off. The last thing this place needs is for you to get sick. So take the damn day off and rest for a change. That includes working on your laptop."

"But you don't know what we do for Halloween, we go out. We've got—"

"I think I can figure it out. And if you haven't noticed, you go all out for every holiday. This isn't a news flash to me."

"But Halloween is different. You haven't been here for what we call the holiday season. It starts with Halloween and ends with New Year's Day. Each one over-the-top big. This is the hardest time of the year for the guests. They're missing their families and they know they, most likely, aren't going to be seeing another one. They want to remember the good times, the times from their childhood, when everything was simpler, magical. That's what we make sure we give them."

Ethan sat down on the edge of the bed and brushed her hair back from her forehead. "You are truly amazing. I don't think there's another person like you out there. Your compassion blows me away, every single day."

120 DAYS...

She shook her head. "I'm nothing special. I'm only doing what's right. Being kind to people, trying to help them. That's it."

"Even if it means putting on a Packers' shirt."

"Even then, and don't remind me. I haven't thrown up in ten minutes. I'd like to make it another five."

"I think you should take the rest of the day off. I'm serious here. Humor me."

Her eyebrows pulled together and she frowned at him. "I'm going to be bored. You have to at least let me have my laptop to do some work."

"I think it might do you good to be bored for once because I don't know if you can be trusted with your laptop. I think you'll end up working and not resting."

"No, not me."

"Samantha Rose Truman."

"Fine. How about if I promise." She looked up at him and batted her eyelashes at him. "For every hour I nap, I get an hour of laptop time."

"No, for every *two* hours you nap, you get forty-five minutes on the laptop."

Crossing her arms over her chest, she sighed. "Fine."

He leaned down and kissed her on the forehead. "Don't make me regret this." He went over to the table in the corner of the room near the French doors leading out to the balcony, grabbed her laptop and held it out to her. "Here." He pulled it back toward him. "I'll be checking up on you. So don't think you can pull one over on me." He held it back out to her.

Tugging it quickly out of his hands, Sam said, "I wouldn't dream of it. I'm going to check my email and then take a nap." She yawned. "See, I'll be asleep in no time."

"You'd better be. Get. Some. Rest."

"Yes, sir." She already had her laptop open and was working. "Now go so I can get this done and get some sleep." She looked up at him when he walked away from her and started getting ready for the day. "I am tired and I'll take a nap soon. We have about fifty plastic containers of Halloween decorations, each one labeled as to which building it goes in. Most of the staff were here last year, so they will be able to remember and help you if you need it. The first day we usually organize everything, putting the containers in the right areas and putting batteries in the decorations. Not everything gets batteries, which is good. That would cost us a fortune. Only the decorations in the common areas need to make sure they work. Everything else really is only there for show. I should be better by tomorrow to help start to put them all up."

"First off, you don't worry about tomorrow. Rest today, and we'll see what happens tomorrow. Second, fifty containers? Please tell me they are the small ones."

She laughed at him. "Nope. This happens to be my favorite holiday." She shrugged. "I indulge myself, and the guests always love it. Oh, and there is the occasional guest who isn't a fan of the holiday, or who gets scared easily. You'll have to check the current register and see if we have anyone who marked that on their forms. If there are, we try to go easy in the areas they like to relax in, and of course, nothing in their cabin. Sometimes it helps if they are shown exactly where everything is, in the daylight, or how it works."

"Good to know. I'll check that before we get started today."

"Or I could check it right now for you. I know what to look for." She started tapping on the keys.

120 DAYS...

Ethan strode over to her and put his hand on the laptop as if he was going to close it. "You're already making me regret my decision. Check your email, and take a nap. That's all you should be concerned with right now. Understand?"

"But, it will only take me fifteen minutes."

"No, who cares if it takes me thirty, you need to ease up. Let me do this for you and you get some rest."

"When did you get so bossy?"

"Honey, I've always been bossy, but I never thought I'd find someone who makes me look like a pushover."

"What?"

He leaned down and looked her straight in the eye. "Yes, my dear, you are bossy, but I happen to find it very attractive on you because it comes from your heart. You're only trying to make things better for everyone. Now relax and be quiet so I can do the same for you."

When she didn't say anything, he raised his eyebrow at her. "What, nothing to say?"

"You told me to be quiet."

"And you listened? Well, that was easy." He smiled and winked at her. "I'll have to remember that. Now, I have to get to work before my boss writes me up for being late."

"You got that right, mister. You'd better move it."

He went over and opened the balcony doors for her. With the sun coming up, it was warming up outside and he knew she'd want to hear the birds and breathe in the fresh air. "There, perfect napping weather. I'll check back in a little later."

"I'll be here. Resting. All day."

"You'd better be."

She saluted him as he walked out of the room. Grabbing some coffee, he thought about what Sam had said about the containers and how she had to be exaggerating. Surely there was a better, more efficient way to get it all done sooner.

Five hours later, they finally had all the containers down from the barn and where they were supposed to go. They still needed to check the batteries on the decorations in about half the containers. Ethan was thinking maybe he should have asked Sam more questions. Like how she could have gotten all this work done in one day. Even with all the extra help he was getting, he didn't think they'd be done by dinner.

They took the cart and dropped a container off at each cabin and room in the main house. Since none of the guests had any aversions to Halloween, he didn't have to worry and was able to put everything where it needed to be. Since most of the guests liked the rec center, he thought that would be the best place to start. Looking at fifteen large containers, he shook his head and hoped not every single decoration needed a battery. He now knew why every time they went into town, she was picking up batteries. Between Halloween and Christmas coming up, they were going to go through a lot of them.

Pausing for a moment, he thought about what Christmas would be like at the ranch. There would be no doubt Sam would do everything in her power to make sure the place was magically decorated. He was sure it would be a bittersweet time for everyone.

Ethan frowned as many of the resort's guests started filing into the rec center. He looked around and saw Phil escorting guests to different tables. Once

120 DAYS...

everyone was seated, Phil started talking. "Thank you for coming out. You'll see there are tools and batteries on everyone's table. If you need help or more batteries, let us know and we'll make sure you get what you need. Now, you all go easy on Mr. McGregor here. I think he's feeling a bit overwhelmed today since Miss Truman is out sick. But that's okay. We'll do a great job, right?" There was a round of good-natured ribbing toward Ethan before the staff started making sure each table had a container.

Reading the top of each container, Ethan started organizing them and making sure similar containers were put together. What Sam hadn't told him earlier, there were already an additional seven containers, which had been used for their Beetlejuice viewing, already checked and was ready to go. That meant there were closer to sixty containers left to go through. Looking at his watch, he knew it was almost time to check on her again. She'd been sleeping the last time he went up to the house. On one hand, he was happy she was resting; on the other, he was worried she was actually resting, and he wasn't the only one. The staff told him she hardly ever took a sick day. In fact, most had never seen her take one. Sure, she'd take some personal time off to go into town, but she always combined it with shopping for the resort, so it was never a full personal day off.

Since everything was handled, he took a break and went to check on Sam. He crept through the house quietly, to make sure if she was sleeping he didn't want to wake her, but if she was working, which he assumed she was, he wanted to bust her so he could give her a hard time. Sure enough, the closer he got to the bedroom door, he could hear her tapping on the keys of her laptop.

Walking in, he didn't stop until he pulled the laptop

off her lap, ignoring her protests.

"Anything you want to tell me?" he asked, his eyebrow raised.

"No." Sam raised both eyebrows at him. "Nothing, can I have my laptop back?"

"Let's see . . ." He used the touchpad to view what she had been doing. "I think you have some explaining to do, young lady."

"I took a nap after you left."

"For how long."

She shrugged. "I wasn't keeping track."

"Just like you weren't keeping track of how long you've been working. You owe me a four-hour nap."

"No way." She shook her head. "There's no way I could sleep that long."

"Then you shouldn't have worked so long."

"But . . . but . . . I was in bed resting the whole time."

"Nice try." He clicked the button to save her work and closed her laptop. "I'm taking this with me. You sleep." He walked over and kissed the top of her head while he kept her laptop out of her reach. "I'll be back in a little bit, and you'd better be sleeping."

"How's the decorating going?" She had a hopeful expression on her face.

"You'll find out tonight. You're already over on your work hours."

"Come on, you've got to cut me some slack. I'm not used to not being able to do anything."

"You need to get used to it. Honey, I'm part of your life now. We're in this together, which means you can relax some and let me help you. I know, it's a crazy idea, but you'll get used to it."

She smiled at him. "I like the sound of that, 'We're

120 DAYS...

in this together.' But you have to cut me some slack, too. I'm not used to depending on someone to help me."

"Yeah, I kind of already picked up on that."

"You don't have to be sarcastic."

"Anyway, I have to get back to letting the guests run amok and destroy the place. I'll be back around dinner."

"Ethan!"

"Bye, love!" He quickly ran down the stairs and laughed when he saw a pillow sail out of the room and hit the wall. "Great arm, honey, maybe we should start a softball team." Not able to stop himself from laughing, he knew he had to leave before she got out of the bed and chased after him.

With everyone helping, the rest of the work for the day went quickly, and they finished right before dinner. Ethan jogged down the path toward Sam's house. He wanted to see how she was doing. Last time he'd taken her laptop away, so he was sure she was going stir-crazy. He went to the resort kitchen to grab something for dinner. He didn't want her to think she had to cook for them.

As he approached the house his stomach grumbled; he could smell dinner cooking. Sam must be feeling better, a lot better if the aroma coming from the open kitchen window was any indication. He could see her dancing around and as he put his hand on the screen door to open it, he heard her singing. He smiled. She was back to her normal self.

"Hey, Lucy, I'm home." He tried for his best Ricky Ricardo impression.

"Dinner's almost ready. Tell me how the rest of the day went? I felt so bad for staying home, but I must admit, you were right, I feel so much better now."

"Whoa, wait." He staggered to the chair. "Let me sit down." He let his legs fold under him and looked up at her with his eyes open as big as they could go. "Did I hear correctly? Did you just say I was right? Come here." He reached out, and took her hand, and put it on his forehead. "Do I have a fever? I must have a fever to hear you say that. You must have gotten me sick."

"Stop." She gently pushed his head back. "Keep it up and no dinner for you."

"Well, it does smell wonderful. I think I'll let it go, for now." He winked at her. "Is there anything I can do to help?"

"Nope, you can go get cleaned up. Dinner will be ready when you are."

"Perfect." He stood up and gave her a kiss on the cheek as he passed by. "I'll be back down in about fifteen."

"I'll be waiting." She turned and went back to the sink humming.

Ethan stood there for a moment, trying to memorize everything. It was a good day, all of the guests were doing well. He'd been there long enough to know the signs of when the end was approaching; although everyone was different, and sometimes they snuck up on you, if the cancer was growing fast. But for the most part, they usually had a couple of days' warning before the guest was going to need round-the-clock care which came at the end.

Sam looked so beautiful—she always did—but there was something different about today. When he'd first come to the resort, she'd been all business, not hard, but she didn't let many people in or get too close to her. He could barely remember that version. The Sam before him let him see her weak, let him help her. And he had to admit, he was in love with her. He wished he could pinpoint the exact second he fell. It was something you didn't want to forget, but he couldn't. It was a culmination of things, building on one another until he couldn't deny it any longer.

Turning, he took the stairs two at a time, plotting what he was going to do next. He'd never been in this situation before and didn't know how to handle it. He had to find a way to make her see she was in love with him. There was no way she couldn't be, and they needed to spend the rest of their lives together. There, at Last Resort, making their dreams come true.

Chapter 19

DAY 49

ETHAN-

I'M STILL NOT FEELING TOO WELL, SO SAM TOOK ME TO THE DOCTOR. I WAS HOPING I'D BE DONE WITH THEM WHEN I CAME UP HERE, BUT AS SAM SAID, WE HAVE TO DO WHATEVER WE CAN TO EXTEND MY LIFE, AND THAT INCLUDES GOING TO THE DOCTOR WHEN I HAVE A COLD. SHE'S RIGHT, BUT I DON'T HAVE TO LIKE IT.

EVAN

Sam got up as quietly as she could and made her way to the bathroom. This was the third morning in a row she had gotten sick. With shaking hands, she reached over and grabbed the wet cloth to wipe her face. She was beginning to get worried. While it was mostly only

120 DAYS...

first thing in the morning, there were still times throughout the day when she was nauseous. The last thing she wanted was for Ethan to worry about her. For so many years, it had just been her. She had no one to rely on, and at that moment, she couldn't depend on Ethan. She hadn't been completely honest with him, really with anyone. She knew that once she and Ethan became close, she should have opened up to him, but she didn't know how to. What words could she say? She was kicking herself for letting things get as far as they had.

Sitting for a few moments to make sure her vomiting was over, Sam admitted to herself there was nothing she could have done. There was no way either one of them could have stopped what was going to happen. There was no choice involved with who or when you fell in love. At that point, all she could do was hold on and hope for the best when she finally told him everything.

Her phone rang from the bedside. Quickly, she went to answer it, hoping it hadn't woken Ethan up yet; he still had a half an hour to sleep. "Hello," she whispered and walked out of the room.

"It's Kris," said Phil.

"I'll be right there." She disconnected the call and turned to go back into the bedroom to get dressed and ran right into Ethan. "Geez. You scared me," she squeaked.

"Everything okay?" His voice was gruff with sleep.

She shook her head. "No, Kris isn't going to make it much longer."

"Dammit."

"Yeah, well, I'm not sure when I'll be back, so–"

"So nothing, I'm coming with you."

"Ethan . . ."

"Don't 'Ethan' me, you know I'm going. For Christ's sake, Sam, he's the first guest I checked in. I made sure he had the best time at the football game. It's something I couldn't do for Evan, but I could do for Kris. This is different."

Sam's heart went out to him. She knew not being there for his brother had been eating at him, and that making sure Kris had an experience of a lifetime, helped in some small way. "I know, Ethan, but this isn't going to be easy. It's going to be harder than any before."

"I know. Patty was hard, and this one will be too. It wouldn't make it any easier if I wasn't there, if I walked away and did something else." He took her face in his hands. "Samantha, I'm here for the long haul. Doesn't matter if things are smooth sailing or rough weather. I need to do this."

"Will you let me help you?" she asked him.

"I'll always need you."

He pulled her up in his arms and they held tightly onto each other, knowing another guest would be leaving within the next day or so, and there was nothing they could do but be there for him.

The tumor in the back of Kris's head had grown so large he had no control of anything from his neck down. Ethan had helped feed him when he wanted something to eat and joked with him when he was awake, but most of their time was spent in silence since the pressure on his brain was too much.

Sam would come in every hour and stay for a little bit, but Ethan wanted the responsibility. He knew it was hard for her. Sam felt it was her duty to take care of everyone who came to the resort. But that time, it was Ethan's and she didn't know how to completely let go.

She had just left and it was only Kris, Ethan and Phil, the nurse on duty. Ethan looked at the clock. It was eleven at night. It was Ethan's second night by Kris' bedside. He hadn't left the night before, wanting to make sure someone was there for Kris if he woke up.

"Hey," Kris's soft voice slurred from the bed. "Make sure my girls get the ball."

Ethan didn't have to ask him to explain. He knew exactly what he meant, the game ball. "You know I will."

"Make sure they know . . . I'll be looking out for them." He tried to raise his hand to point up, but couldn't.

"I will. They'll know you'll be there for them." Ethan leaned in closer to the man he'd grown so close to in such a short time. "Listen, buddy, I can see you're holding on, but it's time to move on. It'll be okay. I'll stay with you."

"I don't want to leave," Kris whispered.

"There's something better waiting for you. All that's left for you here is pain. You've done what you were put on this earth for. Now it's time for your next journey."

"I don't know how."

"Just let go." Ethan bowed his head. "Yea, thou I walk through the valley of the shadow of death, I will fear no evil; for thou art with me; Thy rod and thy staff, they comfort me. You are not alone, Kris. He is waiting for you."

Silently, Ethan held Kris's hand and continued to pray for the man as he slowly let go. His breathing became shallower and there were times it stopped altogether, then would start up again, before finally going silent.

Ethan didn't leave his side as all the machines were turned off and phone calls were made. When he looked up and saw Sam standing in the doorway, he nearly lost it. He wasn't sure how it could get any easier. Was it really something he could do, day in, day out? Sometimes, they ended up having a couple of deaths a week. He wasn't naïve; he knew people came in and out of people's lives all the time. But to be surrounded by death, even doing something so good, took its toll.

Sam came over and sat down in the chair on the other side of the bed and picked up Kris's hand, saying her own silent prayer for the man they'd just lost.

Chapter 20

DAY 50

ETHAN—

CONSIDERING I'M DYING, THE DOCTOR SAID I WAS DOING REALLY WELL. I'LL TAKE IT. DOESN'T IT ALWAYS WORK THAT WAY, AS SOON AS YOU GO TO THE DOCTOR YOU START TO FEEL BETTER? THAT'S ME TODAY. WE'VE GOT ANOTHER NEW GUEST TODAY, BRUCE. HE'S AN AWESOME OLD GUY, AND CAN STILL RUN CIRCLES AROUND ME ON THE BASKETBALL COURT. I BLAME THE FACT I'M NOT 100 PERCENT.

EVAN

Sam always hated to go down into the city so soon after someone passed. There was something about the resort, working it, helping other people that healed her after another death. She'd learned quickly that

120 DAYS...

when she went into the city, it was almost as if the trip sucked the life out of her. The hustle and bustle, everyone only thinking of themselves, shoving people out of their way to get what they want. But she couldn't put it off any longer; she had to visit the doctor.

Sitting in the cold exam room in one of those dreadful gowns, she kicked her feet back and forth to the rhythm of the music they piped in to help you relax. She never understood why they made you sit like that for so long. At least in the waiting room, she could people watch, or read, or do something besides look at inspirational posters.

There was a soft knock on the door and Dr. Sanders opened it up and peeked his head in. "Hey, Sam, didn't expect to see you so soon." He came all the way in and shook her hand. "You aren't due back for another four months."

"I know, but I've been getting sick, throwing up every morning. Since it's something out of the ordinary, I wanted to get in to talk to you about it since it isn't going away."

"Hmm . . . How long as this been going on?"

"About a week."

"Have you been able to eat?"

"Not in the mornings, but after about ten I can."

"What about any medication, have you been able to take anything?"

Sam blushed. "See that's the other thing, I haven't been able to take them in the morning. I know we don't want me to go too long without taking them."

"Samantha–"

"I know, it's just the nausea is so bad."

"Hmm . . ." He turned from her and started tapping

the keys on the laptop. "Well, that's interesting . . ."

"What? What's interesting?"

Dr. Sanders sat there tapping his finger on the edge of the desk before he turned to her. "Are you sexually active?"

She raised an eyebrow at him. "Umm . . . yes."

"You need to take a pregnancy test."

"But . . . but . . ." Her mind couldn't form the right words.

"Sam, let's get this taken care of. This is the easiest thing to either rule out or confirm. I'll have the nurse come in to get you, and in about fifteen minutes, we'll have a better idea of what we're dealing with."

She didn't notice him leave the room. *Pregnant.* She couldn't be. There was no possible way. When the nurse came in, she let her lead her to the bathroom where she went through the mechanics of taking the test and tried not to laugh, or cry.

There was no way she was going to be able to sit down. As soon as she got back to the examination room, Sam paced back and forth in the small space while she waited on the results. When the door finally opened, she all but leapt at the doctor to rip the piece of paper out of his hands to read it herself. She cursed the fact that the doctor had a good poker face.

"Have a seat, Sam."

"I don't want to."

"Well, I want you to." He folded his arms across his chest. "How long have we known each other? Give an old man a break and sit down so I can."

"Fine." She plopped down on the exam table. "Happy."

"Yes. Now, I'm sure you're wondering about the results." He fiddled with some papers in his file. "It

120 DAYS...

seems like you are going to have some serious thinking to do, Sam . . . because you're pregnant."

"No, no." She shook her head as a smile spread across her face. She'd always wanted children. "But you said I couldn't get pregnant."

Dr. Sanders shook his head. "I said it would be extremely difficult for you to get pregnant, about a 1 percent chance. Not that it was impossible."

It took her a few minutes to process what he was saying and go back years to when he'd first said it to her to realize he was right. "What do I do now?"

"First thing, discontinue any medication you are taking. The nurse will go over with you if there is anything you need to decrease the dosage, and those that you can stop cold turkey. You're going to stop everything until you decide exactly what it is you want to do and know what all the risks involve for you and the baby."

"What are they?" Her hands shook. Deep down in her heart she knew.

"Best case, you stop your meds, you and the baby are fine, and you both live long, wonderful happy lives."

"And the worst case?"

"Without the medication, the cancer grows and runs rampant throughout your body, killing you for sure and most likely your baby too. We'll keep an eye on you, run as many tests as we can which won't harm the baby, and make adjustments, but you may have to make some hard choices to keep yourself alive."

"What do you think I should do?" She looked up to the man before her. He'd treated her parents, and she trusted him.

"I've got a name of another doctor up in Sacramento. He deals in high-risk pregnancies and cancer patients. If there is anyone who could work a miracle for both you and your baby, it would be him." He handed her a card. "But don't wait too long. I've already called him, and he can see you tomorrow."

"Thank you." The first tears fell down her cheeks.

"Here." He stood up, opened his arms and she stepped into them. He had always been so nice to her, helping her understand everything that was going on with her parents, and then with her own cancer and opening up the resort. She cared for him like she would a favorite uncle, and for the first time in years, she cried on his shoulder.

As soon as Sam parked the van, she was out the door and walking up the hill to talk to her parents. She needed their advice and wished, like so many other times in the past, they were still there for her. Sitting down on the bench, she told them everything. All about Ethan and how wonderful he was, how much he'd changed, and how happy he was now compared to what Evan had said about him, and how he'd been when he'd first showed up at the resort.

She filled them in on the fact that she loved him, had started thinking of a future with him, or as much as she could give him seeing as there were no guarantees in life to begin with. Then she moved on to what Dr. Sanders had said, and wondered what she should do.

Growing up, their family time together, every memory was still clear, including the ups and downs, especially her teenage years. But the thing that stuck out to her was how proud her parents were of her. How much being a parent meant to them. She remembered watching videos of her mother while she was pregnant, and if she had to be completely honest with herself, she wanted to experience that. She wanted everything. To have a child, to have Ethan. She knew with the right attitude she could do this. It was something she wanted, deep down in her soul. She placed her hand on her belly. Sam and Ethan's love had created something beautiful. There was no way she couldn't seek out all the answers.

Looking at her watch, Sam knew she had just enough time to run down, pack a bag and get on the road to get to Seattle before dark. Her appointment was for late morning. She'd be able to get some rest, go through her morning routine of getting sick, and then head out.

Nodding, she knew she needed to have all the answers before she said anything to Ethan. It was already going to be a shock to him to learn she had cancer, but then to add everything else to that. No, she needed to make sure she could answer all his questions about him becoming a father.

Chapter 21

DAY 53

ETHAN—

SAM SAYS IT DOESN'T HAPPEN OFTEN, BUT SOMETIMES GUESTS LET THEIR FAMILY MEMBERS COME FOR A VISIT. TODAY THAT HAPPENED. ONE OF BRUCE'S GRANDCHILDREN HAD A BABY, THE FIRST GREAT-GRANDCHILD. THEY MADE THE TRIP HERE SO THEY COULD HAVE A PICTURE OF THE CHILD WITH HIM.

WE ALL MADE AN EFFORT AFTER THEY LEFT TO MAKE SURE BRUCE DIDN'T GET DEPRESSED AFTERWARDS. WE SHOULD HAVE KNOWN BETTER. THAT MAN IS A ROCK.

EVAN

120 DAYS...

Ethan slammed the door behind him and stalked around the room. He was pissed enough Sam had left this morning and hadn't told tell him she was going into town, but to then find out she'd come back, packed a bag and left again. It wasn't like her and he was worried. Thinking he was doing the right thing, he let her have her space and didn't press things. With her being AWOL, he knew he should have pressed her for answers.

Her note was crumpled in his shaking fist as he thought of the words she'd left for him. She wrote she had an appointment down in Los Angeles she'd forgotten about, and would be gone for a couple of days. He could tell she was lying about where she was going, even in a note. The feeling of dread wouldn't leave him. He tried to shake it off, but it hung on; its claws stuck deep inside of him.

Looking around her house, part of him wanted to tear though everything and see what he could find, the other, and more logical part, told him he had to do this systematically. He had wasted too much time after his brother left before he tried to find him, and the trail was cold. Of course Evan had wanted to disappear. He also knew what kind of resources Ethan had access to and took measures not to throw up any red flags, so he wouldn't be found. Sam should be easier to find. She only took one bag, so she couldn't be going that far.

Taking out his phone, he made a phone call. He knew his contact would find out exactly what he needed to know, and quickly. Walking upstairs, he thought about what he was going to need to pack. He wasn't coming back without her.

Samantha checked into the hotel and went up to her room. It had been a while since she'd stayed in one and decided to treat herself to some room service. The last thing she wanted was to have to interact with people. She needed to be alone to think. It was a situation she never thought she'd be in. Making sure she ordered something healthy, she ate quickly while her mind flew in circles.

Looking down at her belly, she couldn't believe there was a child growing in there. Something she'd made with Ethan. While neither one of them had said the words yet, she knew they loved each other. This baby was a miracle, a dream she only dared to dream in the darkest part of the night when she was alone—when no one was around to see her tears because it would never happen.

But it had, and with it came hard choices. Actually, for her, the choices weren't hard. She'd already made her decision. She had to see the specialist to see if it was really possible. Although she did have to be realistic with herself. There would be a chance, probably a big one, that she could lose her baby at some point. That was going to be the hard part. Would she be able to handle the loss? Did she have enough strength to carry on when the one thing she'd never thought she could have, may be taken from her?

If she was going to make the choice, she decided to daydream, think positive. What did she want for the future? She wanted Ethan by her side, running Last Resort with her. She wanted a simple wedding ceremony. She wanted him to be her husband, and for him to call her his wife. And she wanted their baby. She wanted to watch her belly grow, hold her child in her arms for the first time, give it its first kiss. Protect the child and raise it, praising every accomplishment and helping them with every obstacle. At some point, their child would leave, fall in love, have a family of their own, and there would be grandchildren for her to spoil.

If there was something she'd learned, positive thinking and prayers made all the difference in the world. She'd seen it over and over again, first with her parents, and then each and every guest who came to the resort.

But then there was also the heartache if she lost the baby. It would be hard enough if she lost it tomorrow. In her heart, she'd already began to plan, to dream, to love the child. But one of the worst things would be if she was further along in her pregnancy and something went wrong. To feel the child moving inside of you, to have it a part of you, and then nothing. No happy ending. Was that something she could really survive? What would it do to her and Ethan, what would it do to him? She didn't even know if he wanted children. It wasn't something they had talked about yet. Maybe he would leave anyway, child or not.

Thinking of her life before Ethan came into it. She knew she could go back to it if she needed to. Would she be as happy as she was? No, of course not, but she could do it simply for the fact that there were too many people she had to help. Her heart, her soul would be empty without him, but she could still make sure everyone she came into contact with knew they were loved. In time, her heart would heal. To a point, she knew everything happened for a reason, and she couldn't control everything, no matter how hard she tried. Life always moved forward. The resort was her life before and it could be her life afterwards.

If she lost the baby, he could leave after that. She knew that would be the hardest, to almost have everything she'd dreamed of, and then have it all taken away. She'd be left alone, with the resort. No husband to share the ups and downs with, no child to watch grow. That would be the worst, but she'd never been a quitter before, and she wouldn't become one now. Before Ethan, the resort had been her baby. She'd watched it grow from an idea to a fully functioning business. Over and over she'd seen guests come in and watched them fulfill their dreams, just because hers might not happen didn't mean she couldn't continue to make them happen for others.

She also knew she couldn't terminate the pregnancy. That was something she could never do. There was no way she could even entertain the idea. The cost to her didn't come into the equation.

Sam yawned so big her jaw popped. There would be no more going around in circles that night. There was plenty of time in the morning. For the present, she needed sleep.

Ethan stood in the lobby of the hotel with his arms crossed over his chest and his eyes glued to the elevators. The staff wouldn't tell him what room she was in, but he sure as hell could stand there until she came out of the elevators. It may not be his town, but people still knew his name there, and knew he didn't mess around, and the staff wanted to keep their jobs. He could buy this hotel and level it within a week if he wanted.

He could have found out her room number, but he didn't want to scare her, and he had a feeling his poker face hadn't made the trip with him. People were steering clear of him, and if he barked an order, they were jumping to make sure it was done as quickly as possible.

Finally, the elevator dinged and she walked out. He

could tell she had been sick; he should have seen it the other mornings if he'd been paying attention and not seeing what he wanted to see instead of what was really there. He was just as pissed off at himself as he was with her.

She froze as soon as she saw him. Since she wasn't coming to him, he strode over to her. "Miss Truman, would you like to explain yourself?"

"Ethan..."

He crossed his arms over his chest and raised an eyebrow at her. "Is that all you have to say?"

"I can't... not now..."

"See, that's where you are wrong. Don't you think I can't see that you were sick again this morning, and the fact that you ran away from me and *lied* makes me wonder just what the hell is going on. I suggest you start talking, and fast."

"Ethan, I can't, not now. I'm late for an appointment."

"Yes, your *doctor's* appointment.... Don't look so surprised. Remember, I have more money than I know what to do with, and it usually,"—he looked over at the front desk—"opens every single door I want opened. You can either tell me what is going on, or I can find out from your doctor."

"You can't do that. There's laws that protect my privacy."

He leaned down so they were eye to eye. "Want to push me a little more and see what laws I'm willing to break to find out what you're hiding from me?"

They stood there staring each other down. Ethan knew he had the upper hand. She lived by the book, one to always follow the rules. He, on the other hand, didn't mind bending them if needed.

"Fine. Here." She stuck out her room key. "I'm in room 388. We'll talk when I get back."

"Why can't I go with you?"

She sighed and her eyes filled with tears. She blinked, trying to hold them back. "Because, for this, I need to go alone." She placed her hand on his shoulder. "I promise, let me go to this one alone, and you can go to every other one in the future."

"Sam, you're scaring me. Are there going to be many others?"

"It'll be okay. I shouldn't be too long. Wait for me."

"Forever and always." He kissed her forehead and watched her walk away from him. Absently, he rubbed his hand over his heart. The dread was back, and its claws had a death grip on his heart.

Ethan couldn't sit still while he waited for her. Pulling his laptop out of his car, he set about doing more research on the gold mine. There had to be some truth behind the rumors. Every rumor had at least some truth to it. Maybe it was only one little fact, but the rumor had to be built on something, and he was going to find out what it was.

He spent a couple of hours going over the ranch's history, the people who spent time there, making notes and trying to figure out what he could to unravel the mystery of the gold mine. He knew it was going to end up being the key to giving Sam the security she needed for the future. Somehow, he knew she'd never just accept his money as hers.

When he heard the electronic lock click, he stood up and went to the door, holding open for her. He couldn't help himself; he lifted her up in his arms and walked over to the bed where he sat down and kept her on his lap. He couldn't believe how much he missed having her in his arms. Everything seemed all right with the world when she was there with him.

He could feel her body trembling and it scared him more than anything. Leaning back from her, he looked at her face and sure enough, her eyes were huge and her chin quivered. "Oh, honey." He hugged her tightly, not knowing what monsters he needed to slay for her. All he knew was that seeing her distressed was killing him. "Tell me."

"Just a few more minutes. Please. I need a few more minutes like this."

"Sure, sure." He rocked back and forth, hoping to calm them both.

She started playing with the buttons on his shirt. "After my parents died, I had some tests done. I wanted to be prepared for what might be heading my way. If there was any way I could shrink my chances of getting cancer, I was going to do it, no matter what it was. There is genetic testing you can do, where they can see if you have cancer markers. I did. Colon cancer, just like my dad. I couldn't just cut my colon out and not worry about it, so we watched, and they were able to put me on what we call preventative chemo maintenance. Every six months, I go in and have scans done to make sure nothing is showing up."

Ethan felt like his world was crumbling around him. "But you have your hair, and you don't get sick."

"Not everyone gets sick on chemo, and it all depends on the cocktail they give you if you are going to lose your hair or not. And honestly, I did get sick in the beginning, but we found the perfect dose for me. It hasn't impacted my life, but for a couple of hours every few weeks."

"Does anyone at the resort know?" The thought of the staff knowing and not saying anything to him was going to seriously piss him off.

She shook her head. "No one knows. I can't have them treating me differently, treating me more like a guest and not the owner."

"Tell me the rest." If he knew everything, he might be able to fix it.

"A few years ago, a few spots showed up on my colon; they were cancerous. But because of the scans, we caught it in time and it was, all things considered, a minor surgery and they were removed. They adjusted my chemo, and all my tests have come back normal since then. Last Resort has helped me just as much as it's helped others. Based on my medical history, I shouldn't be here now. If I hadn't taken those proactive steps years ago, things would be different now. If I didn't have all those people depending on me, I wouldn't be here. Because, every single guest who came to me to help them live a few extra weeks, they've given me extra years."

"But why are you seeing a specialist?"

She got up off his lap, walked over to the window and looked out. "Between the radiation in all of the scans and the ongoing chemo, the odds of me being able to have children was slim." She gave a humorless laugh. "I thought it was impossible. Turns out I wasn't listening close enough." Turning back toward him, she fidgeted with her fingers. "I'm pregnant."

"Wait . . . what?" Slowly, he stood up.

"I'm pregnant with your child."

He pointed toward her belly. "What about all the medication? Is it possible? Healthy?" His vision tunneled until all he saw was her. There were too many emotions flowing through him to identify.

120 DAYS...

"As it stands right now, yes. I haven't been able to take any of my pills since I started getting sick. And this was my week to go in for the juice. At this point, there shouldn't be any adverse side effects."

"At this point . . ." He felt like he couldn't keep up, wasn't fully understanding her words over the sound of his own frantic heartbeat.

"Yes, that's why I went to this specialist. If there is anyone who can make sure both our baby and I survive this pregnancy, it's him."

"Wait." All of the blood drained out of his head and he sat down quickly. "Explain. What do you mean *both* of you survive?" He felt like he was on the edge of a cliff and the rocks started shifting under him.

"There is a chance one or both of us could die."

"No. No." He shook his head. "I don't accept that. How in the hell do you think I'm just going to accept something like this? You can't die. Dammit, no. I can't lose you." His body started to shake. "Give me a minute." He stood up and tried to concentrate on putting one foot in front of the other as he went over to his laptop. "I can figure this out. I can fix this. I can't lose you." His voice shook with emotion he couldn't hide.

"Ethan," Sam said quietly from next to him.

"No, my brother wouldn't let me do anything to help him. I'm not going to sit by and do nothing for you." His words sped out of his mouth, tumbling into one another. "This doctor, you may think he's the best, but we'll see about that. I don't care what it costs, or where we have to go. I'm not going to lose you. I'm not going to lose either of you." Frantically, his fingers flew across the keyboard.

"Ethan." She placed her hand over his. "Stop. There's nothing you can do right now. We have to take each step. Right now, I'm fine."

He turned haunted eyes toward her. His life had been ripped from him, again. First his parents, then Evan, and now Samantha, and their baby. My God, there was a child growing inside of her, the awe of the fact that they'd created something so wonderful together amazed him. But then maybe the cancer would be growing as their baby did. Cancer could be spreading throughout her body this very second. The thought of burying everything and everyone he'd ever loved hit him like a sledgehammer and he dropped hard to his knees in front of her. Wrapping his arms around her, he rested his head on her belly where their child grew, and cried at the thought of what was to come.

Chapter 22

DAY 59

ETHAN—

I'M TRYING NOT TO GET EXCITED, BUT TOMORROW IS DAY SIXTY. SUCH A SMALL NUMBER THAT MEANS SO MUCH MORE TO ME NOW THAN IT DID BEFORE I FOUND OUT I HAD CANCER. EVERY DAY IS A GIFT.

GROWING UP, I ALWAYS LOOKED UP TO YOU. AS MY BIG BROTHER, YOU WERE LARGER THAN LIFE. I SWEAR I THOUGHT YOU HAD SUPER POWERS, EVERYTHING ALWAYS WENT YOUR WAY. EVEN AFTER MOM AND DAD WERE KILLED AND WE LOST THE HOUSE, WHAT YOU DID TO MAKE SURE I WAS TAKEN CARE OF AND PROTECTED... AS AN ADULT, I CAN APPRECIATE EVERYTHING YOU DID FOR ME. BECAUSE OF YOU, I AM THE MAN I AM.

THANK YOU

EVAN

120 DAYS...

They lay wrapped in each other's arms on the bed, Ethan absently playing with a lock of her hair. He needed her close. He felt completely empty, completely void of emotion. There was nothing left for him to grieve. Once Sam started crying, he'd stopped. He knew tears weren't going to help anything and he didn't want to make it harder on her than it already was. All he wanted was to go back to how things were two days earlier, forget the last three hours had happened, but that wasn't an option. They both had their moments to wallow in sadness, but now, they needed to plan.

"What happens next?"

"Tests, tests, and more tests." She sighed. "The doctor said that was pretty much going to be my life until the baby comes."

"Which is when?"

"June ninth."

"June. Eight months." He rolled over and looked down at her. "You are one of the strongest people I've ever known, but I have to ask, are you strong enough for this? Don't brush me off. Seriously, I need you to think ahead. What if we are in May and something goes wrong, and the baby doesn't make it. Can you survive that?"

Sam bit her lip and nodded. "I'm not going to say it won't wreck me, and I don't know how long it would take me to recover, get back to my normal. I've made myself go there, to that dark place, to feel what it would be like. Ethan, I have to do this. No matter what the outcome, I can't terminate this pregnancy. It's not in my makeup. This child is already a part of me. A part of us."

"You're willing to die for this child, if it comes down to that?"

"Yes. There is no other option."

"You've thought about this. You've had time to process everything. I haven't. Since you're set in your decision, then you're going to live with mine. You're going to have to deal with the fact that I'm not going to settle for second best of anything. You will have the best that money can buy. I don't care what we have to do, or where we have to go. I will do *everything* in my power to make sure you both survive this, do you hear me?"

"As long as you understand this child's life is more important than mine. We are both alone in this world. This can be my way to leave more than just a handprint behind."

He recoiled from her. "Where the hell do you get off saying one life is more important than another one? No, you'll agree to the fact that the doctor's will know if it comes down to one or the other, they choose the one who has the best chance of surviving. Period. No arguments." When she didn't say anything, he continued. "Look at it from my perspective. If I have the chance to make sure at least one of you lives, I'm going to take it. I'm going to make sure the doctor's do. I'm not going to have them ignore you and try to save our child when they could have saved you and the child still dies. Please give me this. Think about it, so much of this is out of my hands, with nothing I can do, and there are no decisions that are mine to make. It's your body, you decide. Let me do what I can to make sure if I can't save the both of you, at least one of you lives."

Slowly, she nodded. "I can understand that, but we've got to think positive. We'll both make it."

120 DAYS...

"That's what I'm praying for. I think I've said about a thousand prayers already."

"Good, then we'll bother Him so much, he'll make sure they are answered."

"So . . . tests, that's it for the next eight months? What happens if those tests show something we don't want?"

"Then we'll have to see what is best. Really, there are so many things that could go wrong in a normal pregnancy, let alone with someone like me. We can't dwell on the what ifs. We need to try to take each day as it is and do our best."

"You do understand you're going to have to take it easy at the resort. I know you said you didn't want the staff treating you like a guest, and I can completely understand that, but you can't go on like you have. You're going to have to take care of yourself, which means, you're going to have to get a lot of rest and delegate."

She frowned at him. "I hate that word."

"I know you do. You're also going to hate the next thing I'm going to say, so in your words, suck it up, buttercup. You're going to have to have help, and you're going to have some and like it. You are carrying my child." He patted her belly. "And I'm a successful businessman, which means, I'm helping, and you're going to take my money and not say one word. Samantha, if there is anyone who completely understands your vision for Last Resort, it's me. We've already started working on the improvements you want to make. Let me oversee them. I know where you want to take this. I can do this for you so you don't have to worry about it."

"But the money."

"Seriously? This is a few million I'm not going to

miss it. And yes, I have that much money. I don't need you to pay me back, and don't start arguing about how you aren't comfortable taking my money. It's mine and I can do with it whatever I want. You want me to go behind your back? I can. Don't think I haven't thought of anonymous donations. There's nothing you can say about that now, is there?"

"You wouldn't." She narrowed her eyes at him.

"Who's to say I haven't already? Yeah, you think about that. I've been there for how long now? Gee isn't it funny how you've had some extra money coming in lately? I wonder where that came from. The checks will only get larger. Might as well sit back, and relax, focus on your health and growing that child."

"Now wait a minute, I will not be reduced to the stereotypical woman's role just because I'm pregnant."

"If you were *just* pregnant, we wouldn't be having this conversation. We are also trying to keep both you and our child alive. Don't be so stubborn you can't see what I'm trying to do."

"I don't know what you're talking about. I know what my priorities are, and I also know what I'm capable of doing. You on the other hand—"

"Just stop already. We both want the same damn thing. Sometimes I wonder why I love you so much when all you like to do is argue with me."

"What did you say?"

"That you're stubborn and like to argue."

"No you said you love me."

"Of course I do. Do you think I'd be going through all this if you were just a fling?"

"Wow, Ethan, way to charm me."

"You know what I mean. You can't expect me to be

120 DAYS...

all charming when you're sitting there being hardheaded and won't listen to me."

"Hello." She waved her hand in front of his face. "Obviously I was since I'm the one who heard you say you love me. Want to try that again, and this time not be an ass about it?"

Ethan's face softened as he looked down at her. "I should have told you long before this. If anyone should know to not take each moment for granted, it should be me. Samantha Truman, you amaze me. Your strength and compassion is unshakable. Because of you, I feel like I've finally become the man I always should have been. And now this, a child, something so wonderful and precious we created from love. I wasn't sure I'd ever be able to say the words to someone ever again and mean them, but I do. I love you with everything I am."

"I love you, too." She smiled at him. "So much it scares me sometimes. Both of us have had so much loss in our lives. It's scary to take that leap again. But with you, it was one of the easiest things I've ever done."

His arms wrapped around her and he held onto her tightly. "God, I never want to let you go." Closing his eyes, he said another prayer to keep both of them safe.

"Then don't."

Chapter 23

DAY 60

ETHAN-

ONE OF THE HARDEST THINGS I'VE EVER DONE WAS WALK INTO YOUR OFFICE TO TELL YOU I HAD CANCER AND WAS WALKING AWAY FROM YOU TO DIE.

GROWING UP, YOU ALWAYS LOOKED OUT FOR ME, ESPECIALLY AFTER MOM AND DAD WERE KILLED. THERE WAS NO WAY I COULD HAVE YOU DOING IT AGAIN. I WANTED YOU TO REMEMBER ME HEALTHY, LIKE I USED TO BE. NOT LIKE I AM NOW. I LOOK IN THE MIRROR AND CAN'T EVEN RECOGNIZE MYSELF. I DON'T LOOK LIKE HOW MY BRAIN THINKS I SHOULD LOOK. I LOOK LIKE I'M DYING. MY BRAIN HASN'T CAUGHT UP TO THE FACT THAT IT'S ONLY A MATTER OF TIME.

EVAN

120 DAYS...

One good thing about having money was Ethan paid for someone to drive her car back to the resort so they could ride together in his car. He made some snide comment about her non-descript sedan, to which she came back with a comment about men and the horsepower of their cars.

Sam had to admit that it felt good to relax and let him drive them back. Both of them were making a concerted effort to keep things light. They'd spent so much time talking and planning the day before, they needed the small break before they were back at the resort and had to tell everyone what was going on.

He didn't admit it, but Sam was pretty sure he'd been up all night making plans while she slept. Somehow, she didn't think he'd sit around and wait for the next step. He was already planning for the ten ahead. In fact, she worried nothing would be the same at the resort by the time they made it back there. The only thing that kept her from being angry was she knew it came from a good place. He was going to do whatever it took to make sure they had their happy ending. There was no way she could fault him for that.

Sam sat in a chair at the large table in the rec center waiting for the staff to show up. Part of her wanted to run and hide, the other part knew they would help her. They'd be there with all of the positive thoughts and energy she needed to succeed.

"Thank you all for coming on such short notice. I have a few things we need to go over." She stood up and picked up a stack of papers. "First, Ethan and I have been talking about changes I've wanted to make to the resort, and he's generously donated the money needed to make them happen." She passed the papers to her right. "Here, take one and pass it along. We're going to build new accommodations, ones that can house more guests, specifically for those who need more assistance. These will be almost like apartments. It will be built to keep with the feeling of the rest of the resort, so it won't stick out. The main house will be for staff and offices. My goal has always been to help as many people as possible, and unfortunately, we've had to turn too many away. By creating this new area, we will be able to help twenty more guests than we currently do. Also, we're going to be building ten more cabins. I don't want the resort to get so large it becomes an institution, as we are one big family, and that needs to be our main focus, just as it always has been." She nodded toward Ethan.

"Since I have a developer's background, it makes the most sense for me to head this up. I have all the contacts to make sure this goes as smoothly as possible without affecting the guests who are here. We've passed out the rough drawing of how the new buildings are going to look and where they'll be located. Since you work here on a day-to-day basis if there is anything you can think of that would be beneficial to our guests, or to make your job easier, please come to me as soon as possible so we can get your ideas in place."

Sam took a deep breath. "Next, if you haven't noticed, Ethan and I are an item and he is going to be helping me out a lot more around here." Ethan put his arm around her, and she leaned into him for strength. It was harder than she thought it would be. "I need you to treat him as you would me. He has final say, just like I would in any situation. I'm going to be stepping back for a bit and I need to make sure everything is taken care of so I can focus on other matters." She rubbed her hands together and prayed for the right words. "I have some good news, and some potentially bad news. The good news is we are going to have a baby." She held up her hand to quiet the staff down. "You all know the story of my parents. Well, after they died I had genetic testing done. I've been on chemo treatments for years, mostly a preventive maintenance thing so the colon cancer wouldn't grow, or spread quickly. With being pregnant, I won't be able to continue. Best case, which you know we always focus on, I'll go to term and both the baby and I will be fine. The worst case is we both could die."

Looking down, she had to take a moment before she could continue. "I don't want things to change. I can't have them change," she whispered. "I need to be me and not a guest. I can't lose myself."

"You won't have to worry about that." Ethan's voice commanded the room. "We all know what we are going to have to do, all you need to worry about is resting and growing a baby."

"Oh, is that all?" Her lips quivered as she smiled up at him.

"Yep, that should be easy for you. Do you see everything you've already tackled and won? This is a cakewalk."

"I'll remind you of that."

"You do that." He squeezed her shoulder and left her alone with her staff for a moment.

"No tears. No special treatment," she told them. "I need to know you're going to do everything you've always done for this resort, no matter if it is myself or Ethan giving the orders."

Bethany was the first one over to her, enveloping her in a huge warm hug. "Girl, whatever you need, any time of day, or night, I'm here for you." She pulled back and looked Sam in the eye. "You hear me, I'm here for you. Everyone needs help, ask for me."

"Yes, ma'am." Sam smiled at her through the tears. This was just as hard as she thought it was going to be. "You're the one who should be scared. Ethan is going to be your boss for a while."

"Ha, that pussycat? He's met his match in me. I'll keep him in line and keep things running smoothly. Don't you worry about a thing."

"Thank you."

When Bethany moved aside, Phil stepped up and looked at her. She felt like he was studying her, trying to figure her out. "You should have told someone sooner. You needed someone here on staff who knew your history, could help you if you needed it."

"No one needed to know before now. I had everything under control. Now that I need help, I'm asking for it."

"You're going to have to share your records with me." He narrowed his eyes at her.

"I know, and I'll make sure you have everything you need. I promise."

"We'll take good care of you and your little one. You know Ethan will be there for you too."

She tried hard to keep the tears from falling. "I know you will. Now go on before you make me cry."

Tracy came up to her and shook her finger in Sam's face. "You have to let me know what you want to eat. You know I can cook anything. I'll make sure you're hooked up for every single craving you have."

"You'll be the first to know. You might want to stock up on chocolate though."

"Yes, I can do that." Her voice quivered.

"Stop, no more tears, we'll be fine. Now, go and see if you can find a new cake recipe for Ethan to try out.

120 DAYS...

You know how much he loves cake."

"Okay. I'm so happy and sad for you at the same time. You finally have everything you ever wanted, Ethan is a good man. I'll be praying for both of you." Tracy sniffled and walked away.

She spent a few minutes talking to a few other staff members. When Ethan walked back in, everyone went quiet.

In the silence of the room, she took the mold he had brought into the room and placed it on the table. Taking a deep breath, she placed her hand over the cement, and carefully pressed down. It was colder than she thought it would be. She couldn't look up at her staff who were watching her make her handprint for the Legacy Wall. There would have been no way she could have kept it together. As it was, she could hear some of them trying to hold their sobs back. When she was done, Ethan was there to help lift her hand and wipe it clean before she used a stick to write on it.

Samantha Truman
Owner, Last Resort
Colon Cancer
Never Giving Up the Fight

Quickly, she drew a butterfly in the corner before the tears clouded her vision and she stood up and left the room.

The next few weeks were a whirlwind of construction planning and making sure Ethan knew everything he could about the resort. Luckily for her, he picked things up quickly and since he did have a background in business, most of it he already knew. She also appreciated the fact that while he may have other ideas on how to run things, he was learning the way she wanted things done first before making any suggestions.

The amount of rest she needed surprised her, between work and reading up on pregnancy, she didn't have much time for anything else, and Ethan was making sure she didn't overdo it. She almost scoffed at the idea, as if her body would let her. She also realized how much she missed spending time with her guests, not to mention going on adventures with them. As she sat on her porch swing with paper and pen, she tried to come up with a schedule where she could get back to having fun again. There was a reason they said laughter was the best medicine.

When she heard Ethan approaching, she smiled. She already knew he'd have a funny story or two to tell her, and something to eat. The staff had taken it upon themselves to make sure she was overloaded with all the right foods to help not only her baby, but foods which were said to help prevent cancer.

"There's my beautiful lady." He slid next to Sam and put his arm around her. "Come here often?"

"Every day."

"Well then, lucky me." He held a bag up for her. "Look what I have for you."

"Food?"

"Yes, food, but you'll love this."

"I'm waiting." She held her hand out.

"Close your eyes . . . Come on, you trust me. Just

120 DAYS...

close your eyes and open your mouth."

"No tomatoes."

"I know what you like and what you don't. Give me a little credit."

She sighed, closed her eyes and opened her mouth. When he placed something chocolatey and sweet on her tongue, she moaned. "Oh my."

"Exactly. Is it the best thing you've ever had? If I do say so myself, hiring that pastry chef was a great idea. It's also giving Tracy more time to work on the meals, which is where her passion is."

"I have to agree with you, even though I hate to feed your ego."

"You should see what he's planning on making for Halloween. They're going to be creepy looking but oh so tasty."

"Oh, Halloween." She sighed.

"What? I thought that was your favorite holiday?"

"It is, I don't know where the time went. I don't have a costume."

"Seriously? Sam, one of your extra rooms upstairs has only costumes in it. Surely you can find something there to wear."

She shrugged. "I try to do something different every year."

"It's okay, you can recycle, and it's kind of the 'in thing' right now."

"Ha-ha. Maybe you're right." She stood up. "You need a costume too."

"Oh, don't worry about me. You pick yours out. I've got this whole Halloween thing handled."

"That scares me a little bit."

He bent his fingers into claws and laughed like an

evil genius would. "And you should be."

"You're hopeless." She turned to walk away from him.

He came up behind her and gently wrapped his arm around her waist. "Hopelessly in love with you."

Sam smiled and leaned back into him, knowing, no matter what the future held, the moment was perfect.

"Are you ready yet?" Sam asked Ethan through the closed door of the spare room.

"I bet this is a first, a woman waiting on a man to finish getting ready."

"Don't you start with me, mister! I'll open this door right now and ruin your surprise."

"Hey, cut me some slack. This is harder than I thought it would be."

"Do you need me to zip you up?"

"Ha-ha. No, I'm ready. Stand back, I'm coming out."

"Oh my," Sam said as she looked him up and down and then nodded. "Oh, yes. That's working." She gestured for him to turn around. "Let me see if the backside is as good as the front."

"Samantha!"

"Come on, you can't come out dressed like Thor and not expect women to drool over your body. And move that cape out of the way so I can see your butt."

"So you're saying you like my body."

"No, Mr. McGregor, I love your body." She batted her eyelashes at him. "But why Thor? Don't get me wrong, it's working, but I never would have guessed you'd pick out this costume."

120 DAYS...

"Simple, my dear, you know what Thor does in the movies. He meets this beautiful mortal woman. They spend some time together. He falls for her, but he has to leave. He's got these responsibilities to take care of back in his realm." He tucked a strand of hair behind her ear. "But he never forgot her. He wanted to go to her, but his duty to his people was strong and the Bifrost is broken. Then she needed him. She had a sickness in her blood. He did everything, taking her back home to be treated by his people, even asking the brother he no longer trusted to help him save her. He defied his father, the king, committed treason to help her. In the end, he gave up the crown, what he'd been born to do, to rule the seven realms, for her. There was no other superhero I could be for you but Thor, because I'd do all of that and more for you."

The words he spoke touched Sam so deeply she felt every broken piece of her put back together, simply by the love of this good man. "You have no idea what you do to me."

"I think I do, the very same you've done for me. Healed me, made me better, given me back hope." He pulled away and looked her up and down. "Now, just what are you dressed up as?"

"What, it's not obvious?" She giggled. "We must be connected, although a different comic. I'm dressed up as Dr. Jean Grey from *X-Men*. She's powerful, caring, and a scientist." Sam shrugged. "I'm trying to be positive."

"It's totally working." He pulled her into his arms. "Now, let's go have some fun."

"You know, the ladies are going to be all over you."

"Of course. That's the other reason why I picked this costume out." He looked at her with a straight face for all of ten seconds before he started laughing. "Nah, they all know I only have eyes for you."

He swept her up in his arms and danced her back into the bedroom while singing the song "I Only Have Eyes for You" to her.

Chapter 24

Six Months Later

DAY 68

ETHAN—

I NEEDED YOU TO UNDERSTAND WHERE I WAS COMING FROM. FROM THE VERY START, I THOUGHT I'D CREATE THIS JOURNAL FOR YOU, SO IN A WAY, YOU COULD TAKE THIS JOURNEY WITH ME. BUT IT'S ALSO SOMETHING FOR THE FUTURE SO YOU CAN ALWAYS HAVE SOMETHING OF MINE TO REMEMBER ME BY.

THERE'S NO DENYING THE FACT ANY LONGER. I KNEW I WAS NEVER GOING TO GET BETTER, BUT FOR SO LONG I WASN'T GETTING WORSE. NOW I KNOW, I DON'T THINK I'M GOING TO MAKE IT ONE-HUNDRED-AND-TWENTY DAYS.

EVAN

120 DAYS...

Sam waited until Ethan had gone down to the main house before she slowly made her way upstairs to the bedroom in the back of the house. Before they had officially moved in together, it had been an empty room. After she found out she was pregnant, she started sneaking items into the room and organizing them into containers. She tried to look at this as good planning. Her attitude was still positive; they were both going to make it, but she needed to be ready for the worst. Plus she could focus on other things as their child grew up and she'd already have each holiday covered.

Stopping by the first one, she ran her hand over the label, Thanksgiving. At that point, she had been tired, but still feeling well. Good enough in fact she still went down to the office every day and would participate in the less strenuous events.

They had a traditional huge meal gathered around the large table in the rec center and gave thanks that they were able to spend time with each other, share food and laughter. Thumbing through the pictures she'd taken, she swore she could smell the turkey and stuffing from that day. After Halloween, it was her next favorite holiday. She loved all the food and always ate more than she should have.

Putting the pictures down, she picked up the first of eighteen USB drives and looked at the date on it, next Thanksgiving. She wanted to make a video their child could watch every year until they were eighteen. Since nothing was guaranteed and she didn't know how weak she would become, she decided to record the videos sooner rather than later.

Ethan had started making small changes around

the resort during her pregnancy. All were good ideas, and he did them in such a way that the transition was smooth.

Making sure everything was in perfect order, she put the lid back on and went onto the next one, Christmas. The smell of peppermint wafted up as she opened the lid. Inside were eighteen Christmas ornaments for their child along with a letter on the wonder and meaning of Christmas for when they needed to be reminded of it.

Her fingers played with the heart necklace around her neck Ethan had surprised her with for Christmas. It had three diamonds in it, one for each of them. She'd cried then, just as she cried at that moment. Her emotions were overwhelming her a lot, and she spent a bunch of time crying.

Moving to the next box, she smiled. New Year's. Every year they always celebrated with New York City, since most of their guests couldn't make it to midnight. This year as the ball started to drop, she'd grabbed on to Ethan and kissed him as if her life depended on it. She wanted the kiss to carry over from one year to the next. She thought it was best to end one year together as another began.

They had found out the day before they were having a girl, and everything was looking good with her. Sam broke down and sobbed, so thankful she was healthy. So far. They had started trying to figure out names, but couldn't agree on anything, in fact, they still couldn't.

For this container, she decided her daughter should have a new life lesson for the start of every year. Something she wished she had known growing up, or had found out earlier in her life.

Sam also included the fantasy football trophy in this container, she wanted her daughter to know, even

120 DAYS...

though football was considered a sport for men, that didn't mean you couldn't love it and kick the boys' asses. Which was what she did. They'd continued the league through the rest of the season, and Sam had won the most weeks.

With the New Year came a new project Ethan was working on, something secret he was keeping from her along with the improvements on the property. She was spending more and more time with the guests or alone. They wouldn't let her do much of anything, and she was feeling trapped.

Growing up, Sam had always made homemade cards for her parents. She did the same for her daughter for Valentine's Day. She wanted to make sure her daughter never doubted how much she was loved, so made a card for each year, telling her exactly how much she meant to her, how she was more important than anything else.

All the stories and movies she'd watched growing up about the prince coming and whisking the girl off on a romantic date finally came true. Ethan had taken her down into the city where he had an appointment at a day spa set up for her. She spent all day being completely pampered. When she was done, they made sure her hair and make-up were perfect to go with the new outfit he had bought for her. The evening was spent having a romantic dinner overlooking the lights. She could feel their daughter move in her belly as Ethan held her in his arms.

Ethan still spent many hours working and doing research. If there was something out there she could take or do that would help her and not harm the baby, he was tracking down information on it. He was relentless in his pursuit of knowledge and keeping the resort running.

Since they were both of Irish heritage, they made

sure everyone celebrated St. Patrick's Day. Corn beef hash, green beer and bad accents were heavy that day, as was her belly. Sam was more tired than she'd ever been. She knew why, it wasn't only the pregnancy. Cancer was growing in her. At that point, she was praying almost hourly to slow the growth of it. If it could be held under a certain size, she'd be able to deliver her daughter and then have the cancer taken care of. They could still both survive.

Sam made eighteen trinkets, little things from different cultures that were said to bring luck to a person. Her child, her daughter was her miracle. She wanted her to have all the good luck, more than anyone else.

Ethan was checking on her all the time now. They both knew the further along she was the more things that could go wrong. He only left her for short periods of time. Even when a guest was dying, he wouldn't stay away long before he was back making sure she was okay.

Working on all of the holiday containers while he was away became harder and harder. For Memorial Day, she found stories of regular people who went above and beyond for their country, and ended up paying the ultimate price, their life for America's freedom. Sam wanted her daughter to know that men, and women, paid a high price for everything she had, and to never take that for granted. Even though Evan hadn't died serving this country, she still put something of his in there, a little history on her uncle.

She found old books written by the Founding Fathers for the Fourth of July. To understand what we are as a country, she wanted her daughter to know how it all started. For Labor Day, she added more books. These were books which were written for or by the people who had dreams, who followed them with

120 DAYS...

all their heart, so their work was their passion and not a job.

The Halloween container, was actually two. When they were putting all the decorations away last year, she held out her favorite ones, and put a note in there as to why they were her favorites, along with the complete works of Edgar Allen Poe and a dozen of her favorite horror movies.

Turning, she faced the longest wall in the room. Before her were eighteen containers, one for each of the birthday's her daughter would have. She'd tried hard to figure out what she would want for each year and think of something that wouldn't be obsolete by the time her daughter got to open it. The hardest thing was making sure her daughter knew Sam loved her. She hoped with everything she was doing by putting these containers together, their daughter would know she did everything she could to make memories for her. She wanted her daughter to know she loved her and would never regret any decision she made in deciding to have her. This was the only thing Sam could think of to leave her that would continue to show how much she loved her.

Sam was dozing on the couch when Ethan came through the door a little later. As always, he stopped in his tracks and looked at her. His heart sank. She didn't look good; there was no denying it. The doctors said they couldn't believe how well their daughter was doing considering how bad Sam was. The cancer was growing faster than anyone had estimated. Their goal was to try to make it to thirty-six weeks and perform a C-section, and after the child was born, they'd do whatever they needed to do inside Sam to remove the cancer they could, before sewing her up again.

There was no hiding the look in the staffs' eyes when they were in the office to see the doctors every week. They didn't think there was any hope. There were nights when Ethan didn't have any either. He kept that from Sam. She didn't need his worries and heartbreak on top of everything else she was worried about. She didn't think he knew about the back room, but he did. He let her do what she felt she needed to do in order to get through every day and prepare for every possible outcome. Thankfully, she wasn't there the first time he'd found it, because he'd lost it seeing all of those containers lined up, labeled with the holidays. Then he opened one and started crying all over again. She amazed him with her strength, gathering all that for their daughter, while all the while fighting for both of their lives.

Quietly, Ethan went into the kitchen and prepared a snack for them. He found that if they ate together, she'd eat more. Between the baby and the cancer, there wasn't much left of her. She was too skinny, and he hated to admit it, almost grey looking. He'd been at the resort too long. He knew what that color meant and it almost shattered him.

He had some news for her and he hoped it would settle her mind for the future of the resort. He put the tray of food down on the table and looked over at her, smiling when he saw her eyes were open and looking at him. "Good morning, beautiful, did you have a good nap?"

"It seems all naps are good now. It would be nice if they could be a bit longer. I know it's good for us."

"Yes, it is, and so is this. Here, let me help you up." Once she was sitting up, he placed the tray next to her on the couch. "Now eat. Did you do anything special while I was gone?"

120 DAYS...

"No, I did a little reading, and daydreaming. You?"

"As a matter of fact, I finally have some good news to share with you."

"What?"

"Remember how we talked about the gold mine months ago?"

She waved her hand at him and picked up a strawberry. "That's a myth."

"It isn't."

Pausing with the berry almost to her lips, she blinked her large eyes at him. "Excuse me? It isn't?"

He smiled and shook his head. "I've found it."

"No way." She shook her head.

"Oh, yes, since we talked about it I've been doing research and hired geologists to come out, and what do you know, we ended up finding it."

"Where is it?" She sat up straighter and set the berry down.

"Pretty much right under our noses. Going back through the historical records, we discovered the old building we turned into a gym was one of the first buildings here, and there was a crawl space hidden, way back in the corner. It was so dark I always missed it, not like I spent a lot of time down there, but yeah, there it was, the entrance to the mine."

"It's been here all the time?"

"Sure has, and here's the kicker. There's still a lot of gold down there. In fact, there is so much you're going to have more money than I do, a lot more." He smiled at her. "Do you know what that means?"

She shook her head. "I have no idea. I can't wrap my head around that much money."

"It means Last Resort is going to go on for a very

long time. Hell, you could buy all the surrounding properties and expand and still not worry. You could even open up other resorts throughout the country, world even."

"There can't be that much down there."

"There is. Of course, there are no guarantees as to how far the veins of gold goes, but just with the little bit that's exposed, and the going rate, you're seriously set."

"Well, that's good . . ." She leaned back and stared off. "All these years, it's been right here. Oh! What about the tunnels? You always hear stories about tunnels collapsing and swallowing buildings, could that happen here? Should we map them out and make sure there aren't any buildings above them?"

"That's the thing, it's a small tunnel, a few feet wide and about six foot tall, and maybe each section goes out twenty feet from the gym. They were very surprised it was so small considering the stories on how much gold was pulled out of there, but once they got down there and saw exactly what everything looked like, they were very excited."

"Should we worry about people coming here to get their hands on it? I mean, I've gotten offers to buy the land because of it. In fact, some of them have gone so far as to sabotage equipment."

"No, you're not going to have to worry about anything, because between the two of us, we have enough money to make sure we have the best security, both in personnel and equipment to make sure nothing happens to harm anyone here on the resort."

"Wow. I've got nothing else, just wow."

"I know. I've been pretty excited the closer we were to discovering its location, and today, everything was confirmed. It's gold. I was afraid it might have been

120 DAYS...

fool's gold when I first went down there."

She raised an eyebrow at him. "Should I be pissed off at you after the fact that you went down there before the professionals did, you know, the ones who would know if it was a safe thing to do or not?"

Leaning in close to her, he looked her in the eye. "Tell me you wouldn't have done the same thing." When she didn't answer, he kissed her quickly on the nose. "See, you have no room to talk."

"Okay, changing subjects. How was the rest of your day?"

"You won't believe who I heard from today. Peter, you remember, him and Marissa at the restaurant." He watched as her hands stopped the circular rubbing motion on her belly.

"What did he have to say?"

"I guess they're divorced. She found someone new, with more money and left him, but not before taking half of his money."

"I guess, that's good for him?"

"Hopefully. He called to apologize again."

"I'm sure that wasn't all of it."

"No, he has a deal he wants me to go in on."

"Are you?"

"What? No way, I've been quietly selling all my investments as it is. The last thing I want is to get into another one."

"Why?"

"Why what?"

"Why are you selling all your investments?"

"I don't need them." He shrugged. "If I don't have to go down into the city, I don't want to. I've never been happier than I've been since coming up here. I've actually been grooming my assistant Jodi to give the business to. She's really intelligent and doesn't take grief from anyone. She's going to do really well."

"Don't you miss it?"

"Sure, I've spent so many years wheeling and dealing, but Sam, this is my home now, you and our child are my home. All I've ever wanted is here."

"But what if I'm not here."

"Samantha—"

"Don't you *Samantha* me. We have to talk about this. About the worst case scenario. We've been skirting the issue for months. We can't wait any more. Think of everything Last Resort represents, now think of me, can one exist without the other? Can you exist here without me?"

He stood up and walked away from her. "I'm not ready to talk about this."

"Well, you're going to have to be. We have this opportunity to talk things through before it happens, most people don't get this chance. Don't throw it away."

"I refuse to talk to you about you dying. It's not going to happen."

"Go ahead, keep lying to yourself." Slowly and awkwardly, she stood up. "Think of it this way, I like to be prepared for every single possibility that might happen. By being prepared for the worst, most of the time it never happens." She started to walk away.

"Don't go," he whispered. "I don't know. You're in every building, every tree, and every breath of this place. Am I strong enough to be here if you're not? I don't know. Can I expect to see you every time I turn a corner and not break down when you're not there? Can I walk into the Legacy Garden and see the butterflies and your handprint amongst so many others and not fall to my knees feeling my heart break over and over again? Can I hear your voice only to turn around to nothing but the hope you are still here and the ache in my heart that will never go away? I just don't know."

"But you'll have our daughter."

"Hopefully, I will. She's strong right now. Can she be that way for another month? What if I lose both of you? It would be hard enough trying to put one foot in front of the other, day after day without you by my side, but to lose something I've never held before but in my heart? I can't . . ." He placed his hand on her belly. "I love you both so much." He couldn't hide his anguish, his voice shook with it. "Promise me, promise me you'll continue to fight with everything you have, for yourself, for our child, for *us*."

"Ethan, you have to know I'm not giving up. As long as there is a breath in this body, I will fight. I will hold out hope that we will both survive and be able to have a long life with you by my side."

"You have no idea how much I want that." He wrapped his arms around her, breathing in her scent which always calmed his soul.

"We both do, we both do."

Chapter 25

DAY 79

ETHAN–

GOT TO TELL YOU, BRO, THINGS AREN'T LOOKING GOOD. I THINK IT'S MY TIME. STRANGELY, I'M OKAY WITH THIS. I'VE LIVED MY LIFE. I'VE HAD MY FUN AND NOW I GET TO SEE WHAT'S ON THE OTHER SIDE.

STAY POSITIVE. LIVE THE REST OF YOUR LIFE, TRULY LIVE IT, BROTHER OF MINE.

I LOVE YOU,

EVAN

"Here." Ethan held out a package for Sam. "Put this on."

"Why should I?" She crossed her arms over her chest.

"Because we're going to have some fun today."

120 DAYS...

"Why do I have to change? Do you know how much work it is for me to get out of these clothes and put on whatever is in here?" She waved it at him.

He sat down next to her. "Come on, you used to love this stuff." Placing his arm around her, he deepened his voice. "If you'd like, I can help you."

Sam burst out in tears and covered her face with her hands.

"What is it? What did I say?" He tried to pull her hands away from her face. "Come on, honey, I'm sorry. Please let me make this better."

"You don't understand," she wailed.

"No, I don't, so help me."

"I'm fat. I waddle. I look like crap and my body isn't my own anymore. Between the pregnancy and cancer, I'm nothing."

"Oh, honey." He gathered her up in his arms and held her tightly. "You're everything. You have to know I love you no matter what."

"But I can't give you everything you need."

"Stop, stop it right now, you,"—he tapped her chest where her heart was beating—". . . you have given me so much more than I could ever give you. I'd still be that shell of a man if it weren't for you. And this,"—placing his hand on her belly, he rubbed it—". . . this is so special I can't even put it into words."

"But you've spent so much time having to take care of me, sacrificing what you want for me."

"Listen to me. Love is never a sacrifice. Every single thing I do is out of love. I remember my dad saying he'd bend over backwards to make sure Mom was happy, because to make her happy made him happy. And it's never work or a chore if you love that person."

"I wish I could give you more," she whispered.

"You give more than you think. Now please, if you want to make me happy, go change." He picked the package up and handed it to her.

"I don't think that's playing by the rules."

"Oh, it is. Now get a move on. I have to change too."

"Fine. Here, help me up." She held her hands out to him.

"Always." Once she was on her feet, he leaned down and kissed her, hoping to show her that he meant every single word he said.

"Wonder Woman? Why?" she asked Ethan as she looked down at her costume. "And I didn't know they made them for pregnant women."

"They make just about every costume for pregnant women. But don't you get it? To me and everyone else, you *are* Wonder Woman. Even now when you can't do as much as you could before, you still make time for everyone and make sure you are visible around here."

She couldn't help herself, tears welled up in her eyes. She knew the pregnancy hormones had a lot to do with them, but Ethan had been so wonderful to her, always making sure she had what she needed and indulging in her every whim, and taking care of Last Resort when she couldn't.

"Shhh . . ." Ethan wrapped his arms around her. "It'll be okay. We have a fun day planned and your invisible plane, otherwise known as the golf cart, is right outside the door waiting for you."

"Well then, lead on, Thor." Sam took his arm when he held it out for her. She liked the fact he wore the same costume as Halloween, the meaning behind it meant so much to her. "Although, you know walking is good for me."

"Yes, it is, however, if I know you, you're going to be up and down all day at the rec center anyway and you'll get plenty of exercise then."

"True, true." She sat back and enjoyed the ride over the hills to the rec center, breathing in the fresh air and seeing the changes that both she and Ethan had implemented. A sense of pride came over her. For all that she and they had achieved together. It wasn't all smooth sailing. They both had their own opinions, sometimes strong, but in the end, they knew they wanted the best for the resort and were making it their own.

Ethan had started buying up the surrounding properties that were available with the money she had from the gold mine. They had revised their original plan, and based on how much more property they would be able to acquire, would determine how large the resort would become. One of the things she wanted to do was form a children's area, where the child could not only have all of their wishes come true, the families could stay with them.

Their main focus was to make it feel like a community, a large family and not an institution. They were on the same page there. Most of their arguments came from the fact Ethan wanted to put more of his money into the resort, yet Sam wouldn't let him. She knew he had his ways of helping out without letting her know, and she let him.

"We're going to need a bigger rec center," she said.

"I was thinking we could keep this one, add one in the family area, and then maybe a large one for when we do events everyone wants to attend. We could even build a couple of smaller ones if needed."

"True, that might be better. That way each one

could be specialized."

"We'll talk more about it tomorrow. Now, its movie time."

She couldn't help it, and blamed it on the pregnancy hormones, why she always seemed to be able to cry at the drop of a hat. The staff and guests showed her all the time how much she meant to them and how special she was. She realized exactly how she made the guests feel when they came to her resort and it made her happy. She had to admit it was harder to put on the brave face than it had been before. There was so much more at stake, her child's life, her own, and Ethan's love. She wanted the happy ending more than she ever could have dreamed possible.

Ethan kept checking his watch. They'd been watching one Marvel superhero movie after the other, all in order from when they were released in the theaters. It was almost time for the last movie, the one that wasn't going to be released for another month and his other surprise hadn't shown up yet. He was thankful he had a favor he could call in to make this epic evening happen for her.

When his phone chirped signaling a text message, he quickly looked down and couldn't hide the smile. "I'll be right back," he said to Sam. "You stay right here."

"Where else am I going to go? Hey, where are you going anyway?"

He leaned down and kissed her quickly. "I'll be right back."

"Hey!"

He ignored her and walked out of the rec center

120 DAYS...

and down to the main house. There was a black SUV and Devlin Cross stepped out of the driver's side and walked around to open the passenger door where his wife, Lily, stepped out. She went around to the back door and reached in as a boy of about ten scrambled out around his mother.

"Hey, Ethan, how's it going? You didn't have to dress up for me though."

"Great, Dev, thanks for coming. I'd like to see you look so good in this costume."

"Wait until you see me in the movie. You'll be jealous."

"No, you'll both be jealous of me," a British voice came from the other side of the vehicle. "Everyone knows without me there would be no little pack of superheroes." Will Martinsson came into view along with his wife, author Melissa Loring.

"Please," a third voice called from the sports car Ethan hadn't noticed parked behind the SUV. "If it weren't for me, none of this would be possible. I was in the first movie."

Devlin Cross was one of Hollywood's biggest stars and in the new Marvel movie, while Will was the master villain of the franchise. The last man there was Royce Rivers, the cocky movie star who played a cocky billionaire.

Ethan held his hand out to Will, who introduced his wife, and Royce. Ethan hadn't met either man yet and he felt uncomfortable in the costume in front of him but knew it made Sam happy.

"Lily," Devlin said. "Come meet Ethan McGregor, he's magic when it comes to finding the right property at the right time if you're looking to invest."

"Nice to meet you." She shook his hand as the little girl on her hip shyly looked over at him. "But I think

I'm happy with the property in Maine, thank you very much."

"And Los Angeles." Devlin winked at her.

"That's all you. I only come out here when I need to. Leave me with the kids and my artist's studio back home and I'm happy. You go play make-believe."

"It's what I do." He smiled and put his arm around her. "This little sweetheart is L.D., and the boy running around like crazy is Leo."

"Hey, Dad," said Leo. "Look at this place. How cool is this!" He had climbed up on the old ranch equipment Ethan had found and cleaned up. "I could totally use this for ninja training."

"Yes, you could. Now get down before you hurt yourself," Lily answered.

"He wasn't talking to you." Devlin smirked at his wife. "Hold up there." Quickly, Devlin ran over and jumped up on the equipment next to the son he had officially adopted after he'd married Lily. "Oh, yeah, you could totally use something like this. Hey, Mom, we should do something like this in the backyard."

"No, now both of you get down before you get hurt."

"Girls," Devlin said and elbowed Leo.

"Yeah, girls. We need more boys in this family."

"Ha! No . . ." Lily said and gave them both a look.

"Mama . . . down . . ." L.D. said.

"No, sweetie, we're running a little late to begin with. Hold on a few more minutes and you can run around."

"'Kay."

Lily hugged her tightly and spoke to Ethan. "She's so laid back and calm. Nothing like the rest of us. It's a nice change"—she pointed behind her—"from all of that."

"I can see you have your hands full."

"Which is why we left ours at home." Melissa looked at Will. "And don't get any ideas. I'm not ready for anymore yet."

"*Yet* being the operative word, darling." Will kissed the top of her head.

"Besides, you know Hannah is loving having some one-on-one time with the little one." Royce turned and looked at Ethan. "Hannah is my very lucky wife and Lissa's assistant. She decided to stay home for this trip since she's feeling a bit under the weather."

Lily turned around and said, "Come on, boys, it's time to go. And don't . . ." shaking her head, she continued, ". . . jump down."

"All right, let's get this show on the road." Devlin slung his arm across Leo's shoulders. "We're always waiting for these women, aren't we?"

Lily sighed. "Lead on, McGregor, lead on."

Leo was full of youthful exuberance as they walked down to the rec center running up and down the path. Ethan filled them all in on the workings of Last Resort and what their plans for the future were. When they stood outside, Ethan held open the door and let them walk in. Soon enough, the whole room hushed.

"Don't stop talking on my account," Devlin said. "Tell me, how have the movies been so far?"

Ethan peeked in and saw Sam's mouth hanging open. He knew this would get her. Devlin Cross was one of her favorite movie stars, and add that he was in the next Marvel movie made this extra special for her. Devlin saw her start to struggle to stand up and knew he couldn't get to her in time to help.

"My lady." Devlin held out his hand to Sam, which

she took with shaking hands. "I remember when Lily was pregnant. I was constantly helping her up."

"Hi... hello..." she stuttered.

"Hello, Wonder Woman, or can I call you Samantha?" He bowed and kissed the back of her hand.

"Sam, Sam's good." Her wide eyes swung toward Ethan and she mouthed, '*Oh, my gosh. You did this.*'

He grinned and nodded.

"If you'll excuse me." Will stepped around Devlin. "I believe it's my turn to meet this beautiful lady." He bowed at the waist. "William Martinsson at your service."

"Umm..." Sam blinked big eyes back and forth between the two of them. "Too much."

Royce stepped around the other two men and laughed. "I don't know the meaning of too much. Although, if I had known it was going to be a costume party, I would have worn my costume from the movie. Speaking of the movie." He reached into his suit pocket and pulled out a DVD. "Anyone want to watch the new movie?"

The small crowd cheered and Royce laughed. "Well, lucky for me, this is the movie, huh? Here, Ethan, put this on will you, while I have a chat with this lovely lady?"

Ethan handed the DVD to Phil and put his arm around Sam feeling her shake from the excitement and hoping it wasn't too much for her.

"You're such a flirt," Melissa teased Royce.

"Which is how I managed to get Hard-Hearted Hannah to fall in love with me."

"Well, there is that." Melissa stepped over to Sam. "Hello, I'm married to Will, I'm–"

120 DAYS...

"No, no, seriously? I know who you are! You're Melissa Loring, I've read all of your books. Well, I don't have a lot of time to read, so it takes me a long time, but I love your crazies."

Ethan couldn't help but chuckle at how cute she looked, beaming with happiness and practically bouncing around with excitement.

"Then you're going to love this." Lissa held up a tote bag filled with books. "When Will told me he was coming here and I learned what you did here, I had to do my little part. I've got signed copies of all of my books here so your guests can read them, along with copies of my next two releases. You'll get to read them before anyone else."

Sam took the bag and clutched it to her chest. "Thank you so much. I can't wait to read the new ones, oh, and of course, go back and re-read the others."

Devlin leaned over to Royce and whispered, "Why do I get the feeling she's a bigger hit than we are?"

"Yeah, there's a first. The author is more popular than the movie stars. Someone should write about that. We can file that under fiction."

"You two stop it," Lily said. "Devlin, go over there and stop your son from eating all of the chocolate cake and here,"—she handed L.D. to Royce—"Do something useful, charm her. I want to meet Sam."

Ethan ran his hands up and down Sam's arms trying to keep her calm and grounded. He remembered all of the other times guests had something big like this happen for them and the next day they'd crashed. He didn't think that would be good for Sam, but the thought of doing something so special for her greatly outweighed the fact she might end up in bed all day under the watchful eyes of a nurse.

"Hey, Dad," Leo said, "when are we going to start

the movie? I haven't seen this one yet. I can't wait. Is there any popcorn?"

"Manners, Leonardo," Lily reproached. "Sorry, sometimes I think he was raised in a sewer like the Ninja Turtles he loves so much."

"No worries," Sam said. "We have popcorn *and* candy if you want some." She pointed to the kitchen area.

"Awesome!" Leo jumped up and ran over there.

"Devlin . . ." Lily called.

"On it. Come back here, kid, you've already had enough sweet stuff." They walked over to the kitchen area as Leo pleaded his case for more candy.

"Well . . ." Sam rocked back on her heels. "I never expected something like this."

Royce frowned at her. "Why not."

"This is something I do for other people, not for me."

"Which is exactly why Ethan did this for you. He called Devlin who called Will who called me. When we heard what you are doing up here, we all had to come to make this a special night for you."

"That's nice of you." She turned slightly and looked up at Ethan. "I didn't know you knew Devlin."

Devlin overheard the comment as he walked up and took his daughter from Royce. "Since this acting gig is a fickle business, I wanted to make sure I diversified. Ethan found some investment properties for me all around California. I must say, I've made a lot of money because of him. Anyway,"—he put his arm around Lily—"this is my beautiful wife Lily and our daughter L.D. She wanted to meet you."

Lily held out her hand to her. "I can't believe you came up with the idea and were able to make it

120 DAYS...

happen. You truly are Wonder Woman."

"I was lucky enough to have everything fall into place and be able to help so many people."

Ethan knew by now there was no use correcting her. She always downplayed how much work it was to get the resort up and running, not to mention continue to do it as she did.

"We walked by the Legacy Garden on the way here, all those people . . ." Lily wiped away a tear from her eye. "I don't know how you do it."

"Each of them has touched me more than anything I did for them." She leaned back into Ethan.

"Someone needs to tell your story." Lissa looked at Sam thoughtfully. "More people need to know about what you do here."

"Come on, you need to sit down again," Ethan said and guided her to the couch.

"You may be right." She smiled up at him. "Thank you."

"You are very welcome, my dear. Now relax and talk to the ladies while Devlin, Royce and Will go around and spend a little bit of time meeting everyone." The other men had already started talking to the guests and staff.

"Sounds good, oh and can you get me something to eat too?"

"I figured that would be our last stop before heading back to you lovely ladies."

"Charmer."

"Hey, do you see this guy?" Ethan pointed over his shoulder to where the three men were surrounded by the people. "I have to pull out all the stops."

"Well, you've got my heart, so you can relax."

"You heart is nothing to trivialize. It's something I

will spend every day making sure I'm worthy of."

"Ethan..."

"Be quiet, enjoy. I'll be back."

They were lying in bed and Ethan was rubbing her feet.

"Another doctor's appointment tomorrow," she said.

"Yep."

"It's going to be good news. That everything is going well."

"Yes, it is."

"Ethan..."

"Yes, honey."

"Thank you."

"For what?"

"Devlin, Royce, Will and Melissa, I can't believe they spent so much time with us. And Lily, she's so cool. And their kids. Wow. Melissa and Will have a baby, so I was able to get some advice from both of them. It was a really good day, all because of you."

"Nah, you always have really good days. I just helped a little bit with this one. Come on, tell me you wouldn't have loved today, even without the celebrities."

"You're right. It would have been a great day without them, but with them? Spectacular."

"Oh, really." He raised an eyebrow at her. "So you're telling me they were the only reason today was spectacular."

She giggled. "Okay, part of the reason, the rest of it

120 DAYS...

was seeing you in that Thor costume."

"I'm glad you approve."

She grinned. "Oh, I do, I do." Her smile faded. "We do need to talk about something." With her belly fluttering, she didn't know if it was from nerves or their daughter.

"Anything."

"I think I've come up with a name for her."

"Let's hear it."

"Well, I was thinking of both of our mothers, Bonnie and Jennifer. What about Jennie? Jen for Jennifer and n-i-e for Bonnie. Do you think it's too hokey?"

Ethan cleared his throat. "No, no, I think it's perfect. Absolutely perfect, just like you."

"I'm far from perfect. Now since that's decided on. We need to come up with a middle name." She tapped her lips with a finger thinking. "Well, I came up with the first name, how about you figure out the middle name?"

"Sounds good. And the last name?"

"McGregor of course."

"But what about your last name?"

With a quick intake of breath, her stomach dropped. Her mind whirled with exactly what he was asking her. She didn't want to assume marriage and make a fool of herself. "What exactly do you mean?"

"I know this isn't the perfect situation, and if I had my way, I'd plan the most romantic evening and ask you, but we can't do that right now. So instead . . ." He stood up and walked around to her side of the bed and got down on one knee. Picking up her hand, he said, "Samantha Rose Truman, would you do me the honor of being my wife?"

The words stuck in her throat; she didn't know what to say. Almost every girl dreamed about this day, and there it was, the man of her dreams down on one knee in front of her, their child growing inside of her. Along with the cancer.

"Why now?" she asked.

"I didn't want to rush you, or make you think the only reason I was asking you was because you are pregnant with my child. I wanted you to know deep down in your heart that I love you, no questions, no stipulations, and no guarantees."

"I do know that, but can you listen to me?" She winced at the pain that showed in his eyes.

"You don't want to marry me?"

"No, no, Ethan, please that isn't it at all. Under any other circumstances, I'd be jumping in your arms kissing you, but with this situation you have to understand where I'm coming from. I'm not going to marry you just to die. So I'm asking you to wait for me. Wait until after the baby is born, after I'm out of the hospital."

"I know what's behind this and dammit, we've been through this. You aren't going to die."

"You know it isn't in my plan to die. But look at me, I'm not at my best right now. Let me focus on the rest of this pregnancy, and *then* we'll get married."

"It's not in *either* of our plans, but that isn't why I want to get married right now. I want to get married right now because I love you and I don't want to miss out on one more moment without you being my wife. If we end up married for one day or fifty years, it doesn't matter to me. You are what matters."

"What about 'in sickness and health,' Ethan? We've had so little health. I'm not going to have our marriage all about the sickness."

120 DAYS...

"You don't get to decide for me what and when I can deal with all this shit. What do you think I've been doing all this time? It's not going to change if we get married. I need you to know how committed to you I am. I'm not going anywhere."

"I know you're not going anywhere. I know you are committed to me, to us." She placed her hand on her belly. "If that were the case, you would have left a long time ago." Sam's eyes filled with tears. "Ethan, I didn't know a love like ours existed before you walked into my life, and now I can't see what it would be like if you weren't in mine anymore." She smiled at him. "Any other time I'd already be planning our wedding, but right now, I don't think I can handle much more. But, what we can do is go and get our marriage license and I promise, once we have everything ready for Jennie, then we'll start planning our simple wedding."

"There's no changing your mind?"

"I'm a woman." She smiled at him. "There's always a chance for me to change my mind."

"It's always good to have hope."

She watched at Ethan stood up and walked around to his side of the bed and climbed in after he turned the light off. He slid in behind her and wrapped his arms around her like he did every night and she relaxed into him. Hope, hope was good.

Chapter 26

DAY 80

ETHAN-

WE ARE MAKING YOUR BROTHER AS COMFORTABLE AS POSSIBLE. I AM CONTINUING TO MAKE THE DAILY ENTRY FOR HIM. HE TOOK A TURN FOR THE WORSE IN THE MIDDLE OF THE NIGHT. I'M SORRY, BUT IT'S ONLY A MATTER OF TIME NOW. I WANT YOU TO KNOW I WILL STAY WITH HIM UNTIL THE END. I WON'T LEAVE HIS SIDE.

SAMANTHA

"Well, Samantha, your baby is doing remarkably well. You, on the other hand, are not," the doctor said. Her normal doctor was on vacation so they had to see someone else.

"I feel fine, well, as fine as I can."

"You're lying to yourself. Luckily your child is very

120 DAYS...

healthy, the odds of her surviving are good, but yours aren't so good."

"Wait a minute." Ethan's voice was hard. "Don't you talk to her like that. We've been doing everything possible to make sure both she and the baby are fine. We don't need some wet-behind-the-ears newbie telling her she's not going to make it."

"Ethan!" Sam said.

"No, I'm not going to stop." His voice was loud. "Do you know who you are talking to? Samantha Truman, she runs Last Resort. You know that place up in the hills where everyone goes when the doctors have given up on them and said they were going to die within weeks. Do you know what she does? She gives them time. More time than any stinking doctor did. She makes it possible to live their last days with hope and laughter and dignity. Something *you* need to learn how to do. I don't care what you think. I know if anyone can prove you wrong it's her. We'll be back here after she's given birth just to show you how wrong you are. Come on, we're leaving." Ethan went over and carefully helped Sam off the exam table. "We'll be back when you're gone."

They stopped at the desk to make their next appointment. Sam's regular doctor was back the following week, which made Ethan happy. He was still fuming at the audacity of that young punk. What did that kid know, hell, he looked like he should still be in high school.

"Ethan . . . Ethan, slow down."

Sam's breathless voice came from behind him and he stopped looking back. "Sorry, that guy just pissed me off."

"Yeah, I kind of got that. You can't get angry at him. It's all he knows."

"He should be open to other options. If he'd even read your file, he'd know what he was dealing with, who he was dealing with. I can't wait to go back there after Jennie is born." He opened the door for her, helped her into the SUV then took a few deep breaths to calm down before he slid behind the wheel.

"You know we're going to have to prepare for the worst," she said softly.

"No, don't you start thinking that way. We know that positive thoughts and prayers are the way to go. Everyone has proven it works."

"It only works for so long, Ethan, before the cancer is too much."

"You're going to be different. We have this all planned out. Jennie will be born and they'll get all of the cancer out. After you recover, you'll be fine."

"But I might not be." Her voice shook with emotion. "You have to know I will do whatever it takes to survive. If I have to tell God to go away, that I'm not ready to die like my dad did, to buy me some more time with you and Jennie, I will, but it's not up to me. We have to be ready for everything."

Ethan started the engine with a roar. "*You* be ready for every outcome. The only one I know of is where you both survive and we have our happy ever after."

For the rest of the day Ethan kept his anger at bay, even when they were in the office and Sam seemed to be provoking him on purpose. Always going against what he thought was going to be the best for the resort. She kept at him until it was time to take her home for her afternoon nap. Every day she seemed to spend less and less time in the office or with the guests, and it was slowly killing him.

120 DAYS...

Since Ethan needed something physical to help release the tension that flowed through his body, he changed into a pair of shorts, grabbed some earbuds and once again, like he had so many months ago, cranked Metallica as he ran up and over the hills throughout the resort. But that time it wasn't from the grief of losing his brother. Instead, he was running from the fact that he may lose the woman he loved, and possibly their child.

When Ethan got back to the office he picked up the phone and called his old friend, Peter.

Chapter 27

Day 81

Ethan —

Evan has been in and out of it all day long. He was able to tell me a couple of stories about the two of you growing up. It sounds like you were close.

He's a fighter. He's been fighting with everything he had, every single day he has been here.

Samantha

Ethan wasn't sure it was the best thing to do, but because Sam wanted to, they did it. He tried not to shudder as a sea of pink greeted him in the rec center. Absently, he wondered if they'd be finding something pink there for years to come. If everything ended the way he wanted it to, it would be fine. If one or both of them did not survive, then he figured it would be a knife to the gut every single time he saw the color.

120 DAYS...

Walking over to the mountain of gifts, Ethan saw one of the largest was from Devlin and Lily, and the other from Noah Matthews and his wife, Lexi. He wondered what they could be. They needed everything baby related since they still needed to decorate Jennie's room. Sam had been spending hours going over all different decorating ideas for the baby's room; she wanted it to be perfect.

Smiling, he shook his head. The staff had taken one of the Halloween decorations, the throne of skulls never looked as twisted as it did covered in pink paper on the front, but black and dark on the back. His smile faded as he realized that was how he felt. On the outside all positive and happy, but inside, the fear was eating him alive.

Bethany had planned the whole thing and Ethan let her do it all. When Sam was opening gifts, and the group were playing games, Ethan took the opportunity to make sure everything was running as it should. One of their guests, Lydia, wasn't doing well, and it was only a matter of time before she passed. Walking to her cabin, he tried not to think what would happen when it was Sam's time. He knew he had to keep thinking positive, but sometimes, it was so hard.

Sitting down next to Lydia, Ethan picked up her hand. "Hey, you're missing all the excitement. Sam and I are having a baby shower right now. You should see all the pink." He laughed. "I can hear you now making wisecracks about the color, and saying just because it's a girl doesn't mean she has to have girly colors. Did I ever tell you about the time the guests made Sam and I dress up as characters from *Beetlejuice*? I'm sure you get that a lot since your name is Lydia. Anyway, it was a good time. We had fun watching the movie."

The beeps of her monitor slowed. "You've had a

good run. You said you weren't going to let pancreatic cancer take you too soon and you were going to beat what the doctors gave you, which was sixty-four days. Well, you beat that, and then you beat our average. Today is day two hundred and one. I can't believe you've been here for six months." He paused for a moment. "You've fought for so long, but now it's time. Thank you for spending your last days with us. You have loved ones waiting on the other side for you, it's time for you to go home."

Ethan leaned in close to whisper in her ear. "If you happen to see the big man up there, let him know I really need Sam and Jennie to stick around for a lot longer. I've got to confess, I'm a little scared here and could use some help. So put in a good word, okay?"

When the beeps stopped, Ethan said a prayer for the woman and went through the checklist, which he knew by heart since he had taken over from Sam. Waiting for the coroner to arrive, he tried not to think of everyone who had gone before, and who would be going next.

Sam kept looking at the door waiting for Ethan to come back. She knew where he was, and knew what had happened. As owner, she was still informed of everything that happened at the resort. She said her own prayer for Lydia.

When he finally came in, she breathed a sigh of relief. With effort, she stood up and everyone quieted down. "Thank you all so much for this wonderful baby shower. I can't wait to get home and have Ethan set everything up. It's all perfect, except for one thing. Ethan . . ." She held out her hand to him and when he took it looking puzzled, she smiled at him. "I'm not sure I'm going to go about this right, but you have to promise me you'll let me finish."

"Sure, sure, I can do that."

"I never expected someone like you to walk into my life and change it so completely. Before you, I thought my life was perfect. Well, I was wrong. It wasn't. It was in a holding pattern waiting for you to join me. Because with you, I can do anything. With you, my life is perfect." She rubbed her belly. "And now with Jennie coming, I couldn't be happier. I can't think of one thing I'd want that I don't have this very moment in time."

She placed his hand on her belly. "Ethan, I know I didn't handle it right before, but I'm hoping this will make up for my mistake. I should have said yes when you asked me to marry you. I should know better than anyone to embrace life and not hold back because of fear. Together, we can do anything. So, will you marry me?"

"Silly girl." He pulled her into his arms. "I'd marry you right now if I could."

She laughed. "Well, you can. Pastor Larry is here, and he can marry us right now. See, it was a good thing we went down and got our license."

"There's nothing else I'd rather do than to marry you Samantha."

Smiling up at him, she knew this was one of life's little perfect moments.

Chapter 28

April 8th

Day 82

Ethan —

It's not going to be much longer now. We've prayed for him and now it's in God's hands.

Samantha

Ethan knew something was wrong when he tried to get Sam to wake up and she kept falling back to sleep. After the baby shower, they'd spent the next couple of days going through all their gifts and ordering the rest of what they needed. Sam finally had a plan for the baby's room and they were going to start working on it that day, but she was so tired.

120 DAYS...

Going downstairs, he called the doctor. After a brief conversation, he knew it was either take her to the hospital or wait for the ambulance to arrive to take her down. Since he would be faster, he went upstairs and picked her up, easily carrying her down the stairs even though she was almost thirty-one weeks pregnant.

All the way down into the city, she slept and his anxiety grew. He didn't care what happened to his car as he parked by the doors and raced around to get her out. Again he carried her in and up to the desk.

"Please, someone help me. She won't wake up. Dr. Anderson should have called ahead. He deals in high risk pregnancies. This is Samantha Truman, I mean McGregor. It could be under either name. Please you have to help her."

"Sir, if you could fill out this form, we'll get to her as soon as we can."

"You don't understand," he yelled. "She's pregnant and I can't wake her up. The forms can wait, and right now, you have to help her." His voice broke.

"Sir, that's not how I do things here. There are protocols that have to happen before she can be seen. Now, if you will take this"—she held out a clipboard to him—"and have a seat and bring it back up when you are done, we'll help you then."

"Do you not see? I kind of have my hands full with my pregnant unconscious wife."

"You don't need to take that tone with me—"

"Excuse me, Mr. McGregor? I'm Ms. Simpson, the head administrator with the hospital. I wish we were meeting under different circumstances. If you could follow me, we have a room ready for you."

Ethan followed the woman without looking back at the unhelpful clerk at the check-in desk. "Thank you."

"I'm sorry I wasn't able to meet you, but you made

it here quicker than we thought you would. Her doctor should be here within the next fifteen minutes. Until then, we'll get Samantha settled and start gathering the information the doctor wanted. Here." She stepped into a private room and motioned toward the bed. "You can place her there. If you'll step out for a moment, we'll get her all hooked up to the monitors."

"Why do I have to? She's my wife. I should be with her."

"Mr. McGregor, please, give us this time with her. You'll be able to speak with her doctor privately as soon as he gets here." She turned and left him there.

Leaning up against the wall, Ethan let his head fall back and it hit with a thud. He embraced the pain. Looking up at the ceiling, he relived the last time he'd felt this hopeless. It was after his brother had disappeared. He wasn't sure if he was strong enough to do this and he prayed harder than he had ever done before.

"Mr. McGregor."

Ethan opened his eyes and saw Sam's doctor standing in front of him. "Doctor."

"We don't know what is going on right now, but I need for you to be calm. As long as you are calm, you can stay with her."

"I understand." His heart sank. It was so hard to be positive when everything you loved with every ounce of your being stood on the brink of death.

"I will do everything I can to make sure they both survive, but it could go either way, with both of them. You need to stay in control."

"I know." His mouth was dry and his tongue thick; he was so scared.

"Then let's go."

120 DAYS...

Ethan followed the doctor into the room. He could hear a fast heartbeat and a much slower one. Not waiting for an invitation, he went over to the side of the bed, which didn't have as much equipment, and picked up Sam's hand. He needed to be next to her, he needed to touch her to make sure she was okay. He was surprised at how cold her hand was. "Can she have a blanket? Something? I think she's chilled."

"Sure. Let me see her now. Samantha, Sam, can you hear me? Come on, I need you to wake up now." The doctor looked down and was reading the chart.

He barked out some orders for some kind of medication Ethan didn't catch. "Is that safe for her and the baby? What is it?"

"Yes, Ethan, it is safe for both of them. I am hoping it will help Sam wake up so we can talk."

"What's wrong?" Ethan didn't like the way the doctor was so serious and it was as if he was controlling every word that came out of his mouth. Dread settled in his stomach and his anxiety spiked even further when the doctor's eyes met his in what seemed like a warning to start preparing for the worst.

"We'll wait a minute and see if this works."

He didn't want to ask the question, but he knew he had to. "And if it doesn't?"

"Then you have some decisions to make."

Ethan closed his eyes and willed himself not to cry. He needed to keep a level head. He thought back to everything he had to deal with in his life. The death of his parents, raising Evan, starting his own business and rising to be one of the richest men in the city. Losing Evan, finding Samantha, and now this. He had to take emotion out of the equation and deal with the facts, what Sam would want and go from there. He needed to pray.

"Eth... Ethan?"

He quickly released his breath and hope took hold of him. "I'm right here, honey. You're in the hospital. You wouldn't wake up this morning, and you kept falling back asleep."

"So tired..."

"I know. The doctor has some questions for you."

"Not that young punk..."

Ethan laughed since she seemed like her normal self. "No, not that young punk."

"Good."

"Hello, Samantha."

"Hello." Her head slowly tipped to the side so she could look at the doctor.

"Do you know what's going on?"

"Yes."

"Can you tell me?"

"Cancer spreading... not good for me... or the baby."

"We're going to have to take the baby out via C-section and hope for the best."

"Yes... everything for her."

The doctor held up his hand to Ethan. "Don't worry, Mr. McGregor, we'll also be doing everything for Samantha."

Slowly, Sam's head turned toward him. "I'm sorry..."

He was doing everything he could to stay calm for her, but the dread he'd been filled with since she couldn't wake up this morning came barreling back to him like a runaway freight train. "No, no, don't be sorry. Fight."

"I am... just... so tired..."

120 DAYS...

"You can sleep afterwards. Right now you fight for our daughter and you fight for us." He was struggling so hard not to sob in front of her.

"I . . . will . . ."

"We need to get her up to the operating room right now. Mr. McGregor . . . Mr. McGregor . . . Ethan! Go with the nurse. She'll get you ready."

"Samantha, I'll be right back okay?"

"Sure . . ."

"I love you." His voice broke on the last word.

"I love . . . you, too . . ."

Ethan turned away, leaving a bit of his heart with her.

Sam watched as Ethan walked out of the room and turned back to the doctor. "Jennie, the baby . . . it's all about her . . . I know . . . Seen this too many times . . . I know my body . . . too much cancer . . . She needs to live for him . . . since I can't . . ."

"We can't know for sure how bad the cancer has spread since we haven't been able to do any scans." The doctor patted her shoulder.

"I know . . . I know . . ."

"Either way, we've discussed this. I know what your wishes are."

"Thank . . . you . . ." She closed her eyes and placed her hand on her belly having a last moment with her daughter, knowing there wasn't going to be many more. She hoped everything she had done up to that moment would be enough for her daughter to know how much she loved her, and to never think less of herself because her mother chose for her to live while she died.

They gave Ethan a chair so he could sit next to Sam's head. He had one of her hands in his and the other was stroking her hair. There was a large sheet in front of them so neither one of them could see what was happening on the other side of it. That was for the best. He only wanted to focus on Sam.

"Hey, beautiful," he said.

"Don't make me laugh."

"But you are the most beautiful woman in the world to me."

"Hush . . . Hey, did you ever come up with a middle name?" Her words were beginning to slur.

"I sure did. You want to know?"

"What do you think?"

"Her name will be Jennie Samantha McGregor. Named after three of the best, most loving, and strongest women I've ever known."

"I love you so much." A tear slipped down the side of her face.

Ethan wiped it away. "I love you, too. Now don't cry. You're going to be meeting our daughter soon."

She gripped his hand tightly. "Ethan, please, you have to know I love you, always remember that, even when I'm gone."

"Shhh . . ." He didn't want to have this conversation with her. He wanted her to be focused on fighting.

"No, let me finish . . . if I'm wrong, you can throw it back in my face later . . . I will always love you, whether I am on this Earth or up in Heaven, you are the one for me . . . the only one for me. God brought you into my life when I needed you most . . . now he's taking me back, but leaving you with our daughter . . . Love

120 DAYS...

her, raise her, and make her a better woman than I am . . . Never forget me . . . but don't be afraid to move on . . ."

His heart was racing so fast he wasn't sure he was hearing everything she said. "Samantha, please . . ."

"Love our daughter . . . never for one minute let her think this . . . my death is her fault . . ."

The voices and blood rushing through Ethan's ears made it hard for him to focus on her when that was all he wanted. It felt like a nightmare he wanted to wake up from. He wanted to physically hurt himself somehow so he could wake up, but he was too scared it was real life and they'd take him away from Sam. Vaguely, he could hear the doctors and nurses talking, but their words didn't register.

One of the nurses came around the other side and leaned down to talk to them. "We are breaking with protocol. Give us a minute with your daughter and then you can see her, but only for a moment. We need to get her to the NICU. We'll already have her on oxygen, so don't be alarmed. She's early so she needs it to survive."

"How are things looking?" Ethan asked.

"Let's just concentrate on one thing at a time, okay?" The nurse stood up and walked away.

Ethan looked back down at Sam who was staring at him.

"I'm sorry," she said. "This isn't a nightmare . . . I don't want to leave you . . . but it's not up to me . . . He's given me all the extra time I can have."

"No . . ."

"Yes, my love. When the time comes, you have to let me go."

A soft mew came from the other side of the curtain

and they both went still as the beeping from the monitors slowed even more than they had to begin with. Quickly, their daughter was brought to them and laid on her chest. He couldn't keep the tears back any longer at the first sight of his tiny daughter, so small and perfect. Reaching out with a shaking hand, he cupped her small head, and for a brief moment, the three of them were a family.

"Oh, my precious," Sam said, tears running down her face. "I know this is all new to you . . . and you're so little . . . but you have to fight . . . You have to take care of your daddy here . . . He's going to need you." She raised her head and kissed her daughter. "I love you, baby girl . . . Mommy will always love you."

The nurses came by, picked up their daughter and took her away. Ethan looked down at Sam and her tear-filled eyes met his.

"She's . . . so . . . beautiful . . ." Her breath came in shallow rapid gasps.

"Just like her mama."

"Please . . . please . . . take . . . care . . . of . . . her . . ."

"You know I will, and you can help me." He needed her to live.

"No . . . I'm . . . sorry . . ."

"Fight, damn you, fight." There was no hiding the tears. He had a hard time talking around the sobs. His wife was dying right in front of him and there was absolutely nothing he could do.

"No . . . more . . . left . . ."

"Samantha . . ."

"Love . . . you . . ."

Their eyes locked together, each telling each other what they couldn't say with words until the light went out in her eyes and the beeping slowed and then stopped.

"No, no, no, no," Ethan said. "Please, please, God, she can't die . . . I need her . . . I don't know what to do . . ." Again, like when his parents had died, Ethan had no idea what came next, what he should be doing. He was lost, and as of that moment, alone, when just minutes before the three of them had been a family. Their daughter was fighting for her life in an incubator, all alone; she'd lost her mommy, and the one constant in her life had been ripped from her. The love of his life had been taken from him. How were they both going to survive without Samantha?

Ethan laid his head on her chest and listened to the silence, hating every second of it. He'd give every single dollar he'd ever made to have her heart start beating again. He'd never felt this kind of pain in his whole life and he wasn't sure it was ever going to end. Too soon, the staff were telling him to leave. If his heart was whole, this would have broken it, but there was nothing left of it to break.

Chapter 29

Ethan picked up Evan's well-worn journal and turned to the last entry.

Day 83

Ethan —

Evan woke up briefly, he looked at me and said, "Tell my brother I'll be waiting for him with Mom and Dad." He slipped back into unconsciousness and took his last breath at three-eighteen in the afternoon.

I know these words are inadequate, but I am so sorry for your loss. Evan was a very special man.

Samantha

120 DAYS...

And now Sam was up there with his family.

After all of this time, it was so strange for him to be spending so much time back in his house. He'd made arrangements for Samantha to be cremated and was having a tree planted next to her parents. The plan was to go back up to the resort that weekend. There was no one else he would allow to dig the hole to plant the tree in but himself. It was one of the few things he could focus on.

The other was his daughter, his precious little daughter. She was a fighter, just like her mother. He was so conflicted. On one hand, he didn't want to let Jennie out of his sight; she was all he had, and he had to protect her; she was so tiny. The other was the fact that he was scared to death of what he was going to do next. Once again, he went back to that young man who'd lost his parents too soon and had no clue how to raise his brother, or even live.

Sam had only been to his house once, but she still lived there. There was nowhere for him to escape her memory. He hoped the first night was the worst, but a week later, he still wasn't sure it was ever going to get better. Every night he came back exhausted, and dropped into bed, only to wake a few hours later with thoughts of Sam. He never went down the hall to his office. Every time he saw the butterfly painting, his loss slammed into him once again. The next morning, he'd get up and head back to the hospital to check on Jennie.

He was a lost soul, always wandering, searching for something that was never there. In one brief moment, he'd lost his purpose, but gained a new one. One he had no idea what to do with.

They say babies didn't know where they were, they couldn't miss someone. But he was pretty sure Jennie was grieving along with him. The nurses were wonderful, but Ethan could tell she knew when he was there. She always tried to find him when he talked to her, and she'd grab on tighter to his fingers than the nurses.' The two of them were all the other had.

Sighing, he turned his back on the view he was sure Sam would have loved. There was a storm out over the ocean, a deep dark blue against the orange of the bridge. He knew he was stalling. Going to another lawyer's appointment in a year because someone he loved had died was almost more than he could take. He took a shower out of habit and put one of his suits on, surprised it hung so loose on his hips. Eating had become a necessity, and only if someone put something in front of him.

Ethan couldn't take joy in anything. He was breathing in and out, and that was about it.

Ethan laid his head on the steering wheel and took a few minutes to let everything the lawyer had said wash over him. Sam had left him everything. The resort was his. He never expected her to leave it to him, let alone change her will eight months before her death. She'd changed it before she knew she was pregnant. He felt so unworthy of her belief in him—that he could continue to run her resort after her death.

Turning his head, he saw the small group of items she'd wanted him to have. They were personal items from her and her family, things she wanted passed down to Jennie. She'd been mailing them to her lawyer for safekeeping along with a note for each. She wanted to make sure he knew how important they all were and she didn't want them lost after she died.

There was a USB drive containing a video she'd

recorded for him. That one scared him the most. How could he play it? See her looking so alive, talking to him, knowing she was dead and he'd never be able to hold her again? She said he had to watch it before he buried her.

"Oh, God, please give me the strength. I can't do this," Ethan said in the silence of the car.

When no one answered him, he put the car in gear and headed back to the hospital. The need to see Jennie overwhelmed him; he needed to be close to Sam.

With Sam's funeral the next day, the video remained unwatched. For some reason, Ethan wanted to watch the video with Jennie. He knew she was too young to know what was going on, but he thought she should be there. Since she couldn't leave the hospital, they allowed him to bring in his laptop and gave him some privacy. He knew they were still right there, monitoring everything, but at least he couldn't see them.

His shaking finger hesitated over the touchpad. There would be no going back after he watched this. It was as if by doing this, he was making her death all the more real.

Stalling, he turned toward their daughter. "Hey, Jennie girl, Daddy's here. Looks like you're getting stronger. They say you are doing better than they thought you would. We need to fill them in on who your mama was. There was no one stronger . . . I have a video here. It's of your mommy. Think we should watch it?"

He left his hand in the glove that went into her incubator where she gripped his finger, her only human contact. He tried not to think of how scared and alone she was in all that medical equipment. So different from the loving, warm womb she'd been in.

Clicking play, he watched as Sam's face filled the screen and felt like someone had punched him in the stomach. He could tell by how she looked she'd made this video a while ago. Her cheeks weren't sunken and the dark circles under her eyes was light. As she started to talk, he was surprised when Jennie squeezed his finger. He looked over at her and there she was, her little face turned toward the sound of her mother talking, her legs and arms moving.

Admittedly, he didn't listen to what Sam was saying. He was in total amazement watching Jennie respond to Sam's voice. It wasn't until he could hear the change in Sam's voice that he looked back at the screen. It was obvious, this portion was made after she'd been pregnant for a while. She told him about the back room and what she wanted him to do for Jennie as she grew up and how much she loved him. They might not have had much time together, but the time they had was remarkable.

The last thing she said to them was, "Everything can change in a moment. Live hard. Laugh hard. Love harder. I love you both so much, never forget that and don't waste one moment."

Relief filled Ethan's chest after watching his daughter react to the sound of her mother's voice. The words Sam said touched him. He needed to refocus and really be there for Jennie. He hated leaving her to go up to the resort for the weekend, but he had to. The tree was delivered and he needed to bury his wife.

Walking into Sam's house for the first time almost

120 DAYS...

buckled his knees. It still smelled like her; her scent hung on everything. In his mind, he could see her laughing at something they were talking about in the kitchen, or reading a book on the porch swing as the breeze gently blew her hair and she'd impatiently tuck it behind her ear.

Slowly, he walked up the stairs, passing the room they shared and going to what was going to be Jennie's room. They had everything from the baby shower in there and Sam had finally picked out the colors she wanted. The need to prepare for Jennie overwhelmed him, sending him on a mission. He needed to get her room ready for her. There was no way she was going to come home for weeks, so he had the time, but that wasn't the point. The point was he needed something positive in his life. He needed to move forward.

He tried to organize the room the best he could, but he'd never been around babies and had no idea what half of the stuff was. He knew he was in over his head, and was going to need help.

It was past midnight by the time he finished everything. He lay down in the middle of his daughter's room and closed his eyes, hoping for some dreamless sleep.

It seemed like Ethan's life was full of new levels of pain. Burying his wife next to her parents was right up there. The staff and guests left him alone to dig the hole, but he knew someone was watching when they all turned up when it was time to plant the tree. Everyone did what they could, either by helping him move the tree into place or taking a shovelful of dirt and putting it into the hole.

One by one, every single staff member and guest

said something about Sam. It wasn't anything he didn't already know. There were no women like her out there.

Once he was alone again, he sat down on the bench. His voice was gone. He had nothing left to say.

Chapter 30

The next eight weeks flew by for Ethan, between being at the hospital for his daughter and running Last Resort, he had no time to dwell on losing Sam. He knew it was better that way, but he still felt as if he was betraying her. She deserved more than a passing thought through the day. Although he knew she'd be the first to tell him he shouldn't be worried about it. Jennie needed him, the guests needed him. She'd tell him she wasn't important, but he knew she was everything.

He had a moment of panic when the nurses handed him Jennie and told him to put her in the car seat to take her home. After all this time, he couldn't believe they were just going to let him leave with her. He didn't know what he was doing. He didn't have the first clue even though the nurses were kind enough to teach him the basics of taking care of her, yet he still felt lost.

All the way up to the resort, he kept looking in the rearview mirror at Jennie, who he could see thanks to the other mirror he'd installed on the back of the backseat, trying to see if she was okay. He had been torn between hiring a driver so he could sit in the backseat to make sure she was fine and driving himself. Since he didn't trust anyone else's driving with her, that option won out; although he did stop a couple of times and checked to make sure she was okay.

Sam would be the first to tell him not to hang on so tightly, that he couldn't think of every situation and plan for it so Jennie wouldn't get hurt, but he had to try. It was a father's duty to protect their children, and he was going to try to be as good as his father had been.

His fingers ached when he pulled into the driveway from clutching the steering wheel so hard. Finally home, he worried if he'd be able to make it through the night, the only one to care for Jennie. He tried telling himself not to be such a wimp, he wasn't the first, and wouldn't be the last man to do this.

When he opened the door to the house, he could smell dinner and for a moment, he forgot Sam was gone. He thought it was one of those rare days when she finished up work early and came home to cook for them.

He remembered she wasn't here before he could call out to her.

The staff had made sure he'd have something to eat. He knew they were worried about him. They always found some excuse to push food on him, knowing he'd be too polite to turn it away. He knew they meant well, but for him it was simply nourishment so he could put one foot in front of the other.

He set the baby carrier down in the living room and turned on the stereo to the station Sam liked. One of the things that had changed since she died was he never liked the house to be quiet. Soon enough though, Jennie's cries made sure he wasn't surrounded by silence. As quickly as he could, he made her bottle and then picked her up. He went over to the rocking chair Sam had purchased just for this event and sat down.

Looking down at his daughter, the new love of his life, he was amazed at the fighter she was. So far she'd beat all of the odds and was stronger than the doctors thought she would be. On one hand, he was scared shitless of being the only one there for her, and on the other, he knew this was the most important thing he was ever going to do in his life. Raise his daughter.

Looking out over the hills of the resort, he fed his daughter for the first time in their home, not a hospital, feeling the connection between the two of them, which was one of the best feelings he'd ever had. They were going to be there for each other.

Ethan watched the Fourth of July fireworks from Boston on the television while Jennie napped on his chest. It seemed like he was exhausted all the time, but being there for her and watching her grow was amazing. She had started out so small and defenseless, and had grown so much. She could easily get her point across if she wasn't happy about something.

Peter had called him. His house in the city had sold. It was the last piece of property he owned. He had asked him to start looking into a buyer for the last of his privately held properties while Sam was still pregnant. Ethan knew he wasn't ever going to be going back there.

Anything his company held he gave to his assistant Jodi, he thought she was running things just as well as

120 DAYS...

he did, and she deserved to reap some benefits for taking care of everything for over the past year. The thrill was gone and he couldn't see himself going back to what used to hold so much pleasure for him.

There had also been some interest in the resort. Since he had bought up so much of the surrounding properties, it had become a huge parcel of California land, which also happened to have a gold mine on it, the amount of money being thrown in his direction was staggering, even for him. He started constructing a wall around the whole place. People were sneaking in, trying to find a way to either get him to sell, or a way into the gold mine.

Since Sam had died, he had been pulling back from everything until his life was only him and Jennie on the resort. Nothing was the same, everything seemed duller, not as brilliant without her around. The only thing that brought him joy was Jennie. They were in this together.

Ethan felt he'd been doing so well, every day was a little bit easier for him. Sometimes he couldn't tell how much, but he knew it had to be something. When the package came in the mail for Jennie, he didn't think anything about it. He opened it up and there was a little baby-size Wonder Woman costume for her to wear for her first Halloween.

He sat down right where he was and cried.

In Sam's mind, Halloween started the holiday season. Ethan knew it was only going to get harder.

The staff tried as much as they could, and Ethan

knew they were missing her too. He tried as best he could for them and Jennie, knowing they all needed each other.

Not a day went by that he didn't thank his lucky stars the resort ran so well. He couldn't devote as much time as he needed to, or had been able to in the past. He still tried to meet every guest when they arrived, but he hadn't been able to be there when they passed away. He'd tried, but he couldn't. It was the first time in his life he felt like a failure.

Ethan knew Sam would have said he went overboard for Christmas, but it was their daughter's first, and he felt like he had to make up for the fact that he was the only one there for her. The house looked like it should have been in a Hollywood movie, not to mention all of the gifts under the tree. So much more than an eight-month-old needed.

Overall, he thought he was handling things well, but every once in a while something would happen and it would throw him for a loop. He had been reading *'Twas the Night Before Christmas* to Jennie and when he read the part about the mom and dad being tucked in the bed, he couldn't continue reading. There was no mom and dad for this family, only dad.

They spent the day with the guests, eating, singing carols and opening presents. He couldn't deny the fact that it felt good to be around the staff and guests again. Sitting there with Jennie on his knee, he looked around and knew she was going to have a very special upbringing, surrounded by so much love.

He also knew it was time for them to join the living again. It was what Sam would have demanded he do, and it was what Jennie needed.

Epilogue

April 8th

Ethan held his daughter's hand as they walked slowly together through the Legacy Garden. Jennie may have been born fifty-nine days early, but she was ahead of all the other children her age. Already Jennie knew where to stop. Looking up at her daddy, she smiled and placed her hand over her mother's handprint.

"That's right, honey. That's your mama's handprint." Ethan leaned down and placed his hand over hers, making sure she knew he was there for her. "I know she's wishing you a happy birthday right now. Oh, see?" He pointed to the butterfly that had just landed on the rose bush, which had one of its branches coming over the wall. "There she is. She came to wish it to you personally."

"Ohhh . . ." Jennie's little voice rang out.

"Come on, let's say hello to Uncle Evan while we're here." They walked further down and did the same

120 DAYS...

thing there.

"Ethan?"

"Over here, Bethany." He picked Jennie up, set her on his hip and walked over toward his office assistant.

"Mr. Simpson is fading."

"Thanks, I'll head on over. Jennie, should we go say good-bye to Mr. Richard Simpson? I think he's done an amazing job not letting the lung cancer get him down. He made it one hundred and seventy-three days. I'll have to check my figures, but I think the average number of days someone stays here is going up. Your mommy would be proud of us."

Ethan hugged his daughter and looked back over his shoulder to the butterflies dancing in the garden. He knew both of them were thought of by those who had died at the resort. The butterflies always seemed to follow his Jennie around. Everyone who had come before, everyone who was there, and everyone who would be coming, were all connected. All of their stories mattered and the butterflies were a reminder that each one was important.

The very real people behind 120 DAYS...

It felt very strange to be writing about my parents as if they were dead in this book, but I knew I had to get past it. It was their story, their strength and attitude that gave me the idea for 120 days. They needed to be in it. They are the only people, 'guests,' in the book who are still alive. The others were borrowed from family and friends who have lost loved ones to terminal diseases.

These are the real stories behind the guests at Last Resort.

120 DAYS...

Bonnie and Bill Wivell, my parents
Written by M. Stratton

I think I'll remember that day forever. My husband and I were supposed to go out on a date for that night so my mom was going to come over to watch our son. They live about forty-five minutes away, so this isn't a quick trip. We were sitting on the loveseat when she told me, "Dad has cancer." The next few minutes were a blur, I know I cried, I know she cried and I was in shock. But in the back of my mind, I knew something was wrong. I had just told my husband the month before that he didn't look well, but since he was getting older, I played it off as that. It wasn't.

From the very beginning my dad said he was going to beat this, that he didn't care what it took, he wasn't going to be ashes in an urn. The odds of him making it to five years were slim. He went in for radiation and chemo treatments. They were aggressive in their treatment hoping to shrink the tumors before going in for surgery.

He went in and had the surgery, the next day he looked wonderful. If you didn't know better, you would have never thought he had such a major surgery. They sent him home, but things got worse. He had an infection that was so bad, he couldn't move. He went by ambulance to the hospital, where they pumped him full of antibiotics. At this point, it wasn't looking good. My mom and I were really worried we were going to lose him.

I didn't find out until much later but my dad says he saw God at this point, and he told him to go away; he wasn't ready to die. He said, "You finally give me a grandson to now take me away from him? No, I'm not going." And he didn't. He fought back and went home. About a month later, he had another infection. This time they were going to open him back up and see what was going on. What no one knew was he was allegoric to the sutures they used. They put different ones in and he healed.

After that he was on chemo maintenance and getting his rhythm back. He was going in for routine scans when they found a growth on his lung. It was back in for surgery to remove the cancer that had metastasized there. Once again he showed remarkable strength in dealing with all the pain and uncertainty.

Through all of this, my dad went to work. Of course, while he was in the hospital he couldn't, but if he could get out of bed, he went to work. His attitude was so remarkable throughout all of the treatments and surgeries, we knew that was the reason he was doing so well.

Then he was in Vegas for a seminar, and had a heart attack. I was at work when I received the call from my mom. I wanted to get up there, to be there for them, but they wouldn't let me. He had a couple of stents put in and my aunt and uncle came over from California to drive them home since he couldn't fly.

We dodged another bullet.

I should have known better. I remember sitting there at my parents' a year or so later thinking how well Dad was doing. It was almost like everything was normal for us. He had learned to deal with the side effects of the chemo maintenance and everything was good. It had been four years since he was diagnosed with colon cancer. Then my husband woke me up in the middle of the night. I hadn't heard the phone ring. My mom had a heart attack. I couldn't breathe. It was hard, but my husband went down to be with my dad. There was no way I could drive. It wouldn't be safe, and someone had to stay with our son.

I waited, and waited and finally heard that she was going to be okay. They had put a few stints in her

120 DAYS...

heart. By now it was time to get our son up and get him ready for his day. I did that and went straight to the hospital. My mom was pretty loopy from the drugs they had given her, and later I realized it was because she was scared. When they took the chest x-ray, they found a growth on both of her lungs, quite large. Of course she down played it at the time.

Because of the size of the tumors and the fact they were in both lungs, she wasn't a candidate for radiation or surgery, which only left chemo. Her doctor, the same one who has done such a wonderful job with my dad, said, if the chemo worked she'd have a year, if it didn't months.

We had firsthand knowledge of what the right attitude could do, and that's what my mom did. We tried so hard with my dad, never to cry in front of him, and if we did cry, it was only briefly. We weren't going to add any kind of negative thoughts to the situation, even if he never saw us doing that. We did the same thing with my mom, although it has been harder because we both can cry easily.

At one point, my mom told my son, 'Whenever you see a rainbow or a butterfly, that's me thinking of you." Which is why I have butterflies as a theme in the book.

My dad, my husband, and my son all got buzz cuts when my mom lost her hair. I stood there trying not to cry as each one of them sat in the chair for me and I used the clippers to take their hair down to very short, even my mom's. Her hair had started falling out, and her scalp was hurting. We hoped that by taking what was left off would help, and it did.

The chemo shrank the tumors, but she could only be on it for so long, and they didn't go away. Then they put her on chemo maintenance and she had what they called, an allegoric reaction to the drugs. She was laid up for about two months while they figured out what was wrong. Again, like my father, if she could get up out of bed, she went into work. At that point, all parties decided this was no way to live and she stopped the treatments.

I'm publishing this book on August 29th, 2015, my dad's birthday, and it has been six years since he was diagnosed. He is doing everything he can to kick cancer's ass. I picked Jennie's birthday as April 8th, which is my mom's birthday. As of the publication of this book, she is at two and a half years since her initial diagnosis, and says she could live another twenty years feeling as good as she does now.

For a lot of years, it was only me and my mom, then she met Bill and they started to date, and then they married when I was fifteen. As an emotional, bratty teenager, I know I didn't make things easy on either of them. But they've been there for me, and it took me awhile, but I finally started calling Bill, Dad, because he was. He's been there for me for so many years. We joke around all the time about my son, he looks like my mom, but his personality is a lot like my dad's. He might not be his, biologically, but in all the ways that matter, he is his grandfather and my daddy.

We are all firm believers with the right attitude and prayer, you can still have a good life, even after being diagnosed with a terminal disease. It doesn't mean it's going to be easy, or there won't be pain and tears, but it means you are still you. You can still do many of the things you always did before, or even find new ones. You fight for as long as you can, and as hard as you can, until there is nothing left, and then you fight some more.

Everything can change in a moment. Live hard. Laugh hard. Love harder.

120 DAYS...

Sometimes people come into your life and you don't know why they have, all you know is your life is fuller because of them. I have to say Erika is one of those ladies for me. I received a message from her that she was going to the North Shore Author Signing held in Boston in April of 2015 and she always picks a book from each of the authors to read before the signing. My debut novel, 'After the Storm' was her first choice to read. She loved it. We started talking and one thing led to another, and now I am lucky enough to call her my friend. She is truly a wonderful, loving and caring woman.

I loved meeting her at the signing, and dancing with her to her favorite signer, Rick Springfield's "Jessie's Girl." I knew her mother had died when she was young, but I didn't know of how until after I started talking to her about '120 days' . . . The idea to include real people's stories in mine, as a tribute, came directly from Erika, and she doesn't even know it. I wanted to do something special. Cancer touches so many lives, and we all have stories. Here I can take some pages and include a few of them here. I'm pretty sure her mom and my mom would have been great friends too.—M. Stratton

Patricia (Patty)
Written by: Erika Gutermuth

My name is Erika, and I am here to tell you that I was raised by the most amazing mother in the world. My Mom, Patricia, was unable to have children of her own, so she and my Father adopted me when I was a 2 month old infant. My mom always told me I was her greatest gift. My parents got divorced when I was 2, and it was my mom who raised me on her own. I grew up in a suburb of Boston and loved my life! I remained an only child, besides our dog, Chaney. My mom and I were as close as a Mother and daughter could be. Every Saturday morning we would get up and clean the house to Barry Manilow and Olivia Newton-John albums. Music was HUGE for her! One of her favorite Women's Lib artists was Helen Reddy. On the same album that declared to the world "I Am Woman" was another gem of a song called "You and Me Against The World" sung by Helen to her son Jeffrey. My mom forever told me that was our song and exactly how she felt about us.

My mom and I got to my teenage years! We laughed hard, fought hard, and made up like best friends do. We would watch Love Boat marathons while eating take out from our favorite local Chinese restaurant, The Makaha, regularly. My mom took me on vacations to Disney World, Maine, and St. Thomas. My mom always encouraged my singing in the choir at high school, and was at every performance with a boom box to record me. I loved the nights we stayed up late talking about her days as an American Airlines Stewardess, a Dental Assistant, and her current life as an entrepreneur, as she had recently started a small but successful cleaning company. I think I am most grateful for the fact that my mom was the epitome of a bookworm, and from a very young age, instilled that love of reading in me. My mom was my best friend, sister, and the love of my life.

I was 17 and a senior in high school when my life got turned upside down. Starting in the fall my mom started acting very strange. She was quick to yell and even threw me out of the house for no known reason (I was back home within a week). For most of my

120 DAYS...

senior year she had been complaining that her stomach was really hurting her. She went to doctor who said she was just imagining the pain, which it was all in her head! Low and behold, two days after Christmas in 1987, my mom's best friend had enough and brought her to the emergency room. What they found after X-rays and MRI's was definitely cancer, and not just a tumor. It was a huge mass in the wall of her stomach. Even the oncologists knew my mom's case was too far gone to even suggest remission or recovery. My Aunt Barb (my mom's sister) and Uncle Sten (Aunt Barb's husband), came down from Vermont to help 17 year old me navigate this awful situation. The head oncologist told us that my beloved mother had 4–6 weeks to live. We were all stunned! My Uncle had a thriving dental practice in Vermont, and not only could he not spare the time to stay with me in MA, he had many connections at a well-respected hospital in VT, so we had my mom transferred, even though her current doctors thought that would be a bad idea.

The five of us drove up in a minivan, and once settled, my mom had a wonderful team of doctors working with her round the clock. She received Chemo and radiation treatments, and every time I went to visit her, her hospital room was filled with lots of family and friends, since she grew up in Vermont. My mom struggled and was confused much of the time, but in a moment of clarity she confessed to me that she knew was going to die, and I was speechless. I should have held her, but I was a kid and didn't know what to do. I told her I had to go, I loved her and would see her later.

A few weeks went by, and I took the Vermont Transit bus back and forth from Massachusetts to Vermont several times, as I was trying to finish high school, though it was hard to stay focused. My mom suffered through seizures and dementia. We had one more Valentine's Day together and I remember bringing her a card and noticing oxygen tank between her legs on the hospital bed. My mom proudly displayed my senior picture in her hospital room and always kicked everyone out when I came to be with her because she wanted to be alone with me.

About 5 weeks after her diagnosis my mom slipped into a coma. 2 days into a coma she squeezed my hand. That was last sign of life I ever felt from her. She was in ICU on a respirator and many other machines and would not let go. A social worker on the floor approached my Aunt Barb and asked "Is there anything that Pat could be holding on for?" and my Aunt said "Erika's birthday is in 9 days." That was it. These two sad and brave women came to me and told me that I had to go in and talk to her. To let her know I was okay with her letting go.

I went to her room and cleared out the crowd. I took her hand. I told her how much I loved her and hated seeing her in so much pain and that she didn't have to fight anymore. I told her it was okay to let go. I told her she was my everything, and then I sang the chorus of our song: "And when one of us is gone, and one of us is left to carry on, then remembering will have to do, our memories alone will get us through, think about the days of me and you, you and me against the world . . ." I kissed her and told her I loved her one last time, walked out of the hospital and boarded the bus home that afternoon. I got a call from my Uncle the very next night that she was gone.

I was heartbroken, and in many ways still am. I am happily married and surrounded by incredible people, but my mom/is was my world. My husband once heard a cassette tape of me and my mom goofing

120 DAYS...

around and he couldn't believe it was me, I sounded so incredibly happy! He said it was at that moment that he realized that the day she died, my sunshine had been taken away . . . At times that is true. My wedding day, Holidays, her birthday, anniversary and especially Mother's Day are terribly hard for me, but I go on. My mom was 44 when she died, and the first oncologist was right. It was exactly 6 weeks from diagnosis to death. I have already outlived her by a year, and have lived over half of my life without her, but you know what? Patricia and I were meant to be! I may have had her for only 17 years, but I wouldn't trade a single moment!! Our time together was short, precious and perfect, and I will be forever grateful.

Since losing my mom, I have lost my grandfather to lung cancer, my Aunt Barb, her sister, to thyroid cancer, and my Uncle Sten is currently battling brain cancer. Cancer is evil and scary and a cure for all cancers needs to be discovered and celebrated NOW! For anyone who has been on a journey like mine or can relate to me, I feel you and I thank you. And just so you know, along with carrying my mom in my heart, I always feel her near me. It is nice to know that I have a personal guardian angel constantly watching over me. Thanks for tht Mom, I love you.

M. STRATTON

Kris, wow, this was a hard one. With the exception of being a Packers fan, he was an extremely kind man. I met him in 2007 after my husband and I had eloped and his quiet strength always amazed me. As did the fact he hated to go up against me in Fantasy Football, but loved to give me a hard time about my team, the Chicago Bears. This is for you Kris, Go Pack Go!—M. Stratton

Kristopher James Lesky
Written by: Michael Stratton

Kris Lesky was born on March 14th, 1967 in Hurley Wisconsin. He grew up there and attended South Side Elementary School, and J.E. Murphy High School, Both in Hurley Wisconsin. Kris Loved Wisconsin was a huge Life Long Badger and Green Bay Packer fan.

I first met Kris when he came to work for Creative Cabinets in June 2002. He had been living in California prior to that, and needing a change in life, threw a dart at a map vowing to go live wherever it landed. The dart landed on Tucson, Arizona.

Kris and I became good friends very quickly, getting together with my brother and many others for Poker and Fantasy Football. Over time our friendship grew into more like Family and I considered him My Brother, as did my brother Mark and Kris's Best Friend Jeff Toothaker.

Kris left Creative Cabinets in December 2004 and went to work for one of our competitors, Millwork by Design. He was living in a house that I had previously rented, he moved in there shortly after I purchased my first home in February 2004.

120 DAYS...

In early 2005, Kris was diagnosed with brain cancer, after seeing a doctor about his having seizures, similar to epileptic seizures. He had surgery to remove the tumor, the surgery was a success, but over the years the tumor kept coming back, and Kris had two more surgeries to remove a brain tumor.

Kris had come to work with me at Sierra Woodworks on November 26th, 2010. It was very nice to have my dear friend at work again and see him every day, talk about life, family, football and just shoot the breeze.

In June 2011, the cancer came back once again. This time, and his fourth Surgery, they were not able to remove all the cancer, it had spread to the back of his brain and neck, surgery was not an option. Rather than go through Chemotherapy and another round of Steroids, Kris declined treatment of any kind in the interest of having some quality of life in the time he had left. Kris experienced a loss of feeling in his limbs and motor function over the next year as the cancer grew and began to put pressure on his spinal cord.

A year later, near the end of his life, in those last weeks, I visited Kris several times a week. I would bring him whatever he wanted to eat, sometimes it was a chicken pot pie (He loved those things) and other times it was a chef salad from Arby's.

On July 10th 2012, I went to see Kris at his home that evening; it was chef salad from Arby's night. He had lost most of the function in his arms and I sat with him and helped him eat. Many times he tried to feed himself and had difficulty, I began to feed him myself and I could tell he was grateful, but hated it. After helping him to the restroom and back to his bed, we talked about the upcoming football season and what our favorite teams were going to be like. Kris became very tired, took his medication, and I left him to sleep, giving him a hug and telling him "I love you Brother"! He said "I Love you too! Now get out of here and let me sleep."

The next day, July 11th, 2012, I got a call from his ex-wife Emily, who was always there helping him. She said Kris was arguing with her about what day it was. He didn't believe her that it was Wednesday. He told her that he would only believe it if Stratton got on the phone and told him it was true. She held up the phone to him, I asked how he was doing, and he asked what day it was. I told him that it was Wednesday July 11th, 2012. He said "Whatever," as he almost always did, whether it applied or not, it was his favorite saying.

That was the last Time I spoke to Kris, he didn't wake up the next day, and he had slipped into a coma overnight. Many of us gathered around his bed that Night of July 12th, 2012. We sat with him for several hours, talking to him, not knowing if he could hear us, and told stories about our times spent with Kris.

I kissed Kris goodbye on the forehead, and headed home. Shortly after arriving home that night, Emily called to say Kris had passed away.

I will never forget him, he had a huge impact on my life, and I believe he is still with me, there are times when I can sense his presence. Kris took me to my first AA meeting, and always was concerned how I was doing, even when he was dying. May he rest in peace, my brother forever!

Kris is survived by his Ex-Wife Emily, His Step Daughter Spring, and his Daughter Jules.

120 DAYS...

I 'met' Derrick when he auditioned to narrate my audiobook of Bender. As soon as I heard his voice I knew he'd be perfect. And then he performed my character Nutter exactly as I wanted and there was no one else for the role. Thank you Mr. McClain for telling your son to persue his dreams.—M. Stratton

Thomas McClain
Written by: Derrick McClain

My father was Thomas McClain. Is. Was. I'm still not sure what to say.

He died two months before he could claim his pension. Four months after my graduation from college. Two months after my birthday, which was when I noticed he didn't look well, and begged him to see a doctor. He died one week after they removed the softball sized tumor from his colon. One week after they found out it had already metastasized to his liver, enlarging it three times and replacing almost the entire thing with cancer. One week after I had to pin a doctor down in the hall and make him go explain to my dad that yes, this was cancer, and yes, it is terminal. Because while I realized what was happening, Dad didn't, and no doctor had told him.

He died three days before his first chemotherapy session. The session that was going to tell us how likely the chemotherapy was going to be to help. The session that was going to lead to a prognosis.

He died alone. In his favorite chair, watching TV. Alone.

He was my father. He wasn't a saint, or a hero, but he was my father.

M. STRATTON

He was a musician and an engineer. A drunk and a womanizer. An artist and a depressed soul. Above all else, he was a loving father.

Not all my memories are sunshine and rainbows. My parents divorced when I was only two years old, and so I've only ever known spending time with my dad on Summer vacation and school holidays. I remember learning at the age of four how to roll cigarettes for him. I'm pretty sure it was just tobacco. I remember going grocery shopping first thing every time I visited, as his fridge never had anything but beer and condiments. I remember his dining room full of garbage bags of crushed beer cans, collected to one day cash in at the recycling center, but seemingly never accomplished, at least until the bags spread out beyond the dining room into the kitchen and living room and halls. I remember trying to explain to him at the age of seven that whistling at women in the parking lot is *not,* in fact, a compliment. I remember that after he told me the "birds and the bees" he also explained that it was the best feeling in the world and I should do it as soon as I can. I remember being terrified to tell him that I was gay, not because I thought he wouldn't accept me, but because I was crushed to ruin his dreams of taking me to a strip club on my 18th birthday, and shatter what I knew were his plans to live vicariously through my "triumph" of young attractive women.

I also remember the incredible pride I felt when I went with him to his gigs at different coffee shops and bars, when he would sit on one of his old stools, playing his guitar and singing his love songs. I still am more moved by live acoustic performances than any other type of music. I remember when he gifted me a copy of Khalil Gibran's *The Prophet* when I was ten years old. I remember at eleven, when he had blacked out during a movie we had watched together and been looking forward to all week, the next day confronting him about his drinking—I remember that that day he didn't yell at me, but just looked down, ashamed, and said, "Yeah, you're right." I remember the pride I felt for him when he went to AA, and the continued pride when he celebrated his 17th "birthday" shortly before he passed. I remember him taking me to theme parks, never pushing me to go on the roller coasters that scared me, letting me spend a limitless amount of money on the carnival games resulting in bags upon bags of stuffed animals that he then kept forever. I remember his undying, eternal love for me. The pride in his eyes every time he looked upon me, the joy he felt in every accomplishment I achieved, and the continued faith he had in me despite any and all missteps I made.

My father wasn't perfect. But he taught me the most important lessons in life. No, maybe he couldn't teach me how to fix a leaking sink or remove a hook from a fish's mouth. But he taught me what it is to truly love someone unconditionally. He taught me how you can change your life at any age. He taught me how you can pursue your dreams while still working a "regular" job. He taught me how to believe in myself. He taught me how to bring smiles to other people's faces, and he taught me how to find joy in life even when depression pulls at your heart.

I wasn't there when dad died. No one was. I still have some guilt about it, not a crushing life impeding guilt, but just the right amount that I think I should have. We didn't think the end was so close. Heck, right next to his chair, he had a brand new art easel set up, everything ready to start painting for the first time in forty years, but not a single brushstroke yet added. He had plans, plans to live what we thought was going to be his final year to the fullest, to record new songs, paint new paintings, conceive of new engineering feats. To do everything he had been putting off.

He wasn't able to. So now, I am doing it for him. Not living his life, of course, but my own. Pursuing my dreams, despite any common wisdom to leave them for other days. I don't know how much time I actually have left in this life. I know I'm not perfect myself. But I'll be damned if I'm not going to make the best of what I do have, and love every person left in my life while I can. Here's to you Dad, and all our crazy ambitions.

120 DAYS...

As authors we need support groups and Elizabeth and I are in one together. She was one of the first to message me when I sent a call out looking for stories to add. My heart broke when I heard of a mother and son who had lost their fight with cancer at such a young age, and amazed at their strength, their fight to live. —M. Stratton

Elizabeth "Sissy" and Bobby
Written by: Elizabeth James

My sister-in-law was diagnosed with ovarian cancer at the age of 37 and passed away just a few months before her 38th birthday. She was such a wonderful loving person who had devoted herself to the care of her son, Bobby who was also a cancer victim. Sissy was a fighter and when she found out she had cancer, she took it in stride and decided that she was going to fight it and to beat it. She was always positive and upbeat and even on her worst days, always managed a smile.

Sissy was the middle child of five and the only girl. She loved hanging with her brothers and they always were watching out for her. When she was 19, she met Phillip and they fell in love. A year later, they were blessed with Bobby and thought their life was perfect. Unfortunately, when Bobby was 10 months old, it was discovered during an examination that he had something wrong with him. The family was sent to Duke University Hospital and it was then that they diagnosed him with Tri-lateral Retinoblastoma which is a very rare terminal cancer that focuses on the eyes. His unfortunately had also moved into his brain. The life expectancy for Bobby was only another 8 months and the doctors advised Sissy and Phillip to take him home and just give him as much love as possible and also to try to have another child because their child was going to die. Sissy told the doctors that she wasn't going to accept that and for them to try to save him by any means possible. Essentially, his care was signed over to the doctors so they could experiment with treatments to try and save him, which they did.

Bobby went into remission but as a result of his cancer attacking his eyes, he had to have them both removed. He was totally blind but not like any other blind person I'd ever known. He loved video games and was really good at them. His sense of hearing was uncanny and he used it to help himself go about life with very little assistance. He was taught by his mother to be very independent and not to feel he was handicapped by his lack of sight. Sissy mainstreamed him into public school and he blended in so well that one day he ended up being told he needed eyeglasses. The story was that the school nurse was doing vision screenings and so he went along with the class. When it was his turn to read the eye chart, he said that he couldn't 'see' anything. The nurse had no idea he was blind since he'd walked in unassisted and she told him that he probably needed some glasses. He left the office and went to tell his mother. She was floored that the nurse had told him that but after talking to her; she realized that Bobby had been so much like the other kids that she hadn't had a clue that he was blind.

My profession is that I make eyeglasses and I'll never forget the afternoon that he came to my office and proudly announced that he needed glasses to help him 'see.' Sissy was quick to gesture behind him that we should just do what he said. I ended up making him a pair of eyeglasses with plain lenses to satisfy his need to fit in with people who couldn't see. He swore that when he wore them that he could read his Braille

120 DAYS...

much better.

Everything went well until Sissy's diagnosis. It had started with her feeling tired and that led to depression. The doctors gave her anti-depressants and tried to figure out what was causing her issues. Several months went by before it was finally discovered that she had ovarian cancer. Chemotherapy became a weekly thing and Bobby encouraged and supported his mom because he'd already been through it all himself. She fought as hard as she possibly could but it was so far advanced when it was found that it ran rampant despite the chemo. After only a few months, her local doctor discontinued treatment because he felt it wasn't doing any good. She didn't accept that and turned to Duke again since they'd helped save Bobby. They tripled the dosage and it began to take a toll on her. She was so sick and had no energy. Noises were amplified and food tasted really metallic. Nothing was normal and she didn't like it one bit. One thing I did was call her every day and see her every chance I could get. Little gifts and cards were my way of cheering up her days and bring a smile to her face. I also encouraged her to come to visit us for the weekend so she could rest which also gave Phillip time to bond with Bobby. She prepared them for her possible death and it was so sad.

One activity that Sissy and I loved to do when we were together was to do scrapbooking. It was something she could focus on and also she felt as if she were leaving something behind for others. She scrapbooked right up until the month before she passed away and after her death, Phillip called me and asked me to come over. When I arrived, he showed me her scrapbook which had empty pages with post-it notes instructing me to finish them. She had everything planned right to the end.

She began to have issues with her health related to the chemotherapy and at one point had to be resuscitated. That scared her and she told me that she needed to take care of things in case something like that happened again. She asked me to do her eulogy at her funeral and I was stunned. I didn't like that she was talking about final things but I also understood that it could be years before I would have to do it. I wrote her eulogy that day and I'm glad I did. Instead of writing it filled with grief, I wrote it filled with my love for her and my pride at her strength. I filed it away for the day when I'd have to deal with it which turned out to be less than three months later.

Bobby was 14 and doing really well when his mom passed away. He'd become really close with his dad and also with myself and my husband. He loved to come and stay with us just like his mom did and it also gave his dad a break. About four months after Sissy died, Bobby began to complain of pain in his arm. His dad took him to Duke and they found that he had a tumor in his arm that had broken out of his bone marrow. They treated him the same way they had in the past and luckily, the tumor went away. It was scary to think that his cancer could come back after so many years but it went away so quickly and five years passed making a milestone for a cancer patient. Unfortunately, Bobby's cancer came back again when he was 19 but this time, he didn't tell anyone right away.

I noticed Bobby's appetite had fallen off and when I asked him about it, he'd explained it away by saying he needed to lose weight. Finally, he couldn't hide his discomfort anymore and told his dad that he had pain in his stomach. By the time he got to Duke, the doctors found that the cancer was all over his abdomen, liver and lungs. The doctor, who gave him the diagnosis,

120 DAYS...

essentially told him that there was nothing they could do for him. He was sent home with hospice and large dosages of morphine. Once again, I made it my mission to make every day he had left special for him. I saw him every day and when he asked me for a birthday party, I was more than happy to make it happen. Friends and family gathered to celebrate the bittersweet event that was his 20th birthday which we ended up having a week before his actual birthday. He was on oxygen and very uncomfortable but had a smile on his face as we surrounded him with love and his favorite thing, presents. We tried to make his day as special as possible but knowing all the while that it wasn't going to be long before he would die. He celebrated his actual birthday at home lying on his couch and of course, I went to see him. He was tired but still tried to entertain me with a video game challenge. I knew he was failing fast and it made time with him even more precious. The day before he died, I had the crazy idea that I didn't need to go over there to see him. I reasoned that he was probably sick of seeing me but when I called, I was told to come over. It was insisted upon. When I got there, I realized that he was coming to the end of his journey. We sat together and prayed and he had such a sense of peace. It was overwhelming for me and I spent most of the night with tears running down my face. I didn't want to leave because I knew that would be the end of my time with him so I dragged the evening out as long as possible. Finally, he insisted I needed to go home to take care of my pets and I knew that was my cue to leave. I kissed him and told him I loved him and he said that he loved me and for me to tell his uncle that he loved him too. When I got to the door and turned to leave, I simply said, "I'll see you." He smiled and said, "Yes, you will."

He died at 5am the next morning. I treasure the

memories I made with Sissy and Bobby and will for the rest of my life. They inspired me to follow my dream to become an author and I believe are in my corner watching over me.

They both showed incredible strength and faith and had genuinely beautiful hearts. I have no doubt that they are walking the streets of Heaven and Bobby is pointing out the beautiful sights to his mom. They live in my heart and always will.

120 DAYS...

I love Amalie, she is so funny and caring, I secretly stalk her on social media and am going to fangirl when I meet her, and she is that awesome. When I heard she had not one, but two names my heart broke for her. Her father and her best friend. The more I learn about Amalie the more I am amazed at the person she is.—M. Stratton

William Kenneth Johnson
Written by: Amalie Silver

William Kenneth Johnson was my father. Throughout my life, he'd always been a source of comfort. I won't say he was my rock, mostly because that was Mom for me, but he was always there to help, to offer a bad joke, or show me the proper way to grill a steak.

He was a warm soul, a smile in the middle of chaos, and a good man.

When his cancer took a turn for the worse, my fiancé and I stepped up to the plate and bought his house, the same house I grew up in. My parents were able to retire and buy a home up north on a lake, and Dad lived comfortably for nine months living out his dream until he died a year after they moved.

Colon cancer took him at the young age of sixty-one.

Love you, Pops.

1947–2008.

Elizabeth Munns
Written by: Amalie Silver

Elizabeth Munns was my best friend. She had a rough time battling some personal demons, but she always kept a bright smile on her face. Her entire life was devoted to God and his good, but she never judged anyone. And she never judged me. Not when I smoked. Not when I drank. Not when I came out. And not when I told her I didn't believe in religion.

She was beauty in every definition.

Her diagnosis came out of nowhere, and for a short time I didn't believe her. I remember having to look up the word melanoma and its prognosis, because I wasn't even sure what it was.

God took her home in 1998 at the age of twenty. She passed eight months after she was diagnosed.

Miss your smile, babe. I miss everything about you.

1977–1998.

120 DAYS...

RJ is another author friend. As with all of us, talking, or writing about our loved ones who have or are going through cancer is difficult, she wanted to do this until she is able to write her mother's story. Thank you for sharing her with me. —M. Stratton

Dolores
Written by: RJ Van Cleave

My mom. Ah yes, where do I start? My mom, Dolores, was born in 1936 in Bayside, NY. She was the second of two children and grew up in a very eclectic neighborhood full of second generation immigrants. While Mom's ancestors came from Hungary, she was exposed to Jewish, Polish, German, and Asian cultures and embraced them all. She was blessed to have many friends, but tragedy struck her family when she was 12. Her father died unexpectedly, hemorrhaging to death after surgery for TB, which he had contracted from a co-worker. My grandma held down three jobs to support her children, and my mom took on two jobs once she turned 15. Mom met Dad through her brother when she was 16 (he was 22, fresh out of the Navy). She graduated high school early and got married 15 days after she turned 18—for no other reason but love. Two years later, in 1956, my parents packed all of their belongings into their car. With only $500 to their name, they set off for San Diego, CA, where Dad's ship had docked briefly. They had no job, and no place to live when they arrived, but by the grace of God, they quickly found both.

Mom's greatest joys in life were her family, and then her career. She put work on hold to raise her kids, but went back to school and got her AA degree at the age of 55. She eventually found a niche in the construction trade and loved her job as an office manager. Fast forward to 2011- Mom had four grown children, nine grandchildren, and her first great-grandbaby on the way. She got sick, for the first time in *decades*, with pneumonia. Then pancreatitis hit—or so the doctors thought. Her pancreas was inflamed, but normal treatments did nothing to help. In and out of the hospital, rapid weight loss, and mental confusion quickly took over. Excruciating pain in her back and abdomen, plus fluid filling her chest cavity eventually kept her in the hospital—a place she hated because of her father's death. Numerous doctors saw her (EXCEPT oncology) and had 'pissing contests' as to who had the correct diagnosis. The pulmonologist was convinced it was TB, due to her exposure to it 63 years prior! Twenty-one days after her second long-term admittance, she was transferred to the ICU because her blood pressure had plummeted. Inexplicably, lymphoma cells had also been found for the first time in the fluid drained from her chest, and the doctors told us there was nothing more they could do. We removed the epinephrine that had kept her alive and maxed out her morphine. Three hours later, on June 2, at 11:12 PM, she took her last breath. As a Biologist, I *had* to know what happened. We were all stunned when the autopsy report said it was non-Hodgkin B-cell lymphoma (specifically Primary Pancreatic Lymphoma—so rare that only 0.3% of people get it) and it had metastasized. It had taken over her pancreas, her spleen (which contradicts PPL according to my research), abdominal linings, her left kidney/adrenal gland (the back pain), and both lungs. They couldn't tell us how long she had had it, but we suspect it was the cause of her pneumonia. At the age of 75, and after 57 years of marriage, my mom was gone . . . yet another victim of cancer.

120 DAYS...

Crissy is a reader who happens to love my books and we've become friends. Not only has she given me her grandfather's story, she also beta read 120 days . . . for me. Thank you for your story and the feedback on my story.—M. Stratton

Richard Simpson
Written by: Crissy Sutcliffe

His Life

Richard Simpson was a kind and loving person. He always tried to be funny, even if his humor was lost on others. Along with my grandmother, he took me in when my mother was young. It was too hard for her to care for me. He worked hard, no matter what job he had. Most of his younger years were spent working as a trucker. As time went on, he became a commercial fisherman and loved that job. I think it was one of the things that made him happy in life.

His Illness

One day he started having chest pains. After a month of us hounding him to get it checked out, he went to the doctor. The diagnosis was something none of us expected. Stage IV lung cancer. He was given six months to live.

In the months that followed he tried to stay upbeat. He went through radiation like a champ! The chemotherapy was a different story. It took everything out of him. He was losing weight rapidly. It got to the point where it was very hard to watch. Three months and sixty pounds later, he ended up so sick that we had to take him to the emergency room.

All of his loved ones, family members and friends, gathered by his side to spend the final twenty hours of his life with him. He passed on June 26, 2012.

120 DAYS...

I met Rebecca when she came up to my table at a signing and said "Dorks over forks!" I must admit, I think I squealed. The motto in my street team is Dorks Over Forks, she had been told by an author friend, who is in there, Chelle C. Craze, to come up to me and say that. She took a bloody fork (swag from one of my romantic thriller series) and we've been friends since.—M. Stratton

Lydia
Written by: Rebecca Marie

There are some people you just know on first glance are angels walking the Earth. They're the ones who give freely of everything they have and everything they are. They're the ones who always put others first and never have a negative thing to say . . . I was lucky enough to spend my first 18 years of life with such an individual.

A true walking angel, my Grandma, Lydia, was the greatest woman on the planet, I'm certain. I never wanted for anything, if she could help it. I was always her first priority, the one she put on a pedestal (which I know I did not deserve to be). Aside from just being my primary caregiver, she was my closest ally. In a world filled with darkness, she was light. She was a true positive energy, always focusing on the good, and teaching me that I shouldn't dwell on negatives and should always make the best of every situation. There are not enough words in the English language to describe how amazing this woman was.

Even when devastation hit, she made sure I didn't know until it wasn't able to be hidden any longer. She suffered from the lethal bastard, pancreatic cancer, in silence. Once again putting everyone else's lives first, she didn't want to be a burden. Knowing there was no cure and she would soon be returning to be a heavenly angel, she elected to live her final days here on Earth focusing on the positives, ensuring she had set up for my continued success, and letting her light quietly fade away. She was the greatest thing to have ever blessed my life, and without her I wouldn't be the person, nor the mother, I am today. She taught me so much, and she was the greatest role model there could be. Cancer may have robbed us of time, but it can never take away all the memories . . .

120 DAYS...

I met Tabitha shortly after I published my first novel. She is one of the sweetest people I've ever know and I'm very lucky to call her my friend, and now I know where she gets her strength from.
—M. Stratton

Edward Willbanks
Written by: Tabitha Willbanks

My Daddy was a very special man. He worked 60 hours a week to provide for our family, until he was ready to drop, and then he'd call my mom and say "I'm taking vacation pack up the girls and be ready to go when I get home." That's just how he was. It drove my mom nuts, but she didn't complain too much.

When I was six, he was officially diagnosed with Hodgkin's disease. He was in the Navy, in Vietnam, and chemicals used over there to kill the dense vegetation were being found to cause cancer in soldiers all over the US at the time. It was a life changing blow. But it didn't hold him back. One very distinct memory I have is Dad had promised my sister and I we would go to the county fair the day one of his chemo treatments was scheduled. Mom warned us not to get our hopes up, because Dad always felt awful after his treatments. But he was bound and determined to keep his word, and took us to the fair. He felt terrible, and was throwing up, but he muscled through. That's just the type of man he was. When he was first diagnosed, the doctors really didn't give him a good chance of survival. But he fought, and fought hard for ten long years. I will forever be grateful for those ten years. I really got to know my Daddy, and the amazing man he was. He eventually passed on

M. STRATTON

December 20, 1999 with my sister and I right by his side.

120 DAYS...

I met Jade when I put the call out for stories. Since then we've talked in length via message about my story and hers. It is sad, but we can say we are all connected because this disease that affects so many touches our lives. We can babble with each other and understand the pain and loss we are all going through. Somehow the tragedy brings us closer.—M. Stratton

Bruce Blucker
Written by: Jade Reel Fox

My grampy, Bruce Blucker, was the best grandpa a girl could ask for. He was a fitness buff, doing countless push-ups and sit ups. He loved to box, but never got in the ring. He just did it for fun and fitness. He line danced and played basketball. He loved to garage sale so that he could find the antique gem he could fix up to its former glory and sell. Even into his early 80's he was active and would work around his acreage. He also gardened and was proud to share the fruits of his labor. I was very close to my grandpa. He was an important part of my growing up as he lived in the next town over. We had taco dates once a week when I lived in town and a few times a week when I visited. We had phone conversations 3–4 times a week. He taught me to love, to pray, to be responsible, and to live by doing what was right. In September of 2013 he was diagnosed with lung cancer. Even up to the very end, he handled his illness with grace and class. He never complained and never shared his bad days with his family. He died five months after his diagnosis. There is not a day that goes by that I don't miss him.

I don't have Cameron in my book, he's Carey Haywood's, and he inspired her book Better. If you liked 120 days . . . you should read her book. I was lucky enough to beta read this book. Because of my parents this book gutted me, but in a good way. Her words brought me to tears and helped me to deal with the fact at the point when I first read it, both of my parents had cancer. I love you lady, thank you for sharing Cameron with me and everyone who reads this book.—M. Stratton

Better is available on all platforms

Cameron
Written by: Carey Heywood
Cancer and Harry Potter, the inspiration for Better.

You wouldn't think cancer would be the first thing someone thinks about when thinking of Harry Potter, but for me, it always will be.

I had not read the book when the first movie came out. It was just before Christmas 2001. At the time, I lived in Phoenix, but I was back home in Alexandria for a visit.

120 DAYS...

My father was ill, having had a stroke earlier that year. Being home was hard, and seeing him like that was surreal. I had an escape though—my friend, Cameron. Cameron was one of those guys that it took me too long to figure out just how wonderful he was.

We met in seventh grade French class. My mother met his mother the night before, and she made a point of telling me that Cameron and I should be friends.

When I saw him, I disagreed. While he was always handsome, he had a quirky fashion sense that I did not get. It was middle school, and I was trying so hard to fit in. He didn't seem to mind standing out though, and he was always wearing this ridiculous trench coat. We became friends.

To this day, I'm not certain that I have ever known someone as truly sweet and generous as Cameron was. I say was because Cameron died. That's where the cancer comes in. I'll get back to that.

At the end of and after high school, I was in an extremely toxic and abusive relationship. During one of our breakups, I went out on a couple of dates with Cameron. Looking back, I wish I had been ready for him, but I wasn't. My head was not in the right place to deal with accepting my attraction to the guy with the mohawk when I was still all messed-up over a guy who was nothing but a thug. Cameron was too different.

I moved away, and when I came back for a visit, we went on another date. He took me to the little Chinese place next to where the Blockbuster was. Over dinner, he told me he had cancer.

He learned this during his freshman year of college. He kept having stomach pains and went twice to the student clinic, only to be sent away with painkillers.

The next time, his mom told him to go to the emergency room. They found a tumor.

I remember being shocked over dinner but not scared. Nobody I knew had died of cancer. He would be fine.

We kept in touch while I was in Arizona, talking on the phone maybe once every couple of months. Just as I suspected, the cancer went away. He beat it. He even went back to school and worked up the nerve to ask some girl out. I was jealous.

He never got a chance to go on that date. The cancer came back, and he moved back home to Virginia.

The next time I saw him was December 2001. He looked different but not bad. We went to see Harry Potter and the Sorcerer's Stone. He had already seen it, but he took me anyway.

That was his way, always looking out for me. We swam together during high school. I remember my coach wanted me to join this other team. I was scared because I wouldn't know anyone. Cameron decided to join too.

He looked at me, so serious. "We'll carpool."

And then, through that awful relationship, I remember him putting his hands on either side of my face, trying to convince me I deserved better, wanting to beat up my ex for hurting me.

That December in 2001, I was home one week, and I saw Cameron three times.

I was busy when I first got back to Arizona. I didn't call him right away. When I did, it was just after New Year's. He was in the hospital. I spoke to his younger brother. He told me Cameron overdid it when I was in town. I didn't know.

Cameron called me when he got out of the hospital. It was the first time I actually considered that he might die. I remember saying that he couldn't die, that I was putting my foot down, like I had any power. I made

120 DAYS...

him promise me he wouldn't die, and he did. He promised. When we hung up, I was certain he would beat it again. That was the last time I ever spoke to him.

When my caller ID flashed his name, I answered all happy and excited to talk to him. But it wasn't him. It was his dad.

The second he said, "This is Cameron's dad," I knew.

We didn't talk long, and I honestly don't remember anything after he said, "Cameron is gone."

At the time, I was a smoker. I went out on my front porch to cry and have a smoke. I lived in Phoenix. It never really got windy unless there was a monsoon, which between you and me, I never understood what the big deal was. It was just rain. It rained all the time in Virginia. Either way, it was windy, really windy, and there wasn't a monsoon. It felt like Cameron was coming to say good-bye, using the wind to wipe the tears from my face.

After that night, I began to associate wind with feeling Cameron's presence. I would lie in bed at night and turn the ceiling fan above my bed to the highest setting to imagine it was him. He was the wind.

Harry Potter helped me grieve. It gave me time to rest in my memories of Cameron. I bought each book as they came out and saw each movie.

When the second movie came out, I went by myself on opening weekend. It was packed, standing in line with little kids dressed up as wizards. I had people, strangers really, sitting on either side of me. They probably thought I was off when I sobbed through the opening credits. I just wished Cameron were there with me. That familiar opening melody broke my heart.

By the third movie's release, I had a boyfriend. We

were pretty serious, but he understood why I went to that movie alone. I told him about Cameron. When we became engaged, he started to come with me. He would hold my hand while I cried.

The last two movies were hard. The books were all out. The end was in sight. During Harry Potter and the Deathly Hallows: Part 1, I came close to inflicting bodily harm on the people sitting behind me who were laughing during that scene at the end with Harry and Dobby on the beach. Didn't they know? Couldn't they understand these movies, this experience, meant so much to me? The last movie was the hardest for me.

I am now married to a wonderful man, and we have beautiful children. I understand how blessed I am. I mourn the what-if with Cameron, and even if nothing had ever come of us, I feel sad every day because the world lost such a beautiful soul.

So, for me, Harry Potter will always make me think of Cameron and the cancer that took him away.

I want to say thank you, thank you to everyone who has helped me when my Dad was diagnosed with cancer and then my mom. Thank you to everyone who listened to me talk about this project, told me I was strong for writing it and couldn't wait to read it. Thank you to all my beta readers, editor and clean readers for helping to make this story better than I ever could have imagined possible. And last, but not least, thank you for picking up my book and reading it. I hope, in the end, you remember more than all the tears. I hope you remember to love harder.—M. Stratton

Other works by M. Stratton

The Storm Series (Romantic Thrillers)

After the Storm—Book One

Alexia "Lexi" Hanson moved across the country to rebuild her life after the attack which almost destroyed her. She enjoys the simple things in her beach cottage. Life is finally complete.

Noah Matthews is Rock & Roll's hottest star and on top of the world. After years without a break, he finds the solitude he craves at his beach house. Enjoying his early morning coffee, Noah is surprised to see his neighbor sneak into his garden and crawl around.

They never saw that fateful morning coming. Someone was watching them. Someone who thought Lexi belonged to him and would stop at nothing to have her.

Lives are changed forever when they meet amongst the blooms in his garden. Even when things seem darkest, there is always light After the Storm.

Eye of the Storm—Book Two

Evie Taylor loves her life in Boston, running her bookstore and café, but an accident has made it so she needs to return home to take care of her grandmother. With extra time on her hands, she decides to start looking for the monster which haunts her best friend's nightmares, and a chain of events begins which no one could see coming.

When the last person she ever expected shows up and rings her grandmother's doorbell, she finds herself in the middle of danger. Bound together in a common mission, they'll search the world looking for answers. But can they find them in time, or will they end up paying the ultimate price?

As the storm rages around them, they find each other and the calm in the Eye of the Storm.

Caught in the Storm—Book Three

What happens when the hunter becomes the hunted?

Kat Snyder has spent years chasing after the man who attacked her and left her for dead. It is her one obsession, and she won't let anyone stand in her way. Now that they are getting closer to finding him, she begins to doubt herself and her need for revenge.

Jackson "Jack" Taylor lost the only woman he truly loved. Now that he's found her again, he's not letting go and will do everything in his power to make her see they can have a life together. Together they search for the monster who has hurt so many women.

The closer they get, the closer they become, until they are both Caught in the Storm.

The Storm Series Box Set
Includes all three above books plus two short stories where you learn more about the darkness behind the books.

The Dana Marshall Files

Volume 1 (Two short stories)

Blown Away

While Dana Marshall didn't have a perfect life, she did have a mother who loved her, a mother who encouraged her to be whatever she wanted when she grew up. They both had dreams of all she could accomplish, what she could do when she left this small town.

Then her mother was killed and everything changed. What Dana Marshall wanted to do when she graduated was something completely different than what her and her mother imagined. Mama didn't have this in mind.

Her life was destroyed when a monster killed her mother. Without protection, she fell prey to her alcoholic father. Taking her time, Dana did her research, saved her pennies until finally the storm blew in and scattered her problems to the other side of the county.

The first kill is always the hardest.

Kiss of Death

After successfully killing two men and getting away with it, Dana Marshall had her next kill.

Adrian Silva started beating his wife, Maria, before the ink was dry on the marriage license. When his stepdaughter became a teenager, his eyes turned to her. After an unsuccessful rape attempt, Yara Rivera took matters into her own hands. She attempted to kill him by putting boric acid in his whisky. He drank it, but lived. Sent to juvenile hall, Yara is unable to protect her mother. She knew there was nothing she could do but get her mother to leave Adrian.

Successfully escaping from him, Yara protected her family with everything she had, leaving her listening for every bump in the night in their small apartment every night.

With her file complete, Dana travels to Upstate New York to give Adrian her own kiss of death.

Stand-Alone Novels—Romantic Thriller

Fade to Black

Devlin Cross is one of Hollywood's biggest stars. He has his pick of the scripts and his pick of the women. While on a break from filming his current movie, he takes a drive through the countryside and stops at a local art gallery. There, the owner isn't star-struck by having him in her shop.

Lily Walker is a single mother who wants nothing to do with men. Her goal in life is to raise her son to the best of her ability and give him the stable home life she never had. With her failed marriage behind her, the last thing on her radar is a relationship, especially one with a famous movie star.

Not every breakup is mutual. Some ex-lovers never let go. Some will do whatever it takes to have that person back in their lives. Dead . . . or alive.

Bender

Since high school, everyone thought Jake Bender would end up behind bars; after all, he comes from a long line of bad boys. He spent years away from the place he called home. When he finally comes back, everyone thinks he's just a punk kid all grown up who's now running a dive bar called The Night Club. What they don't know is he heads a special task force which cleans up neighborhoods and makes them safe again.

Stormy Ryan has always felt more comfortable with her books than with people, and she loves to spend her days within the pages. When her second-hand bookstore is robbed for the third time in as many months, her employees quit leaving her to run the shop on her own. With the pressure of having to deal with her shop and people, not to mention the declining neighborhood, she is at the end of her rope.

When closing up her shop late one night, she is held up and the neighborhood bad boy saves her, putting both of them at the forefront of a psychotic's obsession.

Being bad has never looked so good.

Paranormal Novellas

Constant Echo

Reagan Beckett left her hometown and finished her senior year while staying with her aunt. She built her life in a city far away from her memories, never having contact with anyone who knew her back then. No one would recognize her now. She transformed herself and tried to get as far away from the captain of the cheerleading squad as she could.

She was successful until the letter arrived and everything changed. Now ten years later, she's on her way back to face her demons. The closer she gets, the more she feels herself slipping back to that scared young girl who fled in the early morning light, and she doesn't like it. Her stomach clenches knowing what she was headed back into. Scared of having to go back to the house where her best friend was murdered in front of her.

Sometimes the past isn't ready to let go.

The Moon Series (Stand-alone Paranormal Novellas)
Dreaming in Moonlight

This is a paranormal stand-alone novella in The Moon Series.

Ghosts are real. They are all around us. Most of the time, they are satisfied to watch us go by and not interact. When a couple was cursed to spend three hundred years in death searching for the one living couple who could release their bonds, they hunt for centuries to find a love which will make time stand still. If they fail, they will be sent to Hell to live out the rest of eternity.

Demons are real. They are all around us. Their one goal is to make our lives a living Hell. They will stop at nothing to destroy our minds and bodies. With the curse rapidly approaching its end, the deepest, darkest demon is summoned to make sure they don't succeed.

Kate O'Malley fell in love with the old two-story farmhouse in Maine at first sight. She had to live there. Spending all of her savings, she was able to buy it and moved right in. The very first night, strange things happened, and her dreams weren't her own. Looking for answers, she calls on a friend who puts her in contact with a ghost hunter, Sawyer Hamilton. Neither knows what is in their future. Neither knows if they are going to survive it.

Dreaming in Moonlight, when your sleep is filled with passion and your nightmares are real.

Romance with a Side of Humor

When Dreams Come True
(Book One of The Star Series)

What would you do if one day all of your dreams came true?

Melissa 'Lissa' Loring was a successful author. She was happy living in her home at the base of the mountains in Tucson with her assistant, Hannah Mills. First the phone call came; they wanted to make one of her books into a movie. Within six months, she was flying out to Los Angeles and talking with the studio about the final script and a list of actors to play the roles. Excited about her lunch meeting, she was shocked when her muse for one of the characters walked in and sat down at the table with her.

Will Martinsson was riding high on his fame and loving every minute of it. He traveled the world meeting his legions of fans and could pick which roles he wanted. When the script was presented to him, he read it and was intrigued. Then he found out that the author had modeled the character after him, so he searched out information on her and his interest was piqued. He told the studio he wanted in, but he also wanted to meet her before he would sign on the dotted line.

When two independent, successful people meet and have a strong connection, there is nothing they can do but see where the dream takes them.

Wishing On a Star
(Book Two of The Star Series)

At what point do you stop wishing on stars?

Hannah Mills was content in her life. She was the personal assistant to best-selling author, Melissa Loring. But now Melissa was engaged to the famous actor, Will Martinsson, and they were traveling around the world based on his filming and interview schedule. Hannah loved traveling with them, but she didn't want to run into Royce Rivers, Will's co-star and friend. The same man she called friend, until one night, things went too far. She tried as hard as she could to keep him out of her heart and body, but she knew if she saw him again, she'd lose the battle, and she couldn't allow herself to fall for him.

Royce Rivers grew up in the spotlight, a second-generation actor. When he was younger, he did everything and anything to rebel, becoming a typical Hollywood statistic on bad behavior. It took many years, but he cleaned his act up and was at a point in his life when he could try and enjoy it. Then one Miss Hannah Mills walked into his life and nothing was the same. He knew she was keeping something from him. If there was one thing he was familiar with, it was demons, and she had hers. What started as fun and games with a new friend, soon changed to something more. Royce wanted nothing more than to slay the demons which kept her away from him so they could have their happily ever after.

When two people battling demons meet and can no longer deny their feelings, there is nothing they can do but see if their wish comes true.

How to find M. Stratton

If you don't want to miss a single thing about M. Stratton, please sign up for her newsletter:
http://www.mstrattonauthor.com/#!newsletter-signup/c2otr

While you are signing up, take a moment and check out her website:
http://www.mstrattonauthor.com/

Also, please 'LIKE' or 'Favorite' M. Stratton's Amazon author page. It is the best way to stay up to date on all of her new releases and novels you may have missed.
http://www.amazon.com/M.-Stratton/e/B00G6KLAW0/

M. Stratton's social media:

Facebook:
https://www.facebook.com/MLStrattonAuthor

Twitter:
https://twitter.com/MStratton70

Instagram:
https://instagram.com/m.stratton/

Google+:
https://plus.google.com/u/0/106609044933909708636/posts

Goodreads:
https://www.goodreads.com/author/show/7063095.M_Stratton

Pinterest:
http://www.pinterest.com/mstrattonauthor/

Tsu:
https://www.tsu.co/MStratton

About M. Stratton

M. Stratton is an International Amazon bestselling author in the romantic suspense and mystery suspense categories for her Storm Series and Bender. She lives with her husband and son in Arizona, which is a big difference from where she grew up north of Chicago Illinois. As an only child she learned to tell herself stories to make the long winters go by quicker while dreaming of summer vacations. Now as an adult she still makes up stories to pass the time, but now she writes them down to share with other people.

Stratton is a self-proclaimed dork who loves to make people laugh. Her inner rock star is always on stage performing to a sold out crowd, but she quiet and shy on the outside. She spends her days plotting new ways to surprise her readers.